~ *Protecting Dallas* ~

A Military
Reverse Harem Romance

Krista Wolf

KRISTA'S VIP EMAIL LIST:

Join to get free book offers, and learn release dates for the hottest new titles!

Tap here to sign up: http://eepurl.com/dkWHab

~ Other Books by Krista Wolf ~

<u>Quadruple Duty</u>
<u>Quadruple Duty II - All or Nothing</u>

<u>Shared</u>
<u>Snowed In</u>
<u>Unwrapping Holly</u>
Protecting Dallas

<u>Chronicles of the Hallowed Order</u>

Book one: <u>Ghosts of Averoigne</u>
Book two: <u>Beyond the Gates of Evermoore</u>
Book three: <u>Claimed by the Pack</u>

Protecting Dallas - Krista Wolf

One

DALLAS

I woke in the darkness, a cold shiver bolting through me. It ran down my spine, prickling every single one of the hairs on the back of my neck.

You're not alone.

The thought came instantly, without even a moment's consideration. It was a gut feeling. An instinct.

It was terrifying.

Dallas, get up!

Slowly my eyes adjusted, and the ceiling faded into view. I remained frozen however. If I were being watched, or stalked, or anything like that, moving would only—

My heart skipped a beat as I saw him: a dark figure, standing at the foot of my bed.

"WHAT THE—"

He bolted upright, and I let out a bloodcurdling scream. It gave him only an instant's pause, this man in black.

4

This man dressed like the night, head to toe, blending in with the shadows.

An instant was all I needed.

I rolled from bed, one foot landing on the cold floor before the other. Then, without stopping my momentum, I swung the other leg upward...

... and kicked him square in the balls.

"Unnnfff!"

It was a strangled cry, but still just as satisfying. It stopped his charge mid-stride, driving him upward and backward. I could hear him sinking to his knees behind me, but I couldn't see him because I was already through my bedroom door and flying down the hallway.

"HELP!"

I fumbled for lights along the way. I think I even hit a switch, but for some reason, everything remained dark.

"HELLLLLP!"

Your phone!

Damn. It was still back in the bedroom. I could've grabbed it, I could have it in my hand right now. It would've only taken an extra second, maybe two. Time I definitely had, considering how hard my foot had connected with my invader's groin.

"HEEEEEELLLLL–"

My third cry was cut short, as a hand clapped itself tightly over my mouth. It stopped my momentum abruptly, clotheslining me as I flung myself into the kitchen.

"Shhhh!"

It was a hiss, somewhere close to my ear. A second attacker. Someone *else* in my house... someone who now had both arms wrapped around me as I flailed and kicked and struggled to break free.

"EASY," the voice in my ear buzzed. "You don't have to—"

I bit down.... *Hard.*

"SHIT!"

My new attacker released me reflexively, shoving me away from his body. I whirled to face him, just as the warm, coppery taste of blood filled my mouth...

CRASH!

I threw both arms over my face protectively as my kitchen window suddenly exploded inward. Glass and broken bits of the frame rained everywhere. It scattered across the floor, glinting over my countertops like jagged diamonds in the moonlight.

"GRAB HER!"

Another man took hold of my arms, from somewhere off to one side. Like the man I'd bitten, he wasn't wearing gloves. Wasn't wearing black...

"Get her out of here! Now, before—"

He never got to finish his sentence. The man from the bedroom came crashing over him, tacking him from behind. I saw kicks and punches, as the two figures scuffled across the floor. One of them pulled a knife. The other... a sleek black pistol.

Dallas!

I twisted hard, but I was too wrapped up. Whoever held me was strong — *amazingly* strong — maybe even stronger than my brother, Connor.

Only my brother wasn't here. And that's because my brother was dead.

CRACK!

A shot rang out. It was loud and impossibly obnoxious in my tiny kitchen, the yellow starburst from the pistol's muzzle flaring brightly. For a second it illuminated the entire room, and I could see two *more* men. They were scuffling as well, throwing each other up against the wall even as the others writhed around on the debris-strewn floor...

CRACK! CRACK! CRACK!

Darkness reigned again for a moment, and then suddenly I was outside. I could feel the cool desert wind, the bite in the air. I was still struggling, still kicking and screaming, but it was already too late. I was being dragged. Dragged down my side lawn...

... to where a large black truck was waiting, doors already open.

"NOOO!"

I kicked again, this time directing my foot downward. It stomped hard on the boot of the man who had me, and I felt his grip relax ever so slightly.

"LET GO OF..."

Another stomp, and this time I remembered to pull back with my toes. The bone of my heel cracked down hard, hopefully shattering the metatarsus of whoever owned that big, military-style boot.

"OWW... *FUCK!*"

The hands gripping my arms grew tighter, the fingers screwing into painful claws. Suddenly I was no longer attached to the ground — I was being lifted into the air, carried that last ten or twenty feet before being thrown, like a sack of potatoes, into the back of the ominous-looking truck.

"Motherfu–"

I bounced inside, just as two more men came sprinting from the house, chased by the men in black. They slid in quickly, one right beside me, the other into the passenger seat.

Both swung the doors closed, divorcing us from the chaos outside.

"GO GO GO!"

With the screech of tires and a shower of gravel, we took off down the street. I was surrounded by my captors now. The three of them and me.

This is it, the voice in my head told me. *You're finished.*

I resisted one last time, trying to twist free. Once more, I was pinned. Grabbed by the wrists.

You'll never see home again.

My teeth gnashed together as I spat on the floor. The inner voice was making me angry! Making me defiant.

Dallas...

Somehow I managed a look back over my shoulder,

8

and all the fight drained out of me at once. I could feel a fist-sized lump forming in my throat. My heart, breaking...

My whole house was engulfed in flames.

Two

DALLAS

"Everyone okay? Anyone hit?"

The man in the passenger seat wiped his sweat away with one giant forearm. He slicked back a mop of thick blond hair and turned to look at us.

"Negative," said the man sitting beside me. "But I think I got one of them a few times, center mass." The driver merely shook his head.

"Vests?"

"Oh yeah."

"Then damn."

The blond turned his gorgeous blue eyes on me, looking me up and down. Taking stock of me. Maybe even trying to determine if I was hurt as well.

"My house!" I snarled. "Why is my house—"

All at once I was set free, and my arms were my own again. I started by rubbing my wrists, which hurt like hell, while staring venomously back at the guy with the goatee sitting next to me.

"Dallas..."

I tried not to squint at the mention of my name, but it was too hard. Glancing back again, I could see dark smoke rising in the distance, blocking a whole big swath of the bright, twinkling stars.

"Dallas listen," the blond said, his voice placating. "I need you to know—"

It happened in a flash, and exactly the way I planned it. One moment I was distracting the guy next to me with a hand near his face, the next I was pulling his gun from its holster.

"Hey... HEY!"

I flipped the safety off the Glock 19 in one smooth motion and slid my finger through the trigger guard. From there it was only a quick swing of the arm... and I had the barrel jammed up against the back of the driver's head.

"PULL OVER," I said sternly. "Or I paint the windshield with this guy's brains."

Goatee put his hands up slowly. The blond guy did too.

"Easy, Dallas. We're on your sid—"

"Fuck that!" I stammered. "If you were actually on my side you'd be back at my house, helping me put out that fire."

They looked at each other, then back to me.

"Trust me," I said. "Safety's off. And if you think I'm kidding—"

11

Faster than my eye could even follow, the blond in the front seat disarmed me. His hands slid over mine, turned my wrist sideways until it hurt, and plucked the pistol from my open grip.

Shit.

Unbelievably, he pulled the slide back until it clicked, then handed the gun back to me.

"There," he said. "One in the chamber now. Safety's still off, so be careful."

For a half-second I just sat there gaping in astonishment. Then I put the gun to the back to the driver's head, this time pressing the barrel into the flesh of his thick neck.

"PULL. OVER."

To my surprise, he did. Slowing down smoothly, he brought the truck to a stop on the shoulder of the road.

"Dallas," said the man in front again. "We're not here to hurt you..."

My teeth were clenched. "My house is burning!"

"We didn't do that," the man said.

"Then why are you abducting me?"

"We're not abducting you," the man with the goatee offered. "We're *saving* you."

I laughed out loud. It came out maniacal. "Saving me from *what?* The power you cut to my house? The fire you set to kill me?"

"Like I said, that wasn't us," said the blond. "Think

12

about it. We're the good guys. Now, who are the bad?"

My mouth twisted begrudgingly. I didn't answer.

"The ones in *black* were the bad guys," goatee went on. "The ones dressed head to toe in tactical nightgear, with infrared optics."

"The ones we were *fighting*," said the guy up front. "The ones we pulled you away from, to get you out of there."

I thought back to the whole damned clusterfuck, starting with the asshole standing over my bed. He was definitely one of the bad guys. Ditto for the one who crashed through my window, also dressed in black.

Not the guy with the hand over my mouth, though. That was one of these assholes.

I glanced at the driver. His hands still rested on the steering wheel. One of them was bleeding. I could see a perfect imprint of my upper teeth...

"Yes, we grabbed you," said the blond. It was like he was reading my mind. "But we did it to get you out. To keep you safe." He jerked his head downward, toward the gun. "Why do you think your hands are free? Or you're even conscious to begin with?" His mouth curled into a half-smirk. "If we really *were* the bad guys, would I give you back a loaded firearm?"

I hesitated... then very slowly lowered the weapon. The second I did, the driver eased off the brake and the truck started moving again.

"You're Dallas," said the man in front. "I'm Maddox. The guy next to you is Austin." He tapped the driver. "He's Kane."

The driver, who still hadn't said a single thing, pulled back into traffic.

"We served with Connor. All of us."

My shoulders slumped as my body relaxed. The way they acted, the way they moved... it all made sense now. They were SEALs! Like my brother...

"Here," said goatee, holding his hand out expectantly. "Give it over?"

KA-CHING!

With the flick of my wrist I yanked the slide back, ejecting the first round upward. It flipped through the air, end over end, until I caught it nimbly in my other fist.

"Fine then," I growled. "Let's talk."

I handed him back the weapon butt-end first, the chamber open and empty. The pretty-boy in front looked on, as fascinated as he was impressed.

"Well shit," he swore under his breath. "I guess she really *is* Connor's sister..."

Three

DALLAS

The big truck plunged deeper into the desert, where the light pollution gave way to a billion stars. I liked to drive out here sometimes, when I had nothing to do. To get away from the Vegas suburbs, or just drive in the opposite direction of the strip.

"Water?"

I shook my head as the guy in front — Maddox, he said his name was — flipped the cap down on some big stainless flask. He tucked it away, and I went back to staring out the window.

Connor.

It was over a year now. More than fourteen months since my only brother had been killed in action. That was the Navy's official report, anyway. Any other answers I'd tried to get from them had been vague and frustrating.

Oh, Connor...

Hands screwing into fists, I waited until my fingernails dug deep into my palms. It allowed me to concentrate on the pain. Distracted me from what I *really* wanted to do, which was break down and cry.

But I wasn't crying in front of these guys. No fucking way.

What the hell happened to you?

Forget about life giving you lemons. Mine was filled with three giant curveballs. Three tremendous "fuck you's" spaced fairly evenly throughout my existence, starting at age ten when my mother contracted cancer. She was dead by my twelfth birthday, and dad died three years after that... presumably of a broken heart.

Our little family of four had been halved just in time for my sweet sixteen, which was about as sweet as biting into a lemon. But through it all, and even afterward, at least I had Connor.

OUCH!

I glanced down, into my palms. I'd drawn blood again. This time on both of them.

Smearing my hands on my sweatpants, I gazed back outside. The moon was just three-quarters full, but it was enough to cast the entire desert horizon in a hazy blue light.

Connor had been the ultimate brother, before and after our parent's death. He'd been a father figure as well. He was old enough to assume guardianship of me, and we were able to stay in the house we were raised in. The house held memories for us. Memories of fun and family. Memories of holidays, and mom, and dad...

My brother didn't really raise me, we raised each other. We were a team — totally inseparable. Bound by blood, but also through our baptism by fire. Everything I'd been through, he'd been through... and vice versa.

Graciously, unselfishly, Connor put aside his dreams of enlistment until after my eighteenth birthday. He was twenty-one when he made it to boot camp, and aced the physical screening tests so easily that he was fast-tracked through the Naval Special Warfare pipeline.

Connor became a SEAL, and I became solely independent. Not that I wasn't independent before, but now I was completely, entirely on my own.

I still had my brother though. We still talked and texted and Skyped each other every chance we got. Sometimes he'd even come home, between deployments or stints away. Between the incredibly dangerous things he did that he never really wanted to talk about, and the places where I wasn't able to reach him.

Those were my favorite memories of all — the times where we'd sit home watching old movies. Talking about mom and dad, while burning different meals together. The two of us were both terrible at cooking. Luckily, we were both great at ordering out.

When you're a blackjack dealer, nothing really appeals to you about the strip anymore. It becomes work. It becomes standard. The only times I ever really enjoyed going out in Las Vegas was when Connor was home. Because when we got bored of reminiscing — or chasing the ghosts of our past around the house — the two of us would go out and paint the town red together. Or however the hell that expression goes.

But now...

Now Connor was dead. Gone forever, like everyone else in my life. It was something I would never recover from, nor did I want to, nor was I even trying. But somehow, I still woke up every day. I still dragged myself to work, dealt cards for nine hours, and put up with varying degrees of pit-boss bullshit only to come home and crash out in my bed.

And now my *bed* was gone too...

I forgot all about my hands. The tears started streaming, regardless of whether I wanted them to, and the next thing I knew I was sobbing into my blood-covered palms.

"Hey..."

A big hand fell to my shoulder. I shoved it off.

"A—Are you alright?"

No, I wasn't alright. I was pretty fucking far from alright. My parents were gone, my brother was dead, and now everything I owned was a pile of smoldering ashes. I could see it now; the flashing lights, the sirens, the EMTs and firefighters and police... all standing around, scratching their heads. Trying to figure out whether I'd been in there or not.

Shit, I may as well have been.

"We're here," the driver said, his voice reaching my ears for the first time. He turned to glance back at me, all rugged and masculine... but the look on his face was gentle and kind.

"I'll put on some coffee."

Four

MADDOX

She sat in the center of our kitchen, but not like some frightened puppy or helpless kitten. No, Dallas Winters dominated her space. The same way her brother would've, had he been here.

"You call this *coffee?*"

She spat back into the mug we'd given her and pushed it away. The black liquid sat at the edge of the table, sloshing back and forth with the momentum.

"It's fresh," Austin protested.

"It's *freeze dried*," she practically sneered. "It's a bunch of crap you dissolve in boiling water."

"So?"

She laughed, but I could tell it was one of those laughs to keep from displaying something else. A cover up. A plug, keeping the rest of her emotions in check.

"Never mind," she said, more to herself than us.

"Three grown men. *Military* men. And not a coffee maker in sight."

I sat across from her, taking it all in. Dallas *Winters*. In the flesh. In our *kitchen*. Holy shit.

On the other side of the room, Kane leaned against the counter, arms folded. His gaze was fixated on her. Staring at her just as intently as he had a thousand times before, only never in person. Never this close...

"So out with it," said Dallas. "How'd you know?"

"Know what?" asked Austin.

"Know when those guys were gonna break into my house at two in the fucking morning."

We looked at each other, one by one. No one said anything. We hadn't prepared for this moment.

"You knew, obviously," said Dallas. "That they were coming?"

More silence.

"You didn't just *happen* to be rolling down the street, all three of you? Pointing at houses?" she asked smugly. "Wondering if maybe *that* house needed help from armed intruders who could see in the dark? Men dressed in black, wearing... what did you call it? 'Tactical nightgear'?"

"Okay, okay," I said. "So we knew."

"Yes, but *how'd* you know?"

"Because we were watching you."

The words came from Kane. He said them slowly, evenly. Without the hint of apology.

"*Watching* me?"

"Yes," replied Austin. "And it's a damned good thing we were, because—"

"And just how were you watching me?" asked Dallas. "No wait..." she sat up in her chair. "Could we start with *why* were you watching me?"

Austin was standing, but now he pulled up a chair. He flipped it around and sat down on it backwards, resting his arms on the back.

"We were watching you because your brother told us to," he said.

Dallas flinched visibly at the mention of Connor. Her face twisted into a scowl.

"My brother is dead."

"Yes," said Austin, trying to be patient. "But he told us *before* he died. His last message to us..."

He glanced at me and I shook my head just the tiniest little degree. I did it almost imperceptibly, hoping Dallas wouldn't notice.

"Anyway," Austin went on, "he told us to look after you. To make sure you were alright, because he might..." He fumbled. "Because he might..."

"He might be killed," said Dallas sullenly.

Austin nodded. "Yes."

The kitchen fell silent for a long moment. Then, almost as if a light bulb went off, Dallas's whole demeanor changed.

"So then you know what happened to him," she said hopefully. "You can tell me what... when he..."

I could see her struggle. The search for answers, the undying curiosity... pitted against the little voice in the back of her mind, screaming that she didn't want to know. Not *really*. Not truly.

Because once she crossed that threshold, she could never, ever go back.

"Wait," Dallas said. "When did he tell you this? He's been gone a year."

Austin stopped talking. Kane cleared his throat.

"Are you saying you've been watching me *for more than a year?*"

I folded my arms across my chest. At this point, honesty was the only real option.

"Yes."

"You've been watching my *house* for a year? Driving by in the middle of the night? Looking for signs of trouble, waiting for someone to roll up in my bedroom while I was sleeping, only to—"

"It's not like that," said Austin. "We don't drive past your house because we don't *need* to drive past your house."

She looked confused. Entirely uncertain. But I could sense an anger too, building inside her. Welling up, just beneath the surface.

Uh oh.

"There are cameras," said Kane, nonchalantly, "set up in your home."

He didn't even seem phased when Dallas's head whipped in his direction. Her jaw dropped to the floor.

"We've been watching you remotely."

Five

DALLAS

"You've been *WATCHING* me?" I shouted, leaping out of my chair. "In my *HOUSE?*"

"Easy," said Maddox. "It's not like—"

"For a whole *YEAR?*"

I was shocked. Stunned. Absolutely livid. But also...

Also I was confused.

"I can't believe you put cameras in my house!" I cried. "I can't believe—"

"Not your *whole* house," Austin said, his hands out defensively. "Not in your bedroom of course. Bathroom either."

"That makes it *okay?*" I asked incredulously. "Are you serious? That's your rationalization: not in my bedroom, not in my bathroom... just everywhere *else?*"

"And we didn't place the cameras there," he continued. "Your brother did. They were already installed — a security

24

measure, put there by Connor."

I searched my memory. It came up blank.

"Connor never told me about any cameras," I said.

"He didn't get the chance," said Maddox. He leaned forward too fast, and a flop of blond hair fell over one crystal blue eye. "Your brother put them there shortly before... well..."

I looked down, into my lap. Thankfully he didn't continue.

"That still doesn't give you the right to tap into them," I finally sneered. "Just because they were there, just because—"

"Dallas, stop."

We all turned at once. The guy they were calling Kane was still leaning against the counter. He still had his arms crossed. But now, he was staring back at us.

"Hear them out," Kane said in his deep, gravelly voice. "Your brother was our brother too. Much more than you know."

He caught my gaze, and for some odd reason it calmed me. There was truth in his eyes. And also something else...

Something like sorrow.

"Your brother *wanted* this from us," Kane went on. "Looking after you was his last request."

The words came out slow and even. They were almost haunting. Mechanically, I sat back down.

His last request...

"But I—"

25

"We haven't just been looking out for you," said Maddox. "We've been monitoring the outside of your property for signs of *them*."

I cocked my head. "The guys in black?"

"Yes."

Now were getting somewhere. "Who are they?"

"We're not entirely sure. But we know they had something to do with Connor's disappearance. Something to do with what ultimately happened to him."

I pointed at the door. "So why the hell are we even here? If they have the answers, why'd we run in the first place?"

"Because we were outnumbered," said Maddox. "And probably outgunned. We jumped out of bed and flew out to your place as fast we could," he explained. "The very second Kane noticed them on the monitors, gathering outside your house."

"Still..."

"We fled also because of you," said Austin. "We had to get you out. Make sure you were safe. That was top priority."

The rest of the group nodded together.

"We owed Connor that much."

Suddenly I wanted to go back — to face the men who'd broken in and burned down my home. I wanted to shake them violently. Make them tell me who they were, and what they wanted.

Most of all, I needed to know what happened to Connor...

"We'll deal with them," said Austin, shifting in his chair. "Trust in us. But for now..."

"For now you need to lay low," said Maddox. "We weren't followed here, and that's a good thing. But these people are persistent. They're well-funded. And they've got access to resources we don't."

My eyes narrowed. "So you *do* know who they are?"

"Not entirely. But we know *some* things. And we're piecing together others."

"Just as your brother was," said Kane, ominously. "When they took him."

I swallowed hard. Suddenly I was very aware of myself and my surroundings. The house was big and old, inside and out. I was sitting in its run-down kitchen, wearing a pair of blood-smeared sweats and a T-shirt. Other than the little diamond-shaped pendant I always wore around my neck — given to me by Connor — it was the sum total of all my worldly possessions.

Thank God I'd stopped sleeping naked.

"How long have you lived here?" I asked.

The question must've seemed random. The guys didn't answer it right away.

"Just over a year."

"Since Connor died..."

Slowly they nodded. "Yes," said Maddox.

"So you've been doing this..." I gestured around, "just for me?"

27

"We're doing it for Connor," said Austin. "Each one of us owes your brother a grave debt. But yes, you also. Protecting you is a huge part of paying him back."

The guys stared at me for another half minute, as if getting used to me being there. I realized it must be strange for them, seeing me in the flesh. Having me here among them, after having watched me on monitors for so damned long.

"Think you can sleep?" asked Maddox.

"Fuck no."

He glanced around the room. The others shook their heads as well.

Maddox shrugged helplessly and smiled. "Breakfast it is then."

Six

DALLAS

The guys had shit coffee and shit accommodations. The kitchen even had shit lighting.

But when it came to breakfast...

The first meal of the day had been my brother's specialty, and the only one he could really cook without burning it. The spread placed before me now reminded me exactly of that: piles of scrambled eggs, links of brown sausage, fresh waffles, crispy hash-browns, and a tall frosty glass of orange juice to wash it all down.

It made me wonder how many times they'd eaten this way with Connor, just as I had.

I didn't think I could eat, but it turned out I was wrong. I ate *everything*. I cleaned my plate and helped myself immediately to seconds, and when the seconds were finished I started looking around for bacon.

"You were hungry."

I nodded. There wasn't much else to say. Filling my belly was a welcome distraction from my predicament, and I used the relative silence (knives and forks scraping against ceramic plates notwithstanding) to take stock of my would-be rescuers.

Maddox seemed to be the 'leader' of the three, if you could call it that. He was tall and extremely well-built, with sexy amounts of stubble and thick blond hair much longer than enlistment allowed. That meant he was *ex*-SEAL, if anything. Or maybe he was so high up the Navy's chain of command, they stopped bothering him about his haircut.

As for Austin, his whole demeanor seemed a little more uptight and by the book. He was the one cleaning things up and putting stuff away, even washing and storing the pans the very moment Maddox finished with them. His dark hair and olive skin made him incredibly attractive, and the military precision with which he groomed his impeccably-kept goatee told me everything I needed to know about his daily habits.

That left Kane, who was a lot harder to figure out. He was absolutely *massive*, with a broad, powerful chest and Atlas-like shoulders you could rest the world on. His big arms barely fit through his drab green shirt, stretching the fabric to the absolute limits as he shoveled eggs and sausage into his ruggedly handsome face.

But unlike the others, Kane was silent. He didn't talk the entire meal, content only to eat and listen and observe. At one point he caught me staring at him, and I expected some kind of quick look away. Instead he held my gaze with swagger-like confidence, his mouth widening into the same gentle smile as before.

Somehow, despite everything that happened to me, I found myself smiling back at him.

The sun finally cracked the sky, and one by one the guys disappeared for a bit. They came back fully dressed and cleanly-shaven. Ready for whatever they were about to do next.

"Kane and I have some things to check out," said Maddox. "We'll be out near the city, but we'll be back before sundown."

I rubbed at my eyes. I could only imagine how I looked.

"If you make a list, Austin will pick up whatever you need. Clothes first, of course. Shampoo, toothbrush... whatever other toiletries, just write them down and—"

"I'm *not* writing shit down."

Maddox stared back at me like I'd just spoken to him in Latin. He scratched his head. "Uhh... what?"

"Why in the world would I write anything down?" I asked. "I'll just go with him."

The guys all looked at each other uncomfortably. "You are *not* going with him."

"Oh no?" I laughed. "Everything I ever owned is a glowing pile of ashes now. I have things I need. *Lots* of things. I'll need a new phone, for one. I have to call my boss, see if he can get me a few new uniforms before tonight..."

"Your *boss?*"

"Yeah. At the casino." I folded my arms across my chest. "You've been watching me long enough to know I'm a blackjack dealer, right?"

"Of course," said Austin. "But—"

"You're not *going* to work," interjected Maddox.

My hands went to my hips now, fingers spread. "The hell I'm not."

"Dallas, you *can't* go back to work. These people will find you. Hell, they're probably already at the casino, waiting for you to show up. Just as they're probably sitting at either edge of your block, waiting for you to come by and sift through the ashes... I mean the remnants of..."

His voice trailed off. Austin elbowed him in the ribs.

"Look, tell me everything you need and I'll grab it for you," he said. "I'll do some shopping too. I'll pick up food, groceries, that sort of stuff. Anything you like, just tell me and I'll get it."

"*We'll* get it," I corrected him. "When *we* go."

He sighed heavily. "Dallas, it's not safe."

"Nothing is safe," I said. "Look at my house."

"Yes, but—"

"But nothing. I'm not going to sit around here while the three of you figure this out." I waved my arm around the white-washed, bare-bones kitchen. "How long did you say you've been here again?"

Kane answered this time. "Thirteen months."

After a short span of silence, I laughed. "You're out of your mind if you think—"

"Dallas please," Maddox pleaded. "At least for now, let Austin pick up—"

32

"I need *girl* things too you know," I smirked, throwing an intentional wrench in the works. "Stuff I have to pick out for myself. I'll need different sizes for different shirts, different style pants... oh, and I'll need bras... underwear..."

Austin's shoulders slumped. He looked uncomfortable. Maddox looked worried.

Kane however, had the slightest hint of a grin.

"Feminine products," I went on. "*Lots* of those. And also—"

"But—"

"Look," I said loudly, with a sigh. "I'll put my hair up. I'll wear a hat. I'll wear sunglasses and a phony fucking mustache if you want me to, but I'm absolutely not sitting here alone all day."

Before they could answer I pushed past them, into what looked like the living area. It was big and empty, just as sparse as the kitchen with the walls and floor almost entirely bare. At least they had couches.

"Anyone gonna tell me where the shower is?" I asked over my shoulder. I reached the staircase in silence, and stared climbing. "Or should I just keep opening doors until I find it?"

33

Seven

AUSTIN

She was stubborn as hell, I'd give her that. Strong-willed and intelligent and unable to take no for an answer.

In short, she was exactly like Connor.

I couldn't help but stare at her during the ride back, one leg up on the dashboard as she painted her toenails. Dallas had dragged me to nine different shops, including three grocery stores and a stop for lunch. Three fish tacos each later, we were almost home, no worse for wear.

God, she's gorgeous.

She really was. I mean, we'd known her forever... at first through photos Connor showed us, then through watching her on the monitor for so long. But now she was *here*. Actually here! Sitting beside me in the passenger seat, window down, her blonde hair blowing so wildly it was whipping around her beautiful face.

"Stop for beer?"

I shook my head. We were too close to home already, and she'd already been out too much. As far as keeping things low key went, we'd failed miserably on the first day.

Besides, though we weren't exactly stocked back at the house? Beer was the one thing we had plenty of.

"Got a few cases in the basement," I said, using the conversation as an excuse to glance right. "I'll bring some up for us, when we get back."

Stop looking at her!

It was impossible, though. She was every bit as beautiful as Connor had been obnoxiously good-looking, only with prettier cheekbones and full, kissable lips. She had his eyes though. Those same stunning blue orbs that burned with a distinct inner fire. A burning charisma that converted you without words; a magic that automatically made you want to please her, without her having to say a single, goddamn thing.

Dallas was wearing shorts and a tank top now, and a pair of high-quality mirrored sunglasses that had probably cost us a small fortune. I had no clue, really. I hadn't looked at the receipts on anything. I'd just given her the card — the one we all shared together — and we could worry about the bill later, when it came in.

"How long did you serve with my brother?"

I was surprised she'd waited this long to ask. So far, our conversations had been pretty limited: shopping and the weather.

"All eight years he was in."

She turned to look at me. All I could see was my own reflection in her sunglasses.

"So you knew him well?"

"He was a like a brother to me," I said truthfully. "To all of us, really. But yes. We went through our PST together. Pre-BUDS, BUDS..." I paused. "Do you know what those things are?"

"Basic Underwater Demolition," she replied, looking away. Her gaze swung casually back out the passenger window. "Yeah. I know it."

My eyes wandered again, and I had to forcibly drag them from her legs. Purposefully, I thought about Connor. Guilt flooded in.

"Yeah, we did jump school together afterward," I said. "That's where we met Maddox and Kane. "Tactical communications, sniper school, breacher certification... the three of us went through the whole gauntlet, HALO insertions and all. "

"Were you assigned to the same unit?"

"Yup. Got lucky," I said. "Real lucky."

Dallas switched legs, and I tightened my grip on the steering wheel. This time I was strong enough to keep my eyes pointed forward.

"Everywhere we went, your brother kicked ass you know."

"Oh," she said casually, "I know."

I laughed. "I've never seen anyone in shape like he was. He always made us look bad, no matter what we were doing. The man was a freak of nature."

I could've gone on. I could've told her how Connor

36

Winters always ran faster, went further, and jumped higher than any one of us. That I don't think in all the time I knew him I'd ever seen him out of breath. That he could stay underwater almost a full minute longer than anyone else...

"We loved him," I said instead. "All of us."

Dallas remained silent, adjusting her sunglasses. I could tell my words had hit a nerve, though. Whether it was a good or a bad nerve, I didn't know.

"I– I'm sorry for everything that happened to you."

The sun sank a bit more on the horizon, and the miles stretched on without answer. Not that I needed an answer. I just needed to tell her.

"Fuck it," I said suddenly, pulling off the main highway. "Let's stop for beer."

Off to my side, I noticed my passenger perk up a bit. Her mouth even curled into the slightest hint of a smile.

"The shit in the basement is probably old as hell anyway."

Eight

DALLAS

"Okay, so I need to say a few things..."

We'd finished eating an hour ago, and were just lounging around the table now. The beer was ice cold, and it was going down way too easily. Then again, hitting rock bottom tended to make *everything* go down easily, whether you wanted it to or not.

Buck up, Dallas.

The bad news was that I'd lost everything... and I mean *everything*. Probably even my job with the casino, because I had no clue how long I would need to stay away.

The good news though, was that there was no place to go from here but up.

"First, I wanted to say thank you," I said, trying to be genuine. "I know I was a little rough around the edges yesterday, but I had a bad night. A really bad night."

"Totally understandable," said Maddox. He looked

38

buzzed. His cheeks were flushed red, like he wasn't used to drinking like this. Navy SEAL discipline maybe, and all that jazz.

"Yeah," said Austin. "And you sure as hell don't have to thank us."

"Oh but I do," I went on. "I realize now I'd be dead if you hadn't shown up. That in keeping your promise to my brother, even if it meant *stalking* me for a whole year..." I smiled a little at that part, "the three of you totally and unselfishly saved my ass."

The guys were staring back at me a little differently now. Much more relaxed. Austin raised his bottle in salute, and the others toasted.

"Next, I want to say thanks for putting me up in your place. I know this is probably a pain in the ass, having me here..."

"Not at all," said Austin. "In fact—"

"Give me a few days," I cut in, "and I promise I'll be on your shit list. I'm sure to do *something* to piss you off; clog the shower drain with my hair, leave the toilet seat down all the time... fun stuff like that."

They guys looked on, letting me do my thing. Giving me the floor, so to speak.

"I need you to make me a few promises though," I said, "if I'm going to stay here. And I'll need all three of you to agree."

They looked intrigued now, or at least Maddox and Austin did. Kane just stared on impassively, twisting the cap from his fifth or sixth beer.

"First, I need complete transparency. Whatever you're doing to find who's after me, or who hurt Connor? I need in on that."

Maddox squinted in confusion. "What do you mean by 'in on it'?"

"I mean you share all your intel with me," I said, intentionally using the military jargon. "You keep me in the loop. None of this 'we didn't tell you for your own safety' crap. If you learn something — no matter how bad or scary — I need to know about it. And the door swings both ways."

"The... door?" asked Austin

"Look, I've already decided that no matter what you say I'm helping out," I replied. "I may not have your field skills or your physical training, but four heads are always better than three. You give me your info, your theories, your whatever you have, and together we'll all try to piece together what's going on." I tipped my bottle back and finished it before clapping it to the table. "You might not know from watching me parade around my house in my underwear, but I'm pretty fucking surgical when it comes to the internet."

All three of them blushed instantly, knowing what I'd said was true. After long shifts in a stuffy casino uniform, stripping down to my underwear had always been my way to unwind. Surprisingly enough, it was Kane who turned the brightest shade of red.

I'll have to remember that in the future...

"So are we all on the same page?" I asked.

Slowly they exchanged glances, each nodding some sort of eventual approval.

"Yeah," Maddox said at last. "We're up for that." He paused for a moment, before giving me a bleary-eyed shrug. "Seems only fair."

I nodded for a good several seconds, to drive the point home. "Good. Now onto the next thing..."

"You're pretty demanding, you know that?" Austin quipped.

"I know."

"No offense or anything."

"None taken." I leaned back in my chair. "Now, let's talk about the house..."

It had taken several hours of soul-searching and staring at the ceiling to realize the guys were right; if I didn't stay here laying low, chances were good I was an easy target. The admission hurt, but it was also one I had to swallow and move on from if I wanted to help find Connor's killers.

And I *definitely* wanted to find Connor's killers.

"Don't take this the wrong way," I started off, "but top to bottom this place needs some serious TLC."

"TLC?" swore Austin, lookin indignant. "I'll have you know—"

"Yeah yeah," I cut him off. "I know it's squeaky clean. It's tip-top, as far as cleanliness goes, but not very... homey."

They looked even more confused now, and it wasn't just from the buzz they had going. Basically, they were guys. *Military* guys. As utilitarian as they were, they had no idea what I meant.

"Look around," I sighed. "This place looks like a

41

halfway house. There's barely any furniture. Nothing on the walls. No lamps, no rugs, no anything to make it a home. It looks like you decorated with the Bachelor's Starter Kit. Like you went out and bought a couch and a television and a few bags of pretzels, then you sat down and called it a day."

All three of them said nothing. I couldn't tell if they were shocked or offended. Maybe both.

"I stuck my head in the fridge this morning and my voice echoed. I slid open a drawer and moths flew out."

"So what are you saying?" asked Maddox.

I shifted my gaze to Austin. "That credit card we used today. Whose was it?"

"All of ours," he said. "House account."

"So you're sharing expenses."

"Yes. We share... pretty much everything," he shrugged.

"Fine," I said. "If I'm gonna lay low here all day, I'm gonna need a copy of that card. And that's because I'm gonna need something to *do*."

Maddox scratched at the stubble on his chin. "Do?"

"Yup."

"Like what?"

"Oh let's see..." I said, listing things off on my fingers. "Food, for one. And not just a couple of days worth of groceries, but some stockpiling of necessary essentials."

"What else?"

"Your toilet paper is one-ply." I said, making a face. "*Not* acceptable. Half the light bulbs in the house are out. It's dismal in here. The walls need a fresh coat of paint."

"Which room are you talking abou—"

"Every room!" I cried. "Everything's white. Or grey. Or shit brown. And I don't know about *your* rooms, but the guest room's bedding is scratchy as all hell. The thread count is so low it ought to be criminal."

"Wow," Maddox smirked. "Tell us how you *really* feel."

"Everything's disorganized," I went on. "You moved in a year ago and still have piles of boxes against the walls. You need shelves, you need bookcases, picture frames..."

Austin held up one hand. "Picture frames?"

"Window coverings, better towels in the bathroom..."

Kane laughed. "I told you those towels sucked."

"A stereo system, or at least a couple of speakers so we could stream in some music..."

"That," Austin nodded, "I can agree with."

"A couple of throw pillows. Maybe a few scented candles..."

I ran out of fingers. When I was finished, the guys were all staring at me.

"Look, if you're gonna babysit me for a while, the least I can do is pitch in," I said. "I'm not trying to be difficult. But if I don't have anything else to do..."

I shook my hands anxiously, trying to get the point across. None of this was an act, really. I tended to go stir-crazy a lot quicker than most people I knew.

"Here."

Kane reached into his back pocket and tossed me a credit card, scaling it like a baseball card. All three of them looked surprised when I caught nimbly between my fingers.

"You deal a *lot* of cards," Maddox guessed. "Don't you?"

"You'd better believe it," I said, slipping it in my pocket.

Nine

DALLAS

The next few weeks were interesting ones, to say the least. Even for being holed up in an old house, somewhere out in the desert.

As far roommates went, the guys were extremely chill. I learned tons more about them and they about me, sharing meals and stories and drinks — both in the kitchen and out.

I even learned more about my brother. Much, *much* more. It was amazing, hearing all about the other side to Connor's life. I couldn't get enough of listening to the tales of the exotic places he'd been, and all the incredible things he'd done while there. And the guys never held back. They never tired of telling me.

They never really ran out of stories, either.

It turned out that my brother was absolute *badass*, which I already knew. But apparently he was the King of All Badasses, and after some of the shit he'd been through with Maddox and Austin and Kane, they revered him almost as

45

some of deity or god.

"If it weren't for your brother," they told me on more than one occasion, "none of us would even be here."

They said it solemnly. Soberly. Without bragging or boasting or even a trace of a smile. And while none of them would go *too* deep into the specifics of the actual combat missions they ran with Connor, each of them had their own tales of his sacrifice and unwavering bravery.

I learned that Maddox was retired from service, and doing private-sector work. Austin and Kane were still technically enlisted, but had received a highly-specialized, temporarily leave.

"We're not going back until we figure this out," Austin had assured me gently. "And neither are you."

As for me, I was keeping busy. 'Work' around the house consisted of everything I'd said and more, including painting, redesigning, and putting the place together. The house was bigger and brighter now, with more powerful bulbs and accent lamps that lit up every room with a warm, welcoming light. I'd ordered chairs, tables, rugs. Cabinets and cases and shelves. And of course I'd painted... I'd painted every room and every ceiling — including the guys' bedrooms.

I'd even cleaned out and refurbished the old fireplace, which had apparently been used at one time to heat the entire house. It was a big hit the very first time I lit it; everyone retired to the living room to eat dinner while watching the flames.

There was a computer in the corner of the den, hooked up to the internet through an encrypted VPN. It turned out Austin was the technical guy, and he maintained the cameras and alarm systems as well. He'd been the one who tapped into Connor's security system, where they'd all taken turns watching me. And watching me. And watching me...

Anything I wanted, I ordered. Anything I needed to see firsthand, I was driven into town. The guys took turns watching over me, sometimes two at a time while the third one was out. It was their only stipulation: that I never be permitted to be alone. That, and the phone they made me carry with me at all times. It had no contacts on it other than them, but it allowed them to pinpoint my location and get in touch with me whenever they wanted.

It was strange at first, not having my old life. But as time went on, I realized just how disconnected from the world I really was. I had no family, no job, no boss. Any friends I had were work friends from the casino. Strangely enough, even after three weeks away I still didn't miss them.

"We need to go out," I said, time and time again. "You guys have to take me to dinner, or a maybe a bar, or maybe—"

"Too dangerous," they'd always reply. "These are places where the men looking for you will expect you to turn up. Places they'll have paid people to be watching for you, people ready to call them in at a moment's notice."

That part sucked, always having to stay at 'home'. My only consolation was to keep telling myself it was temporary. The guys were making some headway, even if it was slow going. They were learning more about the type of organization that had showed up at my house that night, and none of the news was good.

"They're military," Austin said one night, clear out of the blue. "And there's a good chance Connor found out about

47

something he *shouldn't* have..."

It made me angry, to the point of tears. Tears I couldn't show however, because I didn't want to run the risk of looking weak. Of looking unable to handle anything they threw my way.

Instead I cried at night, into my pillow. Tears of fury and frustration that, when sleep finally took me, always ended up resulting in some very bad dreams.

Still, I grew closer with each of them as time went on. Austin and I bonded over all things tech, the two of us setting up a killer house stereo system that made me a little frightened to tell them how much I'd paid. Maddox and I shared our deep love for Connor, trading stories about my brother one for one. He loved hearing what Connor was like during our childhood and teenage years. I enjoyed laughing at all the funny stuff he did in the Navy, from playing pranks on guys in his unit to some of the more personal details about my sibling I never really knew.

As for Kane... he and I somehow shared an even deeper, more intimate connection. He talked a lot less than the others, so when he did speak his words carried a lot more weight to them. Whenever we were alone, whatever we were doing, we seemed to communicate on some silent, personal level. There were layers of similarity between us — especially amongst our childhoods — that bonded Kane and I. Sharing the affliction of insomnia as well, it was something we talked about in the wee hours of the morning, on more than a few sleepless nights.

In time the guys went from treating me as a little sister (Connor's little sister at least) to seeing me as more of a roommate and an equal. The wide personal berth they gave me at first was shrinking fast, too. We'd pass each other in the halls wearing less and less clothing, the guys mumbling an apology here and there for being shirtless, or wearing boxer shorts, or even a towel.

And eventually the apologies dropped off too, as even *I* started doing it.

For me it was no big deal; we all shared the same bathroom, so a little skin was practically unavoidable. And physically, there was absolutely *nothing* wrong with my roommates either. On the contrary, all three men were gorgeously built, with lean, powerful bodies perfected by years of the toughest physical training on the planet. They'd converted part of the den into a home gym — the one spot in the whole house I wasn't allowed to re-arrange or remodel. And each of them went through a daily exercise and weight-lifting regimen that made me tired just *watching* them.

And damn, did I love watching them...

It was yet another inevitability; my own attraction to *them*, rearing its ugly head. I was trapped alone in a house with three beautiful men, all ripped and shredded, all built in the most Adonis-like fashion. So if I couldn't help drooling over Maddox's washboard abs? Over Kane's magnificent chest and shoulders, or Austin's strong arms and delicious olive skin?

Well, a girl really couldn't really be *blamed.*

Ten

DALLAS

I dreamed, and in my dream I was back at home. I was young again. Maybe eight or nine. My house was warm and inviting, and somehow filled with all sorts of people I didn't know.

Everyone was talking and laughing, only not with me. And no matter how much I searched, no matter which rooms I wormed my way into, I couldn't find my mother, nor father, nor Connor as well.

I went deeper, further into the heart of my childhood home, and things began to change. Person by person the faces disappeared, the strangers fading away with every step until only their voices remained.

And then their voices went too... and I was utterly and completely alone.

A light caught my eye, and I found myself staring through a window that shouldn't be there. It was less of a window and more a shimmering pool of liquid darkness, filled edge to edge with a billion, twinkling stars.

I saw bright stars. Endless stars, stretching in every direction. But then the stars disappeared too. One by one they all blinked away, whole fields at once, until in the end I was staring at nothing.

In my dream I turned, and my home was gone also. Everything had become a void. A cold, limitless void of pure dark nothing... and when I opened my mouth to scream, the blackness poured into my soul.

DALLAS!

Something hissed my name, so cold and sinister it rippled every square inch of my skin with instant goosebumps. I woke up frozen and shivering, my skin cool to the touch.

It's only a dream, that's all.

I lay there for several long moments, staring at the ceiling, trying to convince myself. Then, teeth practically chattering, I gathered the blanket around myself and sat up.

A dream, or maybe the wind.

Sleep was no longer an option. Not tonight. Maybe not all week, if I was doomed to have nightmares like this...

I jerked my head toward a sound — the wind, rattling my window. I could hear it shrieking loudly outside. Swirling and screaming, against the glass.

A few steps later I was out in the hall, which seemed somehow even colder than the bedroom. I was dragging my blanket. Making my way toward the staircase, my body and mind now fully awake.

Maybe the fire's not out.

It was only one o'clock in the morning. If there were still embers, maybe I could resurrect it. I could curl up on the couch. Try to get comfortable enough to—

My body froze mid-step. Deep in my chest, my heart stopped and then started again.

Someone was standing at the window.

"K—Kane?"

He was at the far end of the hall, staring out into the pale blue darkness. He wore loose-fitting sweatpants. And nothing else.

I held one hand against my thumping chest. "You scared the shit out of me."

He turned as I approached, moving to stand next to him. Then he went back to staring, as the wind howled outside.

"Big storm, huh?"

The massive SEAL nodded, scratching at his chin. Almost on cue a gust of wind whipped up. It rattled the window at its seams, throwing a wave of sand against the glass.

"This reminds me of the dust storms we used to have," he said plainly. "Fierce ones, back in Afghanistan." He was silent for a few seconds. "Somalia too."

I slid next to him, clutching my blanket around my chin. Moving mechanically I offered him one end, and he took it.

"Thanks," he said, sliding one big arm around me. Between the cold, and my lingering nightmare, his touch felt immeasurably good. A moment later I was in the crook of his arm. His bare chest was wonderfully warm.

"Cold night," I said. "This house is drafty."

"It is."

The sand swirled outside, forming tiny dust-devils that danced themselves into existence and fell just as quickly apart. Against the moonlit landscape, the whole thing looked oddly beautiful.

"Can't sleep?" I asked numbly.

"No," he admitted. Then, after a very long pause: "Bad dreams."

I nodded gravely. With Maddox or Austin, I would've needed more. I would've asked all about the details of the dream, and maybe even told them about mine.

Not with Kane, though. Between he and I, neither of us needed to say a word. Instead we just stood there in silence.

Outside, the sand was blowing so much it was difficult to see the horizon, even in the moonlight. The house we lived in was turn-of-last century, at the end of a long, nearly abandoned block. It was a neighborhood that had seen its glory days come and go already, and was now deep in decline. Most of the properties nearby had already been torn down.

"Sleep with me."

The words were simple. They dropped from my lips without thought.

Kane shifted from one foot to the other, then stared down into my eyes. An entire sea of information passed between us, silently, wordlessly...

"Come on," I said, slipping my hand into his. I pulled

him gently in the direction of his bedroom, and he followed.

"Let's keep each other warm."

Eleven

DALLAS

The world beneath Kane's blankets was soft and warm, the presence of his body overwhelmingly reassuring. We were wrapped up in each other's arms. Face to face in the night-blue shadows, basking in our combined body heat.

"This is nice," I breathed, snuggling into him.

He grunted his agreement, sliding one big leg between mine. It was a little crazy, how there seemed to be no barriers between us. How easily we'd become totally intimate, in both physical and emotional ways.

"So..." I whispered. "Am I everything you thought I'd be?"

From his pillow Kane raised an eyebrow.

"In the flesh," I said, poking him. "After watching me for a whole *year* on all those cameras... I was wondering if maybe you—"

Kane's lips closed over mine, and suddenly we were

kissing. Him kissing me. Me kissing *back*. Our bodies writhing together, skin against skin. Our mouths churning, rolling passionately against one another...

Dallas!

His body shifted, and suddenly he was kissing me hard and deep. The instant passion and chemistry was incredible. I could feel the warmth of his chest, pressing against mine. His lips moving insistently, parting my own to make room for his tongue...

Should you really be doing this?

I accepted it into my mouth willingly, even hungrily, sliding my own tongue against his. I moaned softly into his mouth as his hand slid downward, piercing the waistband of my own comfy sleep pants. His palm was big and rough. The contrast was amazing as it slid over one warm globe of my ass...

Mmmmmmm...

Kane's other hand moved up to caress my face, sweeping my hair gently away so he could continue kissing me properly. The hand on my ass was now five individual fingers, clenching and kneading my soft, supple flesh. His touch was commanding and insistent. Deliciously possessive. In response I squirmed even harder into his chest, relishing in the size and power of his massive pectorals.

This is crazy.

It was crazy. It was even *worse* than crazy, because I knew with absolutely certainty I was about to make a colossal mistake.

There are three of them, Dallas. Three.

Kane's fingers probed upward, slipping along my lower back and over my hip. Then then slid their way downward... and over my taut, trembling stomach...

Three of them in the same house.

At best, I was about to cause huge amounts of resentment and jealousy. At worst, I'd be driving a wedge between three men who were forever connected as brothers. A wedge that might even hurt their bond. A wedge that could—

"Ohhhh..."

I gasped as Kane's hand slipped between my legs. One of his fingers pulled my thong to the side. The others...

The others found my warm, wet slit.

Oh God *that's good...*

It was too late. Too late to go back. I'd been without a boyfriend for way too long, sexually frustrated to the point of bursting. I'd lost everything in the fire, including my toys. And for the better part of the last month, I'd been surrounded by three of the most handsome, gorgeous, well-muscled—

"I've wanted you," Kane grunted into my ear, "since the first time I saw you..."

Two thick fingers slid beautifully into me. Or was it one? Jesus, his hands were so big I couldn't even tell.

"Oh yeah?" I squirmed.

He nodded, chewing on my shoulder. Pumping me with his hand. Filling me over and over with those thick, wonderful digits. Curling them gently, to brush my G-spot.

"H—Holy shit..."

My hands clawed the sheets on either side of my body. I was absolutely drenched.

"Holy... holy..."

It was unbelievable, how quickly I'd reached the point of no return. How fast I'd gone from kissing to grinding to totally losing it.

Oh my GOD!

My orgasm usually started in my belly, fluttering its way upward and expanding through my body as I got more and more turned on. Only not now. Not this time.

"*FUUUUUCK....*"

This time my climax surged up like a rogue wave, crashing over me in a split second of pure, white-hot euphoria.

"OH FUCKKKK!"

Kane rolled into me, clamping one giant hand over my mouth to keep me silent. It only made me *hotter.* I bit down against his palm, hard enough to hurt but not break the skin. His eyes flared. They found mine, and we locked gazes, both of us on exactly the same page as to what needed to happen.

"Be quiet," he growled into my face. "Unless you want the others in here."

I nodded numbly, my pussy still contracting around his thrusting, probing fingers. I was at the tail end of a colossal orgasm. Still rolling my hips, grinding down hard into his hand.

Fuck fuck fuck fuck...

His knuckles brushed against my clit with every movement. Over and over they sent delicious aftershocks, rocketing upward and into the pleasure centers of my brain.

Jesus Christ, Dallas...

I reached for him, and my hand closed over something big and warm and hard. Somehow he was already naked. Either he'd kicked off his sweats and wasn't wearing any underwear, or—

Oh... oh wow...

Kane yanked off my bottoms as I stroked him. Tip to base, his cock was long and thick and absolutely incredible.

He's going to hurt you.

Part of me actually wanted him to. The other part somehow knew he'd be gentle.

This... this is—

Kane rolled onto me, pushing my thighs apart easily with one massive knee. He was between my legs now. Ready to take me. I was rubbing the bulbous head of his massive cock up and down my molten furrow, staring down at it in wonder.

It was so *big.* And I was so fucking wet...

The hand over my mouth slid to my cheek. Kane leaned down, pushing his forehead against mine. His eyes were impossibly dark, with long, sweeping lashes.

"Is this what you want?"

His irises were locked onto mine. He was looking into me. Looking *through* me, as if seeing my soul.

"*Yes,*" I whispered.

Our lips brushed and he shifted forward, pushing

slowly inside me. I could feel the head of his manhood, engorged and throbbing. His heart beating through it, as he parted my flower.

"*YES...*" I said again, this time with a nod.

Another inch. Another moan. I was in a frenzy now, desperate to have him inside of me. Bucking my hips downward I tried screwing him into me... only it was Kane who had complete and total control.

"Say it," he growled, pinning my shoulders to the bed. "Say that you—"

"*I WANT IT!*" I seethed into his face. "Kane, please! I need—"

The rest of my sentence ended in a gurgle, as he shoved himself all the way in.

It was like being speared to the core.

"OHHHhhhHHHhhhHHHhhh..."

My hands curled instinctively into claws, my fingernails digging into the meat of his massive back. Then he began pumping. Slowly at first, to get me used to his girth, then more rapidly in and out of my body as the entire length of his shaft was soaked with my wetness.

"Oh my *God...*" I cried. Literal tears were forming at the corners of my eyes. "Oh my God, oh my God, oh my God..."

Kane's hand returned, pressing against my lips. Daring me to bite him again as he crushed me deep into the bed, plowing me to tears as he screwed me without mercy.

This... this is...

I could feel him way up inside me, so incredibly deep it almost hurt. Almost, but not quite.

This isn't wrong, this isn't a mistake...

It couldn't possibly be. This was *wonderful*. Like an insatiable itch being *finally* scratched. Like a long thirst being quenched, so fully and satisfyingly my tears were seeping into either side of his pillow.

"Kane..."

I placed his name in my mouth, tasting it on my tongue. It fit him perfectly. His personality, his demeanor... his whole magnificent body.

"Oh *fuck*, Kane..."

I was mumbling into his mouth because he was kissing me again, our tongues dueling hotly as we fucked. And I was kissing him like a *lover* now. The sort of kiss reserved only for someone who's been deep inside you, filling you up, connecting you at the most intimate and irrevocable of all possible levels.

This... is incredible...

My pussy throbbed as he drilled me deep, rocking the bed beneath us. Every thrust drove the air from my lungs. Every kiss put it back. I was whimpering. Gasping. Crying...

I should've been doing this for weeks.

The voice of reason was totally gone now. Gone because I'd told it to fuck off. Gone because, by this point, there was no way either of us could go back.

"Kane..." I gasped. "I—"

He lifted me abruptly and fell back onto the bed,

pulling me on top of him. I was straddling him now. Riding him as hard and deep as I wanted. My mind spun with all new pleasure as I reveled in the control, running my hands over his amazing, rock-hard chest...

I felt a flash of pain. A growing ache, someplace deep inside me, where I knew he'd reached places no one had before. The admission was stark, even humbling. It only made me grind down harder.

"You feel... you feel..."

His hands cupped my breasts, hefting their weight. He held them lovingly for a moment before smoothing his palms over my stiffening nipples. I was super-sensitive there, and the touch sent shivers down my body. I squeezed my thighs together in response, hugging his flanks as he pounded me from beneath.

"so... so fucking..."

I was totally incoherent. Lost in the moment, to the point of delirium. Rather than say anything else I just closed my eyes and let go, savoring in the feel of his hands on my body...

And just as quickly I was turned over. Flipped, roughly, onto my hands and knees...

In a flash Kane grabbed my hips and re-entered me from behind. It felt like the best thing in the whole fucking world.

"Ohhhhhhhhhhh..."

It was primal, the way he took me. Animalistic. He was using his arms every bit as he was using his hips and ass, pulling me back with those great biceps and triceps to meet every gut-churning thrust. It felt even *deeper*, if possible. The penetration even better. He fucked me like that for a long while, bouncing me off the end of his magnificent cock while I grunted and groaned and muttered a stream of unintelligible curses.

Oh my God this is—

I cried out as he wrapped both hands around my chin from behind. Kane pulled back, forcing my head up. Pinning me against him. Dominating me completely...

Suddenly, abruptly, everything stopped.

Kane's ass stopped clenching. His body stopped moving. He held fast to my chin, his cock buried all the way inside me.

Wha—

My eyes flew open. I found myself staring straight ahead...

... to the other end of the room, where two figures were staring back at me in grave disappointment.

Twelve

DALLAS

Maddox and Austin stood half in the shadows, half in the moonlight. I could see their expressions though. I could read their body language, too.

"Goddamn it, Kane."

The four of us remained frozen, all staring at each other. Me with my chin pulled back, on my hands and knees. Kane pressed hard against my body, still buried inside me from behind...

The other two stood there shirtless, wearing only their boxers.

It was like time had stopped.

For several long seconds no one said a word. No one moved, or shifted, or even breathed. It was almost like a spell had been cast, and even the slightest motion might break it and cause the whole thing to just shimmer away.

Then, incredulously...

Kane started pumping me again.

Holy shit.

My body, which had been warm and flush from our lovemaking, remained utterly still. I stayed exactly where I was, staring at Maddox and Austin. Enjoying the gentle bounce of my lover screwing me from behind, even as the rest of the room remained cloaked in a strange, uncanny silence.

Maddox's gaze shifted from Kane to me. The movement was almost imperceptible. But I knew it had happened.

Dallas... wait—

Heart racing, blood pumping... I motioned him over.

Dallas!

It was the tiniest of movements. A shift of the eyes, an upward jerk of my chin. But he moved. Slowly, unhesitatingly, he walked his way over to the edge of the bed.

Behind me, Kane kept sawing away. He let go of my chin, but kept one hand still wrapped in my hair. The other fell over my hip, squeezing gently, guiding me back and forth against him.

Maddox reached the edge of the bed, where I was at eye level with his crotch. I could see a bulge there, tenting out the material. Struggling against the silk-looking fabric, as he stood there transfixed.

I reached out with one hand... and slipped my wrist through the hole in front. My hand closed over something warm and heavy. He groaned softly as I pulled it out.

Holy shit Dallas...

His cock was beautiful. Long and straight and perfectly cut, I stroked it up and down a few times, getting the feel for it. Staring up into his ice blue eyes, I brought it slowly in the direction of my mouth.

"Fuck..."

Maddox's voice cracked as I closed my lips around him. I heard a sharp intake of air. A hiss of pleasure.

No fucking way you're doing this!

Once again, the voice in my head was wrong. I *was* doing it. And I was going to enjoy it, too.

I sighed softly as Kane picked up the pace again. He'd slowed down temporarily, giving me time to adjust. Allowing Maddox and I our moment together; the eye contact, the physical and even emotional connection as the gravity of what we were about to do actually sank in.

You're fucking two guys. Two guys at once.

The voice in my head was right. I definitely was. And it was just as amazing as I thought it would be. Every bit as arousing and sensual and yes, even beautiful, as I'd fantasized it *could* be... through all the years I'd wondered and imagined it.

Kane rolled his knuckles, his fist going tight in my hair. I felt wonderfully dirty. Incredibly arousing as he applied a gentle forward pressure, pushing my head down around his friend's cock.

Christ, have they done this before?

It didn't matter to me either way. Deep down I'd always *wanted* to try it. I even had a boyfriend who suggested the idea a few years back, toying with the idea several times while fucking my brains out.

Only he'd never followed through. He always chickened out. Our quest for a third had died before it even began, and no matter how many times we screwed while talking about it, the whole thing had always remained a fantasy.

But not now...

No, definitely not. Right now I was living the moment. Enjoying the naughtiness of one lover drilling my pussy while another slid down my throat. I was being slowly spitroasted; the terminology being something with which I was oddly familiar. Spitted between between two amazingly hot men, with incredibly hot—

Maddox pulled himself from my mouth with a wet plop. I looked up, wondering if they were going to switch positions...

... and found myself staring straight into Austin's blue-green eyes.

AUSTIN!

I couldn't believe I'd forgotten about him! But in all the excitement...

My third sexy SEAL had removed his own boxers. He stood just to the side, slowly stroking his smooth, flawless shaft. His cock was dusk-colored, like his mocha skin. Thick and heavy and just as gorgeous as he was.

I shifted in his direction. Maddox stepped to the side, making room for him.

"Holy fuck, Dallas..."

His voice was deeper than normal, practically choking

with lust. He'd been watching us fuck. Waiting patiently for his own turn. And here I was, accommodating him. Accommodating all *three* of them...

"You want her on her back?"

A conversation was occurring somewhere behind me; Kane and Maddox. Discussing me. Deciding my fate...

"No. I want to fuck her just like this."

I felt the bed shift abruptly, and then it was Maddox's hands on my hips. He pushed his saliva-coated shaft against my glistening entrance, and with a single thrust of his hips, plunged himself all the way into me.

"MMMmmMMMmmm..."

If I was trying to form a word, it was lost around Austin. His cock was deep in my throat, gliding smoothly against the back of my tongue. I was sucking hard, keeping my lips tight. Trying to make it good for him.

Then Maddox began pounding me hard from behind, and my whole body went limp with pleasure.

Thirteen

KANE

It wasn't something I'd planned, it just sort of happened. Only it had happened so loudly that it drew the attention of the others, despite it being nearly two in the morning.

And now it was happening with *them*, as well.

I'd thought about being with her a thousand times. Played it over and over in my head, trying to picture how it might go down. At times it was romantic; the culmination of a courtship or a carefully-built connection. But other times...

Other times it had been just like this. Raw and instinctual and full of irrepressible lust.

I watched her now, stretched out cat-like across my bed. Face down, ass up. Screwing her magnificent rear-end backwards in slow, churning circles that made Maddox's eyes roll back into his thick skull...

God, it was so fucking *hot.*

Well, you sure wanted her, the voice in my head chimed sarcastically. *Now you got her.*

Yeah, I guess I did. But so did Maddox. And Austin...

All three of us. Holy shit.

It was a mess for sure. Yet at the same time, it also solved a lot of problems. For one, I wouldn't have to hide what we'd done. I'd been already dreading waking up and keeping a straight face, especially with Dallas. It would've been hard if not impossible to keep the guys in the dark. To exclude them on what we'd done.

Well they're included now, that's for sure.

They shifted again, and Austin moved to take Maddox's place. This time they rolled her onto her back. Dallas's luscious blonde hair spilled over the bed, her face all flush, her lips plump and wet and beautiful.

I bent to kiss them again. To feel the heat from them against my own. Her legs spread wide, and Austin entered her easily as she yelped into my mouth. But we kept on going. Kept on kissing and moaning and sharing the same breath.

How many times had I imagined her in my bed? Hell, I couldn't even count. I thought about all the long, sleepless nights sitting in front of the monitors. Countless hours switching constantly from view to view, outside to inside, looking just as intently at her as I had for signs of trouble.

You fell for her, Kane. Just like that.

Yeah, just like that. Staring at her remotely, even following her to work from time to time. Watching her deal blackjack to thousands of strangers. Seeing her come home alone, sometimes to cuddle up with a book, or to sit in front of the television. And other times...

Other times we'd caught her in more intimate moments. Dallas Winters was the furthest thing from modest, and liked to prance half-naked through every room in her home. And I'd watched. I'd done it unashamedly, unabashedly. I'd done it knowing she was Connor's sister, but unlike the others that somehow didn't bother me.

Maybe that's because I saw her for what she was: *a woman.* A strong, beautiful woman, as sexy as she was independent, and I wasn't about to feel the least bit bad about any attraction I had for her.

"Mmmmm..."

She twisted sideways, as Austin really started nailing her. Then, suddenly, her mouth was on me. It felt incredible, looking down and seeing her beautiful face. Watching her suck on me eagerly, sliding her tongue along the underside of my shaft and winking at me when she finally caught my eye.

God, she's perfect.

I held her steady as Austin fucked her, pinning her writhing, feminine body between us. Her skin was like poured milk. Smooth and perfect. We took turns sweeping her hair back from her face, or adjusting her hips, or whatever we needed to do to take the most possible pleasure in her.

And we were *giving* her pleasure too. I could see it in her half-lidded eyes, all glazed over and full of wanton abandon. She was enjoying this every bit as much as we were, as if she'd done it before, or had been wanting it her whole life. She'd also been the one who motioned them over...

It went on forever, or at least it sure seemed that way.

The wind howled and the skies remained dark and the three of us kept on screwing her, kissing her, devouring her body hungrily. Dallas responded in kind, refusing to be broken. She gave back everything that she got, no matter how many times we swapped places or changed positions. She bucked back against us as we took turns on her, filling her warmth and wetness from both eager ends.

Maddox finished first, losing himself down her hot, greedy throat. I felt a flare of arousal watching her swallow him down, pumping him with her fist, draining him of every last drop. At long last he collapsed backward, totally spent, his lips forming a curse and a grin.

Austin followed almost immediately, pushed over the edge by what we'd just seen. He spilled himself over her beautiful body, spraying her breasts and her neck. Ultimately he allowed her to take over with one slender hand, directing where his come went, and ending by smearing it sexily along her pink areola.

Dallas had one gorgeous leg over my shoulder, and I was balls-deep in her heated folds. I was already close. With the others done and falling away, I had her full attention now. She stared up at me with a wicked, sensuous grin.

Inside me, she mouthed silently.

Holy shit, that was all it took. Her pretty face looking up at me. Those penetrating eyes, locked on mine. The idea of going off *inside* her, of finally exploding after all this time...

"UNGHH!"

I slammed myself home one last time, then erupted like an angry volcano. Dallas's blue eyes went wide as she felt it; my hot come, splashing inside her. Painting the walls of her womb, filling her with a steady, euphoric stream of my warm, runny seed, as I grunted and groaned and craned my face toward the sky.

"FUCK!"

It was white-hot heaven — a million brilliant explosions, — all going off at once. An entire universe of want and need and desire... the culmination of a year's-long obsession, finally come to fruition between her beautiful, outstretched legs.

I collapsed forward on top of her, still coming and coming. Filling her to overflowing, until I could feel our combined wetness soaking against us both. Dallas responded by throwing her arms around me and screwing me back. By enmeshing the fingers of both hands against the back of my head, pulling me into her, whispering so hotly in my ear the whole time I thought I'd go out of my mind with pleasure.

"Yes, baby..." she murmured. "*Fill me up.* Mmmmm... that's it baby. Just like that..."

I didn't care if the others were watching. That one moment was ours, and ours alone. I could feel her body squirming beneath me, her pussy contracting around my cock, milking me for all I was worth.

"YES..."

My vision blurred, the grey edges closing in all around me. I finished in a haze, vaguely aware of Dallas kissing my face. She was holding me now, one hand on each of my cheeks. Adjusting me so that I could look into her eyes, or rather, so she could see straight into mine.

"You okay?" she smiled mischievously.

I nodded, numbly.

"We uh... might've lost you for a minute there."

In the background, I could hear Maddox and Austin chuckle. They might as well have been clapping, I was fine either way. A few cloudy seconds went by, and I was dimly aware of them filing out of the room.

"That was pretty fucking amazing," Dallas breathed, flexing her thighs on either side of me. She kissed me once more, this time on the forehead. "But I think I'm ready to sleep now."

Fourteen

DALLAS

"Morning!"

I walked straight into the kitchen, past Maddox, past Kane. Right past Austin, cleaning his cereal bowl in the sink already.

It was like ripping off a band-aid.

"Umm... Morning," replied Maddox weakly. I noticed his body language had changed already. He looked stiff and uncomfortable as he held up a pan. "Did you want eggs?"

"If you're making them, sure."

I grabbed a mug and poured myself a nice cup of coffee. *Real* coffee. Freshly-ground and steaming, dripped from an actual coffee maker, selected by me.

"We could do bacon too," Austin said hesitantly. "If you were into that."

"Bacon would be cool."

I slid into my usual chair, pinning my hair up as I

went. All three of them were looking down now. Looking up. Looking anywhere except at me.

"So are we gonna talk about it?"

My words dropped loudly in the silent room. They looked even more uncomfortable, if that were possible. Only now they were turning red too.

"Talk about what?"

"About last night," I said, kicking my feet up. "You guys ever do that before?"

I'd decided upon waking there were two ways this could go: the awkward way, or the *really* awkward way. I wasn't sure which one was which, but this path was definitely more my style.

"Do wha—"

"Tag team a girl," I said, cutting Austin off abruptly. "You know, together."

The kitchen couldn't have been more silent if the world outside had ended. For a long while, no one spoke.

"Have *you* ever done anything like that?" asked Maddox.

"No," I answered with a shrug. "But I'd lying if I said I hadn't wanted to. It's obviously been a fantasy of mine... although I always kinda figured it would happen with *two* guys before it happened with three."

Austin let out a short, nervous laugh. "You uh, seemed pretty okay with it."

"Hey," I said. "When life gives you lemons..."

Maddox started cracking eggs into the pan. "We weren't exactly making lemonade last night," he smirked.

"No," I agreed. "Definitely not. But when life gives you three hot roommates who sleep practically naked, and two of them happen to burst into the bedroom while you're fucking the third..."

Kane coughed over his mug, nearly spitting his own coffee all over the floor. Damn, I was foolish to be nervous. I was actually enjoying this.

"Yeah, well Kane fucked up last night," said Maddox, his eyes flitting over to deliver his friend an admonishing glance. "He broke our one rule. The only rule."

I raised an eyebrow. "And that is?"

"We vowed not to get involved with you," he replied. "All three of us."

"Oh," I said, having trouble suppressing a grin.

They looked at each other again, maybe for help. It was kind of cute.

"When you moved in here," Maddox went on, "we all made a vow that none of us would hit on you. None of us would even *flirt* with you. Certainly none of us would ever—"

"Fuck me?" I asked over my mug.

The three of them went silent again. Austin looked like he was trying to swallow a baseball. Maddox was overcooking the eggs. Kane however, appeared as if he were enjoying the conversation every bit as much as I was. Maybe more.

"He should've left you alone," said Maddox,

scrambling for a spatula. "He should never have—"

"Technically," Kane interrupted, "I *kept* my vow." His eyes shifted my way. "Dallas was the one who invited herself into *my* bed last night."

They looked at me and I nodded. "Guilty as charged."

"Still," Austin broke in. "You didn't have to—"

"Look," I said, putting my feet down again. "You guys are soldiers. SEALs. Brothers in arms. You've endured grueling physical training together, seen combat together. You even live together, sharing the same home, the same expenses, even the same common goals."

Austin squinted at me. It occurred to me suddenly he'd forgotten all about the bacon.

"What's your point?"

"My point," I went on, "is that you boys share *everything.*"

My emphasis on the last word dropped like a hammer. The only sound in the kitchen was the pop and hiss of eggs, bubbling.

I shrugged at them. "And now you've shared *me.*"

It was more than a little insane, how logical I'd just made it all sound. Hell, it even seemed rationalized in my own head. Granted, I'd had some time to think about it. Some very dreamy, very fun recollection time, while drifting off to sleep, staring at the ceiling.

"No one did anything wrong here," I said, standing up. "In fact, everything felt kinda... *right.*"

I strutted across the kitchen in my little sleep shorts,

which rode way too high on my legs. The T-shirt I was wearing only came down halfway. It showed off the flat of my stomach. My belly button...

Of course I'd worn these things on purpose, before coming downstairs. But they didn't know that.

Or maybe they did.

"Maybe last night was a one-shot deal," I shrugged casually. "The four of us blew off some steam. Had a little fun."

Kane cleared his throat noisily. "A *little* fun?"

"Okay, a LOT of fun," I smiled. "More fun that a poor homeless girl and three Navy SEALS probably *should* have together. But then again... maybe not. Maybe last night was just what we needed. And maybe it was the beginning of something else."

I approached Austin, using one finger to trace a slow line down his chest. His eyes followed like he was in a trance.

"Something... else?" asked Maddox.

I nodded and bounced over to where Kane was sitting. "Mmm-Hmm," I said. "Something cool. Something fun. Something... just between *us.*"

Spinning on my heel, I let myself fall into Kane's lap. His arms slid around me protectively. I squirmed a bit, grinding my ass into his crotch for a few seconds, before bouncing up again.

"Maybe we'll even do it *again*," I said tantalizingly. "That is, you know... if you guys are *into* it."

All eyes were predictably on me. They crawled up my

legs, panned over my stomach. Followed my every bouncy step. Lingered on every curve.

"Of course we *could* go back to enforcing your vow. That's another option."

Kane reached for me, but I twisted away. I slid over to Maddox now. Running my hand up his shirt I could feel his heart beating thunderously, deep in his chest.

"No need to answer now," I said with a wink. "You guys take some time, think it over. But at least now you know *my* position. You know where *I* stand."

My 'position' had been decided two minutes after slipping out of Kane's bedroom last night. I could still feel their hands on my body, smell the scent of them on my skin. I could feel them inside me! Spreading me open. Filling me up...

Pinning me between them. Crushing me...

There was no doubt in my mind. I wanted it *again*.

Deftly I plucked the pan from between Maddox's fingers. Dumping the burnt mess straight in the garbage, I grabbed a towel and began wiping it out.

"For now though," I said, turning my ass on them. "You'd better let *me* make the eggs."

Fifteen

DALLAS

The guys disappeared for the rest of the day, giving me time to rest and relax. It also gave them time to process what I'd said, and to think about how they wanted to handle our future, all beneath the same roof.

The good news was there didn't appear to be any jealousy, at least outwardly. My biggest worry had been that one or more of them actually 'liked' me, and considering what we'd done, might now be resentful of the others. The last thing I wanted was to come between them. Except physically, of course.

Yet that was always the danger when guys got as close as they were. These men were brothers, in every sense of the word. Brothers fought over things all the time, and I'd vowed it wasn't going to be like that. If what we'd done was actually going to happen again, there was only way to handle it.

I'd make myself available to *all* three of them... or none of them at all.

The other thing I'd been worried about was them treating me differently because I was Connor's sister. That in some strange way, bedding me was a betrayal to my brother's memory. I was glad that didn't appear to be the case either, because I knew these men loved Connor as much as I did. They respected and admired him enough to dedicate the last year of their lives to protecting me, even after he was gone.

How could I not love that about them?

Love.

It was such a strange word, and one with which I was wholly unfamiliar. I loved my parents of course, and I loved my brother more than any other man in my entire life. But as far as relationships went, I'd never truly felt *love* before. I'd had short term boyfriends and even a couple of long term ones. Everything from fuck-buddies to friends with benefits to one lucky guy I actually celebrated a two-year anniversary with.

But it was never *love.*

I thought about all this as I soaked in the claw-footed tub, watching the steam slowly wind its way toward the ceiling. The water was so hot I could barely stand it — one more degree and it would scald my skin. That was the way I liked it though. Showers too.

These guys really loved Connor.

Absently, I rubbed my brother's pendant with my thumb. They did love him, and perhaps that was why I was so attracted to them, even beyond the obvious sense. Physically they were gorgeous, each in his own way. Maddox was the blond-maned hot guy I'd always been attracted to, with abdominals I could get lost in for days. Austin was dark and handsome, as clean-cut and beautiful as a man could be. Even

Kane, with his size and strength and brooding dark nature had me indescribably drawn to him. The way he'd just seized control had me more turned on than I'd ever been in my life, even before the others had joined in.

But beyond the physical, I could feel an emotional connection forming there too. An invisible bond between the three of them and myself. A special kinship... all because of Connor.

I sighed and lifted one leg, running the soapy loofah down over my calf. The guys had turned their noses up at my loofah, immediately upon finding it hanging from the shower spigot. I'd had to explain to them what it was, laughing the whole time.

They're so raw, I thought to myself. *So rough around the edges.*

Maybe that's why I liked them so much. I'd dated men... and I'd dated *men*. The three guys I was living with now were definitely the latter. As soldiers they were polished, disciplined, deadly. But as men...

As men they were big beautiful lumps of clay, ready to be molded by my overly-eager hands.

Yeah, right.

I laughed out loud again in the tub, then wondered if I were going insane. Maybe, I thought. It was definitely possible.

Then again, when you'd lost as much as I had, in such a short amount of time? You had to take whatever pleasures you could.

And I *oh so* planned on taking my pleasures.

Gradually my thoughts drifted back to last night. What the four of us had done together had been unspeakably hot. It would live in my memory forever; the pale blue shadows, the howl of the sandstorm outside...

The three musclebound military men, slamfucking you into oblivion...

Yeah, that too. Definitely that.

The whole thing had been so dirty, so naughty, so unexpected. And it had been *slutty*, too. But slutty in a gloriously powerful way.

They worshiped you. Treated you like a goddess.

They had, really. All three of them had been dominating yet caring. Strong and insistent, yet gentle where it mattered. They'd taken *care* of me. Made sure I was alright, all throughout our filthy little act, and they'd brought me off at least four separate times that I could count, to boot.

I dropped the loofah and let my hand slip beneath the water. It slid down my stomach, my breath catching in my throat as it wandered into the tender valley between my thighs.

You fucked all three of them.

Yes, I had. And it was incredible.

One by one. Two at a time...

I closed my eyes, picturing how I must've looked. Wishing there had been a mirror in Kane's room, so I could've watched myself writhing between them. I wanted a better visual of their bodies clenching and pumping. I needed to *see* myself being screwed hotly from both ends.

Lazily I dragged my middle finger up and down my

warm slit. Yes, maybe it *was* slutty. But slutty in all the best ways.

"Mmmmm..."

My slow purr of satisfaction echoed against the white-tiled walls. I continued exploring myself, delving deeper. My breathing growing more rapid as the heel of my thumb bumped tortuously against my aching clit...

BEEP BEEP!

I sat up at the distant chime of the front door. The double-beep indicating that someone had come in after successfully entering the alarm code.

"Dallas?"

"Up here!"

Maddox's voice was preceded by his heavy footfalls on the staircase. Or bootfalls. Or whatever they were.

"Oh, there you are."

I'd left the bathroom door open intentionally. No need for modesty, really. Not anymore. Not after last night.

Hell, walking around the house in my underwear was back on the menu too.

My back was to the doorway when I felt his presence. I craned my neck over the edge of the tub and smiled at him upside-down.

"What's up?"

He paused awkwardly, trying not to stare. Then he realized he *could* stare, and I saw his eyes begin to wander.

"We uh... we need you downstairs. To talk about stuff."

Shit.

"Is this about last night?" I asked hesitantly. I was hoping against hope they hadn't changed their minds.

Maddox thought for a moment, then his whole expression changed. "Oh no, no! Not about that," he said hastily. "We wanted to talk you about other stuff."

"Other stuff..."

"Yes," he said, taking a step forward. Damn, he looked good. Smelled good, too. Camos and a white T-shirt. Sharp. Simple. Handsome.

"It's about what we *found*," he said, his voice sounding suddenly excited.

My eyes went wide. I reached for a towel.

"It's about Connor."

Sixteen

DALLAS

My hair was still wet as I approached the kitchen table, wearing nothing but a soft terrycloth bathrobe. Little by little, I was acquiring things again. A good robe was just another one of my creature comforts.

"You umm, wanna get changed or something?" Austin said. He gave me a quick look, up and down. "We can wait if you'd like to—"

"Nah. I'm good."

The three of them were at the table, sitting around a laptop. Maddox had some papers in front of him. Photographs too.

"Alright," he said, "so you already know we've been trying to figure out who trashed your house."

I nodded, scooting forward. It was dark outside, late already. Even so I could hear coffee brewing. I could smell it too.

Good boys.

"After the shit-show at your place," he went on, "we checked the all obvious places for loose ends. Police reports. Ambulance and fire. Austin scoured the hospital records for any signs someone might've been brought in injured, maybe with a couple of bullet holes or something equally awesome." He shook his head. "But no, we got blanked on all of that."

"Too bad," I agreed.

"Yeah. That was a longshot, but we had to check it. These guys were pros. They had vests and ballistic armor, probably the latest carbon-fiber flex."

I had no idea what any of that meant, but I got the gist. I nodded for him to go on.

"So we went back and reviewed all the surveillance footage," Austin said, taking over. "The stuff that happened inside the house we obviously missed, because they cut the power from the pole on the way in. But here, check this out."

He punched a few keys on the keyboard, and a series of still photos popped out. I recognized them as an outside view of my house. A street view. At night.

"It was too dark to see much, but we did get a partial license plate." He pointed at very large, very dark SUV. "Riiiight... here."

I squinted hard. I could barely make out anything.

"I can't—"

Austin punched another key, and everything brightened. I could see the dark edges of lettering now. Numbers.

"It's a military plate," said Maddox. "These were military vehicles."

I felt a slow, unpleasant pull in the pit of my stomach. My face must've gone somber too.

"So... Connor was killed by his own people?"

"Well let's not jump to *that* conclusion," Austin said hastily. "All we know for sure is the trucks were military. Based out of Nellis." He laid down a few photographs. Black SUV's, exactly like the ones in the surveillance images.

I was still confused.

"Kane's got connections that pulled vehicle logs for us," said Maddox. "None of these trucks were checked out that night. Which means the logs were scrubbed, or the checkouts were never logged at all."

"Which means someone's covering shit up," I said icily.

"Yes."

They were silent for a moment, as Kane poured me a mug. He set the sugar and cream down before me, and gave me a spoon.

"Did I ever tell you you're the best?" I quipped.

"No," he said, sinking back into his chair. "But I assumed as much."

Austin bumped him with one leg. Maddox smirked before going on.

"So now let's talk about Connor..."

I stopped mid-sip. I sat up straighter.

"Your brother's personal effects disappeared almost immediately after he went missing," said Maddox. "His phone, his laptop, even his car."

"They took his *car?*" I asked incredulously. "*That* old thing?"

"As his next of kin, didn't you ever wonder what happened to it?"

I shook my head slowly. "I— I just assumed they trashed it. I mean, it was really old."

"Not old," Kane said, folding his arms. "A *classic*. You don't trash a classic."

Shit, he looked almost offended. I shrugged again.

"Anyway, your brother's phone records finally came in," said Austin. "More of Kane's contacts were able to clone a digital copy, backed up just hours before..." He stopped himself just in time. "Before the last recorded instance of use."

He pulled out a smartphone and punched it open. It blinked on, and I gasped as I recognized the splash screen immediately.

It was a picture of Connor and me.

"Is... Is that his phone?"

"Yes and no," said Austin. "It's a *copy* of his phone, scribed onto a SIM card, installed into the same basic model." He slid it my way. "It contains all his information, all his contacts, all his text-messages. All his photos too, in case you wanted them."

There was a lump in my throat. I was definitely going to cry.

"W—Why are you giving it to me?"

"Because you said you wanted in on this, Dallas. You said you wanted to help us."

I swallowed hard, and the tears fell. Somehow this time, it was okay. It wasn't at all like it was the first time, where I was trying not to show weakness in the face of three practical strangers.

No, things were very, very different between us now.

"Take your time," said Maddox, "and go over everything on that device." He reached out and closed one hand gently over mine. "Even if it's hard, Dallas. Even if it hurts. No one knew Connor like you did, not even us. Maybe you can find something we missed. Something important."

I looked at him through glassy eyes. There was no pity in his expression now, no placation. Only sympathy. Sympathy and love.

"O—Okay," I said.

They gave me a moment. Kane gave me a tissue. I took both, gratefully, and blew my nose.

"Finally, you need to know this," said Austin. "According to your brother's phone, he's been out to the desert several times. Out in the *middle* of the desert, where there's nothing to see and no one around."

I glanced up curiously.

"And that's not all," he continued. "Your brother had been using a military-grade app to track transponder codes. And a pair of those transponders are somehow attached to two out of three of these SUV's." He tapped the photographs again. "These vehicles wouldn't normally have transponders, unless someone like Connor *put* them there."

My coffee stared up at me resentfully, totally untouched. None of it made any sense.

"These SUV's have been out in the desert too," Maddox broke in. "And they stopped at exactly the same place your brother did, on all the same dates. At exactly the same times."

Another span of silence settled over the kitchen. All at once my brows came together.

"So what are you saying?" I snapped angrily. "That my brother was *working* with these guys?"

Maddox actually looked disappointed. "Of course not," he said. "We all know Connor would never do anything like that."

The others shifted, nodding fervently. I felt foolish.

"Then what?"

"Just the opposite," Austin chimed in. "That whatever was going on out there, your brother was observing it. Gathering intel on his own. Maybe even getting ready to give that information up."

"Whatever it was," said Maddox. "We're thinking Connor was trying to stop it."

I felt a chill go through my body. My hands started shaking.

"And maybe," Kane added ominously, "that's what got him killed."

Seventeen

DALLAS

They left me alone that night, relatively speaking. We stayed in, tore ravenously through some Italian take-out, and probably ate more than our fill. Then we lounged in front of the television for a while, until one by one, each of my gorgeous SEAL roommates retired to bed.

Well shit, that *wasn't what I expected.*

I was left sitting there on the couch, going over the contents of Connor's phone. Flipping through every single photo a half-dozen times, going all the way back to nearly two years ago and more.

Every smiling photograph of him hurt my heart.

Dammit, Connor.

For the first hour or so I resented him. He'd obviously underestimated the men who'd killed him. As a man, a soldier, a Navy fucking SEAL for shit's sake, he above all people knew the strength and value of a team. I hated him for putting himself out there alone, all by himself, in the godforsaken desert.

Why did *my* brother have to be the righteous one? Couldn't he just have left well enough alone?

It was maddening. I found myself staring at the last known photos of us, back two summers when he'd come home for leave. We'd gone skydiving together — something he'd introduced me to as soon as I was old enough to go. There we were, smiling happily. Still wearing our chutes and harnesses. Giving the thumbs up...

My brother...

My only brother.

The tears flowed, and this time I let them go. It wasn't *his* fault, I finally decided. It was whatever evil had ultimately done this to him.

And whoever the fuck *that* was, they were in for a whole world of pain.

Connor...

I sniffled, wiping fallen tears away from the phone's screen. In the photo I'd stopped on, my brother still looked strong, happy, confident. Totally indestructible.

If only that were true.

No, I finally decided. If my brother was in over his head on something, it just didn't make sense that he wouldn't have gone for help. He would've done *something*. Would have had some kind of safeguard against getting caught, especially if he was driving out into the middle of God-knows-where in order to entrap or expose the people who killed him.

Killed. There. You said finally it.

It was a hard acknowledgment — something I'd been avoiding saying out loud, for fear of what it might mean. Killed meant someone had finally found my brother's Achilles heel. That my older brother's legacy of strength and invincibility had been finally stained by the shadow of something — or someone — who'd gotten the better of him.

Killed meant Connor needed to be *avenged*.

I cried some more, curling into a ball. Pulling my legs up against my chest, I threw the phone to the other side of the couch as if it were made of acid.

"Hey..."

My head snapped up, and there was Maddox. He was kneeling before the couch. Somehow he'd made it across the room without me even knowing it.

"You alright?"

He laid a hand on my shoulder, and once again I didn't see it coming. I shrank back for a split-second, until I realized what it actually was.

"What are you a ninja?" I sniffed.

Maddox only shrugged in the darkness. "Maybe."

His goofy grin was the perfect ice-breaker. It made me laugh. Made me eventually throw my arms around him and hug him, when I saw he'd already stretched his arms out to me.

"Come on," he said. "Let's go."

He took my hand in his, interlacing his fingers between mine. The gesture was simple, but incredibly sweet. Meaningful in ways I didn't immediately realize.

We walked the hall, in the direction of my bedroom.

Before we got there however, he swept me into his.

"Shhh..." he whispered. "We're supposed to be leaving you alone tonight."

I followed him inside, practically tip-toeing as he closed the door. It felt like we were kids again, sneaking around the house during a midnight sleepover.

"Why?" I asked.

Maddox shrugged. "I guess because we didn't want to overwhelm you."

My heart softened. "Awww. That's..."

"Stupid?"

"No, actually it's kinda sweet."

A minute later we were beneath the blankets, skin against skin. Maddox spooned me from behind, making me feel safe and warm and protected, all wrapped up in his two very strong arms.

"You're not the only one who loved Connor," he assured me with a sigh. My eyes grew heavier and heavier as I squirmed into him.

"We all did."

Eighteen

DALLAS

"And I'm telling you, your brother *loved* sushi."

Austin pressed the bar overhead three more times, his shoulders screaming with the exertion. I could tell the last few reps had been painful. It was all worth it though. His delts and trapezius muscles looked pumped and beautiful.

"Connor *hated* fish," I reiterated. "He used to scrape it into a bag under the table, every time my mother made it."

At that, Austin laughed. "You told on him, didn't you?"

"Of course. What else are little sisters for?"

"Tattletale."

"Fuck off."

It was a lot of fun, talking about my brother's life with the people who'd spent the most time with him. No matter how many conversations we had about Connor, I always seemed to be learning something new.

"There's no possible *way* he ate sushi," I said. "Maybe by accident, or—"

"Wanna bet?"

I smirked and took another lunge, letting the weights hang loosely from my arms. My thighs were already burning. The pain actually felt good.

"What exactly are we betting?" I asked slyly.

"You tell me."

Hmmm, I thought to myself. *Now this was getting interesting.*

I grunted through the rest of my set, then stood up with a long exhale. Grabbing one foot and pinning it against my own ass, I stretched my quadriceps one at a time.

"I'll bet you anything that Connor didn't eat raw fish," I said.

Austin stopped rolling his arm in his shoulder socket temporarily. He raised an eyebrow. "Anything I want?"

I rolled my eyes. "Sure."

He put out his hand. I sighed and shook it. It was impossible not to be mesmerized by his upper body. Every inch of the exposed skin filling out his tank top was covered in a thin sheen of sweat.

"Remember," he winked. "You said—"

"Hey!"

We both whirled, to find Maddox hanging in the doorway. He looked rushed. Hurried.

His eyes were solely on Austin.

"We uh... we need to move."

Austin stepped forward without hesitation, not even pausing to grab a towel. It was amazing how fast SEALs could move when they really wanted to. I'd seen Connor do it, and it was always a sharp reminder these men weren't just soldiers.

They were *elite* soldiers.

I cleaned up quickly, and headed into the kitchen. By the time I got there all three of them were suited up and almost ready.

"What the hell is going on?" I asked firmly.

Maddox and Kane shot each other a concerned glance. Austin was busy lacing up his boots.

"You know those transponders we talked about?" said Maddox.

"Yeah?"

"One of them moved."

I flew up the stairs, taking them two at a time. I was back in a flash, wearing dark bottoms and a black hooded sweatshirt.

"What do you think *you're* doing?" asked Austin.

"Coming with."

I slipped into my own boots, which weren't all that different than theirs. Connor had turned me on to them years ago.

"Yeah... no."

"Oh no?" I snapped. "And why no—"

"Because it's too dangerous," said Maddox. "We're going after the people who came after *you*, Dallas. We swore to protect you, not deliver you straight to them."

"But you don't even know they want me!" I shouted. "For all we know they wanted something of Connor's. Something still in the house."

"No time to argue," Austin said firmly. "You're staying."

They wore desert night camo, with vests and belts. Sidearms at their hips. Rifles slung, all three of them.

It was kinda hot.

Dallas!

"So you're going to leave me here alone?" I asked coyly. "All by myself?"

Maddox seemed prepared for my statement. He checked the safety and then slid me a Glock — one of the three different pistols they'd bought to replace the one I lost in the fire.

"Set the alarm behind us," he ordered. "Don't leave the house, don't do *anything* except sit tight and wait for our call."

I scoffed at him. "Think that's gonna help if they come for me?"

"They're not coming for you. You've been here for weeks now, and nobody's come for—"

"Yeah, but now you've been *digging*," I offered. "You said it yourself, these guys are pros. They have military ties — the same ties *you* do. And you know what happens when you dig?"

Maddox glanced at his chronograph, then slumped his shoulders in exasperation. "What?"

"You leave marks."

I look to Kane. He was already smirking.

"You know she's probably right."

Maddox shook his head disgustedly. He looked pissed.

"We can't protect her if we're not around her," Kane went on. "And we can't afford to leave one of us behind. Might be best just to—"

"FINE."

Maddox spat the word and left the room quickly. When he came back, he threw something at me: a tactical vest.

"Put that on," he barked. "Then jump in the back, sit *really* low, and keep your head down the whole time. Got it?"

I slipped my arms through the holes and pulled the sleek material tightly around me.

"Yes *sir*," I said, snapping a salute.

Nineteen

DALLAS

It was almost a little surreal, riding along in the back of the truck. Sort of like being in a movie. I was surrounded by fully-armored, heavily-armed soldiers, following a fast-moving GPS signal in the dead of night.

"They turned again," said Austin, guiding Maddox through the darkened streets. "Head west."

I stared out the window as we whipped past Rock Springs and straight through Monterrey. It was exciting. Exciting in the sense that we'd be getting answers, yes. But also exciting to just be a part of everything.

They're a team, I kept reminding myself. *You're gonna need to stay out of their way.*

It was good advice, except that I had a stake in this too. These men in black — if that's who we were even chasing right now — had something to do with my brother's death. They'd left me without Connor; homeless, penniless, and with nothing to lose.

And there was something very reckless, very dangerous about that.

"Slow up," said Austin. "They've stopped."

We were in Summerlin now: a masterfully-planned community with a circular, central hub. An old ex had taken me here a few times. The downtown area was always clean and bright and bustling, but in a way very unlike the main Vegas strip. Less cheesy. More real.

"Remember," warned Maddox. "This could be nothing. That SUV is part of the Nellis base motor pool. It could be it's been taken out by nothing more than a couple of flyboys tonight, for a night on the town."

"Yeah," said Austin. "Except this particular vehicle keeps going to the same three spots, over and over. And this is one of them."

A click from beside me told me Kane had chambered a round. His usual casual demeanor had been replaced by one a lot more frosty. He was silent but observant. Totally aware and alert.

"There."

We were winding through a series of back alleyways when the truck suddenly slowed down. Maddox killed the lights as we rolled to a stop. Everything was quiet. You could literally hear a pin drop.

Up ahead, two vehicles were parked nose to nose. I recognized one of the big, black SUV's from the photographs instantly. The other was a sand-colored Jeep.

"Ready?"

Austin and Kane nodded. Apparently they'd clicked open their doors before the engine had been killed, and now they exited with surgical silence. Maddox remained behind the wheel, his window open, listening.

"What are they—"

He silenced me with a finger over my lips. Straining to see, I climbed defiantly into the front seat.

"You were supposed to stay in the back!" he hissed.

I shook my head. "Fuck that."

I felt his hand on my head, pushing me down. He kept going until all but my eyes were below the level of the dash.

"I hear voices," I whispered.

He nodded.

"What are they sayin—"

"Do you not understand the concept of being *quiet?*"

I blushed foolishly, but Maddox wasn't even looking. He was laser-focused on Kane and Austin, who were now leapfrogging between parked cars as they made their way up the avenue.

It was fascinating, watching them. They glided with practiced movements, each advancing forward with military precision. Both had their rifles drawn. Both were ready for anything.

Long, agonizing seconds ticked by. Eventually we couldn't see anything anymore. Maddox and I sat there, ears cocked, trying to focus on the distant sounds of voices, even laughter.

All at once, the laughter stopped.

"Dallas, I—"

Maddox's whisper was shattered by a staccato of gunfire, as everything seemed to happen at once. Light flared from rifle-barrels. There were men running, yelling. Screaming.

"GET DOWN!"

The truck started up and lunged forward, knocking me back into the seat. I took my spot on the passenger side, Maddox too busy to argue as he jammed the accelerator, racing toward the action.

"I SAID—"

Three men sprinted toward a secondary alley, firing as they went. I could see Kane firing back from a fixed position. Austin advancing to flank them, shooting while running toward the side of a brick building.

SCREEEECH!

Both vehicles sped away. Both moved in different directions. The SUV sailed past us, and Maddox traded shots with it from out the window.

"Go after them!" Austin shouted to Maddox.

A moment later he and Kane were gone, both sprinting full tilt down the darkened alley. Maddox gave me a sideways glance, then tore off in the direction the Jeep had gone.

"Put on your seatbelt," he growled.

"But—"

"NOW!"

Twenty

MADDOX

The Jeep had a damned good head start. Whoever was driving it was quick and decisive, and the size difference between our vehicles made it even easier for them as we weaved in and out of traffic.

"They went left!"

I squinted hard as I gripped the wheel. Having a second set of eyes was always a good thing. Having that second set of eyes as Dallas Winters...

You're an asshole, Maddox.

I could hear it in my head as clear as day. Connor's voice.

You were supposed to protect *her, not get her involved!*

"Piss on that," I spat angrily. "You never told us *anything!* You got wrapped up in something you should've—"

"What?" Dallas was staring at me like I had five heads.

"Nothing."

107

"Who the hell are you talking to?"

"Nobody," I growled. "I was—"

CRACK! CRACK!

I ducked instinctively at the sounds of gunfire. Dallas was staring ahead, mouth open. Eyes transfixed.

"GET DOWN!"

I yanked the wheel hard, swerving left and right. Trying to make us a harder target, while with my left hand...

CRACK! CRACK! CRACK! CRACK!

The pistol rolled in my hand with every bump and jolt. It was impossible to aim *and* swerve. Every angle was bad.

CRACK! CRACK!

I saw the glint of sparks against the Jeep's back bumper, but not much else. Up ahead, I could see the guy in the passenger seat reloading...

"Let me drive!"

Dallas already had one leg over mine. She grabbed the 'oh-shit' handle above the driver's side window, and used it to pull herself towards me.

"ARE YOU FUCKING CRAZ—"

"Let me drive so you can shoot!" she yelled. I was still firmly in my seat. She was sitting almost completely in my lap now.

"But—"

"Move the fuck over!"

It happened out of reflex, like I was obeying an order.

Shit, she'd said it forcefully enough.

"Dallas—"

"NO TIME," she shouted back. She hit a button and the passenger window rolled down. "C'mon!"

Unbelievably, I listened. I yanked the receiver back on my SCAR and stretched my entire torso out the window for leverage.

"Keep it steady for a second!" I shouted. "Give me a good—"

The first round ripped into my shoulder just above the clavicle. The second and third ones were grazing, tearing two streaks in my jacket right along the top of my arm.

I could feel an instant wetness coming from my wounds. It only made me grit my teeth harder as I squeezed the trigger...

CRACK-CRACK-CRACK-CRACK!

The passenger jerked back with the impact, his arms flying forward as he dropped his weapon. It went skidding off along the pavement, even as he went limp against the side of the Jeep.

Almost immediately, someone yanked my target back inside.

"You got him!"

We turned again, this time so sharply I imagined the Jeep flipping over. It didn't, but it came damn close. And somehow Dallas *gained* ground on the turn.

What is she, a professional driver or—

The jeep spun sideways again, this time onto the main thoroughfare. The village center was made up of a big circle, the spokes of which ended in a big central hub. There were people everywhere, walking the sidewalks. I saw crowds, old and young. Couples holding hands...

I lowered my rifle.

"Get alongside it!" I shouted.

My arm stung. My pride stung more. Red had blossomed through my shirt and was dripping down toward my elbow.

"YOU'RE *HIT?*"

Dallas's face was stark white — all concern. She kept glancing at my wounded shoulder.

"It's nothing. I'm fine," I told her. "Hey, keep your eyes on the roa—"

I jerked the wheel for her... just in time to avoid sideswiping a van. Dallas put her head forward, shoulders hunched. I felt the truck surge beneath us as she pressed the pedal to the floor.

Goddamn it, this is crazy...

It *was* crazy. The streets were full of cars, the sidewalks teeming with people. I could hear the screech of the Jeep's tires are it tore around Village Center Circle, nearly rising up on two wheels as we bore down on it.

Dallas's expression was all grim determination. She was slipping between gaps in traffic. Drifting from lane to lane. Every move she made was within inches of disaster. At this point I was afraid to even talk to her, for fear of breaking

110

her concentration.

Holy shit we're gaining.

Coming up on the Jeep's side, our bumpers were growing dangerously close. I pulled my sidearm from its holster. I didn't even know what I was going to do with it...

Dallas brushed the hair back from her face with one quick movement. Her expression was livid. I saw her lips curl back in a snarl, and suddenly I knew what she was going to do.

"Dallas, NO!"

She yanked the wheel viciously, and there was an abrupt and irrevocable connection. Our bumper bit hard into the back of the Jeep...

... and it turned perpendicular to the road going seventy miles per hour.

HOLYSHITTTTT...

I gasped in horror, watching as the vehicle's tires caught. It flipped sideways, end over end... cartwheeling through traffic like some hellish projectile, shedding bits and pieces of metal and plastic along the way.

She pumped the brakes, and we both lurched forward. The Jeep kept on flipping, over and over again. Spurred on by sheer momentum, and the fact it had practically been torn sideways in the span of half a heartbeat.

"FUCKERS."

I glanced over at her as we skidded to a halt. Dallas's eyes were wild and venomous. And they didn't contain even the slightest bit of remorse.

"Dallas..."

She didn't respond, at least not right away. I'd seen looks like hers on the battlefield. Looks on the faces of allies and comrades who'd lost people before, and who were now exacting some kind of payback for their loved ones.

"DALLAS!"

She barely reacted as I took her hand. I placed it back on the steering wheel.

"We have to *go*," I said. Traffic was already piling up around us. In a few moments, we'd be boxed in. "NOW, Dallas!"

She blinked rapidly a few times, and I had her back again. Turning quickly onto the shoulder we zoomed away, riding the curve. We took the first exit, just in time to avoid the lights and sirens: a half-dozen or more emergency vehicles, racing toward the scene of the accident.

My phone started ringing the second I pulled it out again. I punched the speaker button.

"Tell me something good."

"Can't," Austin called back, loud and low. I could hear the disappointment in his voice already. "We lost em'."

Twenty-One

DALLAS

The ride home in the back seat was leather and shadow. All gunpowder and steel, sweat and adrenaline.

Oh yeah, and blood.

Maddox was sporting three separate bullet wounds, but thankfully not one of them was even remotely life-threatening. Two of them were superficial; parallel scratches at the edge of one deltoid muscle. The third was a hole blown clear through his shoulder, but the bullet had entered and exited above the bone, but beneath the muscle.

"Lucky bastard," Kane sneered, from the front seat this time. Austin drove, while I kept pressure on the injury.

"He's always lucky," said Austin with a chuckle. "Remember that time in Kosovo…"

I listened only half-heartedly as they launched into another one of their long stories. There were so many I was losing count. Still, I was happy to hear them in good spirits. Even if our overall mission had been a failure.

113

A mission, Dallas? Is that what we're calling it?

To tell the truth, yes, I was. I'd been in a full-blown combat situation with them now.

Like Connor.

I felt like I'd achieved some sort of right of passage. That I'd been put into a high-pressure situation, and had come out on top.

Then again, I'd caused us to lose the one chance we had of getting some answers. Maybe if I'd shown a little more restraint...

"How'd they make you, anyway?" Maddox was asking.

"Kane's size sixteen feet," Austin groaned. "They probably thought Bigfoot was creeping up on them."

The big man in the front seat scoffed. "You gonna tell 'em about that rock you kicked by accident?"

"That wasn't a rock. It was a tiny pebble."

"It was a chunk of concrete the size of a silver dollar."

"Bullshit."

"You sent it skidding across the ground," Kane continued, "and that's when they looked up."

They continued arguing for several minutes, Kane blaming Austin for their botched approach, Austin blaming Kane for losing the foot-chase.

"You couldn't keep up," he said as he drove. "If you weren't so slow now..."

From the shadowy realm of the back seat I changed out Maddox's bandage for a fresh one. The bleeding had slowed almost to a stop. I'd tried once to get him to see a doctor, but he'd waved me off. The others had too.

Personally I think they just wanted to see his face as they stitched it.

"So the night's a loss then," sighed Austin. "We accomplished nothing."

"No, not totally."

Everyone's eyes turned toward me. Not in an accusatory way, as they had when Maddox told them how I'd pulled a pit-maneuver on the fleeing Jeep. It was more curiosity this time.

"So... about that vehicle we chased?"

"Yeah?" said Kane skeptically. "The one you sent to Jeep heaven?"

I nodded. "I got the plate number."

Everything went silent for a moment. Maddox's wince of pain twisted into a grin.

"Holy shit, really?"

"A7X-271"

Kane let out a long, heated breath. "Well fuck. That's... that's..."

"Pretty damned useful?" I offered.

"Yeah."

A half-mile later we made the turnoff, several blocks earlier than we needed to. Austin wended through side roads until he was satisfied we weren't being followed. Then we headed for home.

"Oh yeah," said Austin abruptly. "Remember the time Connor dragged us all out to that sushi restaurant?"

Maddox laughed. "Which one?"

"The one where he ordered everything on the menu," Austin went on. "And they brought out—"

"They brought out that fucking wooden *boat*," Kane snickered. "All covered in rice and fish. It had masts and sails and everything. Jesus, that thing took up the entire table."

"It sure did," said Maddox, laughing. "Only none of us would touch it. Only Connor."

Smirking defeatedly, my gaze shot over to Austin. He was looking over his shoulder already grinning. His eyes were gloating.

Alright, alright, I mouthed silently as we pulled into the driveway. *You win.*

Kane tried helping Maddox inside, and was immediately shrugged off. They marched through the front door together, standing tall.

"The machismo levels in this house are off the charts," I said, rolling my eyes at Austin.

"You think that's bad? Wait until we stitch him up and he pretends it doesn't even hurt."

I laughed out loud, picturing it perfectly in my mind. It was exactly what would happen, too.

As we took the cracked cement walkway together, Austin's arm slid around me. He pulled me into him.

"Hey, remember our bet?" he murmured. "*Anything* I want?"

He had a velvet voice. A smooth but insistent touch.

"Yes," I answered haltingly. I noticed his scent; musky and manly and delicious. My heart was already beating faster. "Why? Do you know what you want?"

Austin's hand slid downward, cupping my ass. As he pushed his lips close to my ear, he gave it a promising squeeze.

"I want you in my room tonight," he whispered huskily. "Late. After we all turn in."

An electric shiver rocketed through my body. It filled me with feelings of nervousness and excitement. Exhilaration... and anticipation.

"O—Okay."

"After all," he murmured, turning to deliver a smile. "A deal's a deal."

Twenty-Two

DALLAS

The house was deathly silent as I slipped into the upstairs hallway. Maddox was all stitched up, and had taken something for the pain. He and Kane were both slumbering deeply, their doors closed.

It was well after midnight when I let myself into Austin's room. The lights were pleasantly dim. The temperature was warm and welcoming.

"Hey..."

My heart was racing as I closed the door and turned around. Austin was lounged out in a soft, high-backed chair. His incredible body was gloriously naked except for a pair of tight boxer-briefs.

"Lose those," he said casually, pointing with a short whiskey glass. He was indicating my sleep shorts.

"Yeah?" I teased.

"Oh yeah."

Moving seductively, I shimmied out of my shorts and let them drop. Then I hooked two thumbs into either side of my thong, pulling the straps away from my hips an inch or two.

"These also?"

He seemed to consider it for a moment as he took a small sip of the amber liquid. Ice cubes rattled around in the glass.

"No," he said finally. "Those can stay."

I let the straps snap back into place. Setting my hands on my hips, I waited for his next set of instructions.

This is fun...

"You ready to do anything I want?" he asked, raising an eyebrow.

"That's why I'm here."

"Good. Now get on your knees."

I took two steps forward onto a thin Persian rug before dropping obediently to the floor. Through it all, I maintained complete eye contact.

"What now?" I asked sweetly.

"Crawl over here," he said. "Slowly."

One side of my mouth curled into a grin. He was still staring. Still looking through me with those amazing blue-green eyes, which somehow seemed impossibly bright and beautiful against his darker hair and complexion.

"*Now*, Dallas."

I moved. It happened without thinking; one second I

119

was kneeling before the door, the next I was crawling slowly over to where he sat. Austin swung his legs open, revealing two toned, mocha-colored thighs. They were manly thighs — incredibly strong and muscular. Shit, never had a guy's legs seemed so sexy before.

That's because you're at eye-level, the little voice in my head said. *You're practically kneeling between his legs.*

I was, and that was perfectly okay. Especially considering the bulge *between* his legs, straining hard against the fabric of his grey boxer-briefs.

"You wanna touch it?"

He'd seen me looking. Apparently I'd lost our little staring contest.

"You can, you know."

Austin shifted forward a bit, relaxing even more into his chair. I heard the tinkling of ice again as he took another sip of his drink.

I sighed internally, letting my eyes drag over his body. He was quite literally perfect. Silently I thanked whichever SEAL instructors had honed and sculpted his magnificent body, giving it a lean, chiseled strength that made me want to taste every delicious inch of him. I loved the smell of his skin. The cut of his perfect, washboard abs...

He's amazing.

I slid upward along his body, gently kissing that beautiful stomach. I found myself kissing his chest, circling one dark nipple with my tongue. I kissed his neck, reaching that impeccably-trimmed goatee, and then suddenly I was pressing my lips against his. Breathing his breath as I caressed his face, our tongues gliding together.

God...

His mouth was all sweet and delicious from the bourbon or whiskey or whatever the hell he was drinking. Either way I loved it; every square inch of him tasted like *man*. I felt myself going light-headed. My mind, giddy and swimming...

I could kiss him like this forever.

Austin's hand slid over my head and suddenly he was pushing me back down. Firmly. Insistently...

A not so subtle reminder — I was there for *him*.

"There's my girl..."

He groaned as I buried my head in his lap. For a moment I teased him, rubbing my face against his warm, straining member. Cupping and squeezing it gently through the fabric that still constrained it, while kissing my way up and down the insides of his thighs.

"Dallas, I—"

His sentence ended in a groan as I swallowed him.

"*Ohhhhh...*"

It was a simple thing to pull his cock through the front hole of his boxer briefs. Getting it down my throat was a different trick altogether. Austin's manhood was warm and thick, and fit perfectly against the back of my throat. I took him as deep as possible, letting him rest there for a few glorious seconds before squeezing the base and dragging my lips tightly over the entire length of his shaft, bottom to top.

"Oh *fuck me.*"

I chuckled to myself. It was what *I* wanted, that's for sure. But not exactly what he meant by the words. Not yet, anyway.

For the next few minutes I focused on delivering the best blowjob of my life. I sucked Austin expertly, giving it to him from every angle, at every speed. I pumped him hard, down at the root. Fondled his balls gently with my free hand.

He tastes so good...

My mouth went even lower, keeping everything slick and wet and beautiful. Moaning around him as my hair thrashed in his lap. When I caught him looking I held his gaze. Fucked him with my eyes as I kept on going, dragging the flat of my tongue slowly upward along the underside of his shaft.

God, you must look like a total slut!

I felt like one too, and that part was awesome. I was reveling in the entire beautiful act. Taking pleasure in *his* pleasure...

When the throbbing and pulsing began, I knew he was close. I doubled down, sucking and pumping away, but Austin had other plans.

"Your turn..."

Twenty-Three

DALLAS

All at once my lover stood up, lifting me with him. My arms went over his shoulders. My legs slid around his flanks, straddling his waist.

I was admiring his body, his chest, his beautiful face. Trying to figure out where to kiss next, as his cock pulsed and throbbed, trapped firmly between us.

"OH!"

He threw me onto the bed before I knew I was even leaving his arms. I bounced hard, my head settling somewhere up near his pillows. Before I knew it Austin had one big hand wrapped around both my ankles at once.

What the—

I gasped as he pushed my legs high over my head, thighs pinned tightly together. It stretched me out wonderfully. Lifted my ass from the bed...

"OHHHHHHHHHHHHHHHH..."

The air left my lungs in a moan as he pulled my thong to one side... and buried his face in my pussy.

Oh, FUUUCK.

Austin's tongue was everywhere, bathing my sex from top to bottom. I shivered as he planted a series of soft kisses around my swollen clit. Shuddered as his tongue moved up and down in broad, deliberate strokes.

He slipped a finger inside me, and began sliding it slowly in and out. My eyes rolled back. My head tilted on the pillow...

God...

I was enjoying it all; from the feel of his goatee brushing my sensitive skin, to how incredibly tight his finger felt inside me. My legs were still pressed firmly together, my ankles high in the air. I was being stretched out and devoured. Kissed and licked and sucked...

That's so. Damned. Good!

Suddenly I felt a jolt... and gasped out loud as an all new sensation reached my brain. It was a frosty, icy numbness. A blast of cold against an area that was oh so fucking hot. I heard the clink of his glass being set down again, and realized why:

My lover had an ice cube in his mouth.

"MMMMmmmmm..."

It felt incredible, the intensity of the contrast. All new shivers rocked my body as Austin clenched the cube between his teeth, dragging it up and down through my heated channel. He kept on pumping me with his finger. Using the rapidly-melting ice cube to circle and tease the sensitive hood of my clit.

"Oh fuck, baby..."

I writhed and twisted involuntarily, trying to squirm away. Trying to escape the numbing cold, even as my brain told me it felt good at the same time. Soon I was screwing my pussy into him. Welcoming the frigid yet wonderful numbness that had become his lips and tongue, then plunging it back down, where I could feel it melting inside me.

"*YES.*"

I was just getting used to it when he finally let go. Austin's free hand pushed my thighs apart, giving him greater access as he kept on lapping away. One finger had become two, screwing in and out of me. And I was screwing right back into his lips and face. Grinding against his probing, penetrating tongue...

FUCK!

I was halfway to coming when his hands slipped beneath my ass. Suddenly he was flipping me over, flat onto my belly. Spreading my asscheeks with two strong hands, as I clutched his pillow in anticipation of what came next.

Austin buried his face between my legs once again. Only this time... from behind.

Wow...

The feeling was absolutely exquisite. Indescribably *hot.*

"OHH..."

Austin's face was buried in my ass now. His tongue traveled up and down, from the depths of my semi-numb pussy all the way up to my tight little asshole. I could feel him back there, pushing and prodding. Bathing me with heat and saliva, and the smooth, delicious feel of his hot, squirming tongue.

Oh WOW...

The sensations were incredible. Like nothing I'd ever experienced. Like nothing I'd ever *imagined* I'd experience, yet somehow, deep down, I knew I'd always wanted to.

This... this is...

I gasped again as he slipped two fingers back into me from behind. Austin was rimming my asshole and fucking me at the same time. Sliding his wet tongue all over it, while gliding two long fingers in and out of my soaking pussy.

Holy hell this is fucking insane!

My hands were claws, gripping his pillow like talons. My arms were stretched high overhead as I shifted my weight backwards, trying to screw him even further into my dirtiest, naughtiest of all possible places...

"Deeper!"

The word forced its way from my throat. I couldn't believe I'd even said it.

"Just like that... just like that..." I gasped, totally out of control. "Please!"

My lover heard and obeyed. He slid his hands around the front of my thighs and pulled, forcing me backwards. Yanking me harder against his wriggling, writhing tongue.

"OH GOD..."

I saw stars. Literal flashes of white and silver, streaking in from the corners of what little vision I had left.

"OH HOLY FUCK!"

My orgasm was an explosion that began deep in my core. I felt Austin push hard one last time, maybe with three fingers or even four... and then suddenly I was coming... and coming... and coming... all over his face.

Oh Dallas...

My mind left my body, and for a good half minute I lost every last semblance of control. My climax was total — my whole body shaking with the pure white euphoria of ultimate release.

"OHHhHHhHhHHhh.."

I screamed as my pussy spasmed around his fingers, just as the rest of me screwed down around his beautiful tongue. Austin held the pressure, keeping tight against me as I rode out every wonderful contraction. Every last shudder and spasm, every last guttural moan and groan and magnificent cry of victory, or ecstasy, or whatever fucking plane of nirvana my brain had just visited thanks to his talented fingers, mouth, and tongue.

I sprawled on my side, utterly spent, having experienced the first full-body orgasm of my life. Every surface of my skin shivered with pleasure. Even exhausted, I felt charged and alive.

"I..."

My voice failed. I had no words, because there was really nothing to say. I could only stare back at Austin, loving him with my eyes. Sighing softly as my body heaved, my chest rising and falling as my senses, one by one, slowly returned.

"I..." I gasped when I could finally speak again. "I

can't believe..."

"That you've never had that done to you before?" Austin smirked back at me.

I laughed. Nodded. Flopped onto my back, limp and exhausted.

"It's what I wanted," he shrugged, sliding forward again.

I purred with satisfaction as he nudged my legs apart. His hands pinned my wrists to the bed as he mounted me easily.

"*Part* of what I wanted, anyway."

Twenty-Four

AUSTIN

Her breath caught again as I sank into her, stretching her this time from within. It felt like molten heaven. All warm and wet, swollen and snug beyond words.

I stared down at her, shaking my head in pure disbelief. This girl...

Not a girl, a woman.

Okay, fine. This *woman.* This gorgeous, incredibly sexy, beyond beautiful wom—

And not just any woman either, the voice in my head reminded me. *You're staring at Dallas Winters.*

Holy shit.

You're fucking Dallas Winters.

A grunt escaped my throat as I bottomed out, feeling the heat of her innermost depths. It was insane, when I thought about it. Our best friend's *sister.* Our brother-in-arms.

129

It was almost forbidden. Totally taboo. I should've felt guilty, but for some reason I just couldn't. Maybe it was because Connor had been gone for so long. He was still in our heads, still in our hearts...

But his sister was right here, right now, laying in my bed. Staring into my eyes as I crushed her from above, legs spread wide. Moaning softly into my shoulder. Clutching me desperately as I drilled her out.

Dallas...

We'd watched her for a *year* now! Had it really been that long? Watched her and protected her and yes, some of us even desired her. Kane for certain. Me also, though I never admitted it to the others. Even Maddox...

Holy shit.

When I thought about it, we *all* wanted her. And maybe that's why we'd made the agreement, leveled the playing field by deciding not to play at all.

No one goes after her. No one hits on her. No one even flirts with her. Maddox's words. *Everyone stays cool.*

We'd stayed cool, for a while at least. But then all this had happened. We could pin the blame on Kane if we tried hard enough, but that was mostly deflection. In short, we all wanted her. We all knew it. And the reason why was simple:

She was Dallas *Winters.*

I thought about it now as she writhed naked beneath me, clawing my ass to pull me in deeper. Rolling her hips at the deepest point of every thrust, to get me more fully inside her.

Goddamn.

She was the perfect woman. Strong, smart, beautiful. Intelligent and independent but also a sexual dynamo; all feminine curves and soft fragrant hair. Luscious, blowjob lips set against a gorgeous porcelain face.

But even beyond that, Dallas Winters had swagger. A cool confidence and take no prisoners attitude we all recognized immediately, because we'd seen it a thousand times on a hundred different missions.

She was just like her brother.

Only she also wasn't.

We'd loved Connor deeply, all three of us. So much so that the moment he'd died, it was like a piece of us died with him.

Dammit, Connor.

Soldiers were like that, especially as we grew older. Each time we lost someone, it left a hole where that person used to be. Sometimes you could fill that hole, at least temporarily. Other times it was left forever wide, a gaping wound that you could only try your best to ignore.

Yes, I'd wanted Dallas like the others had. I wanted to have her. To *possess* her. To make her somehow fit in that part of our life where Connor used to reside, if only because she was so much like him in so many ways.

I kept plowing away, nailing her to the bed with deep, powerful strokes. Her irises were locked on mine. Her touch was gentle, her movements soft and soothing as she caressed my face.

I could get used to this.

It was sad, in a way. I hadn't had a steady girlfriend in years. And even when I had...

I could even love her.

The thought was dangerous. Warning sirens blared in my head, diverting my attention back to the task at hand. I began fucking her even *harder.* Spreading her legs even wider, so I could take every last thing that I needed from her.

Dallas whimpered softly as I screwed her past the point of no return. My eyes flared, pleadingly. She bit her lip, nodding her consent...

Three strokes later I was flooding her pussy, clawing violently for every last bit of purchase as I unloaded deep in her womb.

FUCKKKK!

I filled her almost immediately, my come bubbling up from the very depths of her womanhood. True to form Dallas kept on screwing, kept on fucking me with the same wild, crazy abandon. It whipped our combined juices into a frothy cream that ran down every side of my plunging shaft.

I'd never been so hot, so crazy for release. So achingly desperate to come.

Maybe that's because I'd never felt so connected before, either.

Let it go, Austin.

I was and I wasn't. Letting go, that is.

She's not for you. She's not for anyone.

I collapsed against her, wanting to believe it. Needing to understand that it was just sex — sex and *only* sex — nothing more than two people using each other's bodies for gratification and release.

Yeah, right.

Dallas clenched me tightly against her, my face buried between her breasts. It was warm and wonderful. Fragrant and safe and full of the steady, comforting thrum of her rapidly beating heart.

"I can see why my brother loved you," she whispered softly, running her fingers absently through my hair. The word hung thickly in the air between us.

"All of you."

Twenty-Five

DALLAS

"Well hello there sleeping beauty," said Maddox, shoving a mug of coffee into my hands. "Grab a seat, you're just in time."

I blinked against the all-too bright kitchen, stumbling in the direction of my chair. Kane pulled it out for me. I nodded gratefully.

Maddox had one arm in a sling. With the other, he was operating the waffle-iron. The others had empty plates covered in waffle pieces and smeared in syrup. I could tell by the level of the coffee maker they were already on their second pot.

"What am I just in time for?" I asked groggily.

"Family meeting."

"So we're a family now?" I squinted, raising one eyebrow.

"Well we're certainly *something*, wouldn't you agree?"

134

Instead of answering I took a sip of coffee. Surprisingly, it was fixed it exactly the way I liked it. Apparently my boys were taking good care of me... every which way.

"Okay, so we were talking about yesterday..."

A waffle landed in front of me, piping hot. Austin pushed me the syrup.

"We've been monitoring the news feeds and calling hospitals, but so far nothing's shown up as far as an accident report," Maddox went on. "Which we all know is impossible, considering what happened. And that can only mean one thing."

"A cover-up."

He nodded and slid into the seat beside me. "You catch on fast."

"Doesn't take Columbo to figure that one out," I said.

Austin leaned back in his chair. "*Please* tell me she just made a Columbo reference..."

Maddox nodded. "She did."

"God, I love this girl."

I returned Austin's smile with a smirk of my own. Columbo had been one of the many television shows we watched together, Connor and I. We'd seen every season, every episode. It was old but timeless.

"Anyway," Maddox continued, "we're heading out today to track down more info. We've already got someone running the plate number you gave us. Kane and Austin are going to hit some of the hospitals and clinics near Summerlin, and I'm heading on base to run some queries."

"You're going to Nellis?" I asked.

"Yup."

"So I'll go with Kane and Austin, then."

"Sorry no," Maddox frowned. "You're staying here this time."

"The hell I—"

"Dallas."

Kane's voice was stern, but not condescending. His stared at me from beneath two dark brows. "This is going to go a lot easier if we're on our own, at least for today. And the quicker we head out, the quicker we get back."

"But—"

"I know you want to come. I know you want to help..." his brown eyes softened mid-sentence. "But for right now, we need you to sit tight. Okay?"

My mouth opened and then closed. Reluctantly I nodded.

"Okay," I said finally. My eyes shifted to Austin. "I'm kinda tired anyway."

Austin's mouth twisted into a half-grin. If the others noticed, they didn't say anything.

"How's your shoulder by the way?" I asked Maddox.

"Shoulder's fine," he said. "Sling's just for support."

"You sure I can't come with you?" I pushed. "I could drive you to the base at least."

"They won't let you on the base," he said. "Not where I'm going. Besides, didn't you do enough driving last night?"

The question was half sarcasm, half admiration. It didn't really require an answer.

"Please don't try something like that again, by the way."

I waved him off. "It worked, didn't it?"

"Yes, but—"

"Yes but nothing. I caught them, I stopped them."

"You obliterated them," Maddox replied. "You didn't *catch* anyone. That Jeep must've flipped ten, twelve... maybe fifteen times."

"So?"

"So someone definitely got hurt. Maybe even killed."

He was studying me now, and I realized they all were. They were watching my response. Waiting to see my reaction.

"You okay with that?" pushed Maddox.

Shoving the syrup away, I bit into my waffle. It was crunchy and delicious.

"Are you *sure* those guys were involved in whatever happened to Connor?"

Maddox nodded gravely. "They absolutely were."

"Then yes. I'm fucking fine with it."

Austin swung an arm across the table and passed something to Kane. Incredulously, I realized it was a twenty-dollar bill.

"Told ya," said Kane, pocketing the money.

"Holy shit, you're *betting* on me now?"

Kane laughed gruffly. "Now?" He crossed two big, hairy forearms and rested them on the table. "We've been betting on you since before you even got here."

I took a moment for the meaning to sink in.

They've been watching you for a whole year, the voice in my head reminded me. *In all that time... who knows what the hell they bet on?*

I tried being angry, or even taking offense. None of that tasted right though. Instead I smiled.

"What other bets you got going on?" I smirked. "Maybe I want in."

Austin laughed outright. Kane chuckled.

"Wouldn't you like to know..."

Twenty-Six

DALLAS

It was a restless, shitty day. The kind of day that always dragged its ass, when you really just wanted it to be over.

With the guys gone and the alarm code set, there was nothing much for me to do but wait. I tried occupying my time by cleaning, starting with the upstairs and working my way methodically through every room of the house.

The problem of course, was that I was living with three Navy SEALs. As military men, everything they owned was already in its proper place. I ran through the dishes, but the rest of the kitchen was annoyingly spotless. A byproduct of Austin being a neat freak, a slight gemaphobe, and having an incurable case of OCD.

I couldn't really blame him. I'd been much the same way for most of my own life — a series of habits picked up through living with Connor. I wondered absently how many of the guys' traits had actually been acquired from my brother. How much, like me, their lives had been molded by living with him.

By noon I was on the couch, flipping channel after channel. The more I sat there the more unsatisfied I became, so I got up and paced the house a bit for good measure.

Maybe I should call one of them?

It was a self-serving idea. Though they hadn't specifically told me not to, I really wanted to leave them alone. Their work was important enough, without me seeming needy. And needy was the last thing I wanted to be.

The computer!

I booted up the machine the way Austin showed me; by logging in through a series of remote connections designed to mask my search history and location. Then I set to work, trying to find out anything I could about what had happened yesterday, in Summerlin and beyond.

You might've hurt someone. Are you okay with that?

I'd said I was, and I certainly meant it. Whoever had taken my brother away from me was *not* someone I should be feeling sorry for, or guilty for hurting.

Still...

I drilled down hard, looking for any record of the accident I'd caused. When the obvious searches came up empty I went after local forums and message boards in the area. Community social media groups, neighborhood watch kind of stuff. I even found an EMT page just for Las Vegas and the surrounding area. Even so... nothing.

These guys are more connected than we thought.

They had to be, which was why going to Nellis seemed so dangerous. Either the people checking the SUV out of the base's motor pool knew how to avoid leaving a trail, or they were of such high enough rank that a trail didn't matter. And I wasn't sure which option was worse.

I shut down the computer mid-afternoon, then started dinner early. Cooking was yet another task I could use to pass the time, only the sun set and the day ended and the food got cold on the stovetop...

... and there was still no sign from any of them.

Fuck it.

I grabbed the phone and was ready to start punching numbers when I saw a flash of headlights outside. They turned my way, heading up our empty block.

Thank God.

Relief flooded through me. Happiness even. It was a little crazy, how much I was looking forward to seeing them at the end of the day. My guys. My SEALs.

My lovers.

I punched off the alarm and flung open the door... but the driveway was empty. So was the street. Everything was darkness.

Stepping out onto the porch to get a better look, a cold feeling swept over me. Warning lights flashed in my brain.

Dallas...

Still, I saw nothing in every direction. The street was silent and empty.

Maybe someone made a wrong turn. Turned back around...

"Where is it?"

The voice was low and gravelly, and carried by the wind. I couldn't immediately tell which direction it had come from. But I knew one thing.

It didn't belong to any of my men.

"I'm giving you one chance," the voice said ominously. "I take it... or I take *you*."

A man stepped out of the shadows. He was ridiculously tall, maybe six and a half feet, with stark white hair and a face that didn't seem to belong with his body.

"Dallas, listen—"

I folded backwards, whirling and running for the safety of the door. Through the corner of my eye I saw the intruder jerk forward. He lunged for my throat...

"DALLAS!"

Somehow I slipped through. I spun in a tight circle, shoving the door closed. Throwing my hip so hard against it that a spike of pain flashed up my body, even as I reached for the deadbolt with my opposite hand.

But I never heard the click of the lock engaging. With growing horror, I realized the door had bounced back.

There was a booted foot stuck in it.

"All I want is—"

Without thinking I stomped down hard, crushing the intruder's toes with my heel. There was a scream of pain, but the foot never left the doorway. It stayed exactly where it was, while I ground my heel even harder against it.

142

"Bitch!"

I shoved again with my hip, and now my shoulder too. The door flexed. It shifted another quarter inch toward the closed position, but it still barely budged.

Then he pushed back... and I was nearly knocked flat on my ass.

Stay strong! The voice of self-preservation screamed. *If you fall down, it's all over!*

Gritting my teeth, I widened my stance. My eyes scanned desperately around for something to thrust through the opening. Anything sharp. Anything long...

But there was nothing... so I stomped again.

"FUCK!"

This time I heard a crunch, or rather I felt it. The foot jerked backwards. The door slammed shut.

My heart was *pounding*. My fingers betrayed me three times fumbling for the deadbolt...

CLICK.

I sighed with relief, slumping against the door. It rattled hard from the other side. I could hear screaming. Kicking...

Then all at once, everything stopped.

The windows!

They were low and wide, easy to break. If this guy wanted in, there was no keeping him out.

Go! Get your gun!

I sprinted back to the kitchen, throwing open the second to last drawer. Silverware flew everywhere, clinking noisily against the tiled floor. My hand reached in, scrambling around to the back...

...and pulled out my Glock.

I sank back against the refrigerator, holding the weapon out before me with both hands. I flipped off the safety. Chambered a round.

The stainless steel was cold against my skin as I waited.

A minute went by. Then two minutes. Three. I strained to hear even the slightest sound; the breaking of glass, the creak of a door or window sliding against its frame. But I heard nothing. I saw no one.

"DALLAS!"

The voice came from the door again. It was pounding. Shaking. The shouting was louder than ever.

"Dallas, OPEN UP!"

I cocked my head sideways.

"*MADDOX?*"

"Yes! It's me!" The door handle shook violently. "Open up!"

I flew back to the door and slammed the bolt home. Maddox entered the foyer with a wild look in his eye, chest heaving, out of breath.

"Are you okay?"

I flew into his arms, being careful to keep the gun pointed away from him. Then I began shaking. Shuddering all over, as I melted into him.

"Hey, hey..." he said, crushing me in his big arms. "It's okay. I got you." He smoothed my hair with his hands. "I got you..."

Gingerly he took the gun and uncocked it before sliding it back into my palm. His hands went to either of my shoulders.

"T—There was this guy," I blurted quickly. "He came from out of nowhere! And he was—"

"I know. I saw him." His eyes did an expert-level scan in every direction. "I chased him three blocks at least, maybe more. He's gone now."

"Okay..."

"Anyone else?"

I shook my head. "No. I don't think so."

"Alright," he said, still looking everywhere at once. "Get whatever you need. We're going. Now."

"Going where?"

"Anywhere but here," he said, sticking close by my side.

Twenty-Seven

DALLAS

Ten minutes and several miles later, my pulse was still racing. Maddox's cool composure however, was calming me down.

"Who *was* that guy?"

"A scout."

"A *scout?*" It must've come off a little bitchy, because Maddox frowned.

"He was looking for you, Dallas."

"I'd say he found me."

"Yeah," he nodded. "He found you and he got a little too excited. Which was good for us."

"Good for..." My brow furrowed. "Wait. Why good?"

"Because if he'd waited for backup first we'd both be screwed."

My hero drove us onward, winding through a nexus of

146

back alleys and sidestreets to make sure we weren't followed. I stared numbly out the window, watching as we headed clear past the strip toward the far end of town.

"They found us because of last night, didn't they?"

"Uh huh."

"So now they know where we live..."

"Yup."

I was still numb, but I regained composure enough to pull out my phone. Maddox noticed immediately.

"What are you doing?"

"Calling Kane and Austin," I said. "Obviously we have to warn them. If they show up—"

"Kane and Austin aren't coming back tonight," he said, closing his hand over mine. "Besides, after tonight we're gonna need all new phones. All new everything."

Before I knew what was happening he took the phone from my hand and tossed it out the window. Then he shook his head in frustration.

"I should've done that miles ago."

It was insane, living like this. I knew what it was like to not have a place, a home, a family. But over the past few weeks, I'd somehow found all of those things again.

"So that's it?" I asked angrily. "We just ditch? We never go back to—"

"I didn't say that," Maddox interrupted. "Let's not get ahead of ourselves." He looked at me for a moment, then squeezed my hand reassuringly. "Trust me Dallas, we'll get this all sorted out. But for tonight? We lay low."

My shoulders relaxed, but only a little. If he was trying to show me there was a light at the end of the tunnel, it looked more like a pinprick.

"So what did he say to you?"

I thought back. Ran the whole terrifying scenario through my head again, trying to remain calm.

"I heard him talking. Saw him screaming."

"I crushed his foot," I said.

"I know. I almost caught him because of that."

"Almost?"

"Yeah," he admitted sheepishly. "The fucker had legs that were four feet long. Every two strides he took were three of mine."

I nodded consolingly. "Should make figuring out who he is pretty easy," I pointed out. "Not many people *that* tall."

"Solid point," Maddox conceded. "So... what did he say?"

"He... I think he was looking for something."

"Something in the house?"

I shook my head. "No. For some reason I don't think so."

"What then?"

I searched my memory a little more, but it was hard. With each passing mile, everything was getting more and more hazy.

148

"It seemed to be something *I* would have," I said mechanically. "Like he was shaking me down. As if I knew where something was."

Maddox gripped the steering wheel as he turned again. I saw his eyes, as always, go to the rear-view mirror. "Any idea what that might be?"

"Not a clue."

"Think, Dallas. It's important."

I laughed, and the laugh wasn't exactly a good one. "What the fuck could I *have*, Maddox?" I sneered. "I came to you practically naked that night, with nothing but the clothes I'd been sleeping in. Everything else in my house was destroyed by the fire."

His mouth went tight. I could see him holding back.

"If there's anything these guys are looking for, it's not going to be mine," I said. "Maybe something of Connor's, sure. But now all his stuff is gone."

We rode in silence for a while, which was probably good. It gave me a chance to simmer down.

"Look," I said apologetically. "I didn't mean to go off like that."

"It's fine."

"No, seriously. I'm not usually like that. It's just... it's just so fucking frustrating."

My chin dropped to my chest, just as Maddox slid an arm around me. He pulled me across the seat, over to his side of the vehicle.

"It's alright," he said, holding me close. There was a

gentle bounce as we pulled into a parking lot. "Let's forget about this for tonight. We're here."

I forced my chin back up. The hotel he'd chosen was a good one; tall and sleek and beautiful. I hadn't stayed here but I knew people who had. It was very expensive.

Maddox noticed me gawking and laughed. "Don't get too attached," he said. "We're only parking here."

I glanced at him strangely. "*Parking* here?"

"Yup," he said. "As a diversion."

I was still confused. "Why do we need a divers—"

"Because they know the vehicle," he said simply. "We can't take the risk."

I sighed in mock frustration. Or maybe it was real frustration, I could hardly tell anymore.

"Fine, then where the hell *are* we staying?"

Maddox held his hand out and I took it. He smiled devilishly.

"I saw a real shitty place about a mile *that* way."

Twenty-Eight

DALLAS

Maddox was right; it *was* a shitty place. A shitty room in a shitty strip of a shit motel, in the shittiest part of—

"Here, go get ice."

He handed me a thin plastic bucket with a crack down one side. I laughed in his face.

"Alright," he sighed, taking back the bucket. "I'll get the ice."

The moment he left the room I flopped onto the bed. We were in one of those theme motels. The room we'd taken was one of the last two left: the 'Hawaiian Getaway'.

I stared up at myself in the mirrored ceiling, then turned my head to see the rest of the amenities. The walls were wallpapered with beautiful beach scenes and ocean horizons. Or at least they *were* beautiful... about twenty years ago. Now they were faded with time and peeling at the edges.

Hawaiian getaway, I laughed to myself. *Holy shit.*

There was a poorly-made Tiki bar at one end of the room. A fake palm tree standing in the far corner. It was so plastic and ratty-looking I didn't know whether to laugh out loud or wrinkle my nose up at all the dust.

Hey. At least you'll be safe here.

That much I was fairly sure of. The Hawaiian room of the *Fantasy Eighteen* was probably the last place on Earth anyone would ever hope to find us, including ourselves. If the bad guys could somehow track us here, they deserved to have us.

"Ice machine's broken," Maddox announced, letting himself back in. He closed the door and engaged the deadbolt. "Vending machine stuff is cold, though."

He held up a pair of bottled waters and half a dozen little bags of pretzels and chips. Shit, it was better than nothing.

"Thanks."

We divided the spoils. Filled our bellies. Ten minutes later we were laying on our backs, staring at ourselves in the mirrored ceiling. We caught each other's eye... and both broke out laughing at the same time.

"We're really fucked, aren't we?" I asked eventually.

"Sure looks that way."

I sighed, grateful for the honesty. "Well at least we're in paradise."

It was a stress breaker. A mood changer. Between this, and the fifteen-minute walk we'd just endured, I was feeling somewhat good again.

"This is hands down the best Hawaiian Getaway room I've ever been in," Maddox quipped. He coughed. "The cleanest too."

I turned to him and giggled. "Yeah, well you haven't seen the bedding yet."

"Oh?"

I nodded. "Even the stains have stains."

He laughed again. "That's fucking disgusting."

"Then why are you laughing?"

He kept on going, unable to control himself. I watching him laugh until tears formed at the corners of his eyes. "Shit, I don't even know."

The whole thing became infectious, and soon we were giggling together like teenagers. In a way it was cathartic. A release of emotions and adrenaline, at the end of a very long, really strange day. He was doing it to cheer me up. To make me feel safe again, despite the horrendous shit I'd just been through.

And it was working.

Eventually Maddox propped himself up on one elbow. The laughter died away, and he looked at me with grim seriousness from his side of the bed.

"Look, Dallas. I want you to know I'm sorry."

My God, he was so *good-looking!* Especially like this. I couldn't stop staring at those high cheekbones. That perfect amount of stubble. The curve of his jaw...

"Sorry for what?"

"For you having to go through all of this," he replied. Slowly he shook his head. "I can't even imagine what it must be like for you, to lose everything. Your home, your things..." He bit his lip before continuing. "Your brother..."

I could see the depth of compassion in his eyes. Legitimate empathy, not pity. But there was an underlying pain there too. A pain I knew all too well.

"You know some of it," I said consolingly. "You lost Connor too. You all did."

I snuggled into him. Everything outside of the scope of our little hotel room was suddenly inconsequential. Everything beyond the silence seemed very far away.

"Yes, but I always had Austin and Kane. I've had someone to share those memories of him, to keep them alive. But you..."

He trailed off, his gaze tracking its way up to mine. "You've had only yourself," he continued. "Not even your *parents*..."

I saw his eyes go glassy. He was actually choking up! Goddamn, it was the sweetest thing in the whole fucking world.

"I want you to know you have us now," he said. "You've *had* us but you didn't know it, and now... well, now..."

I reached out to touch his face, hard yet soft. By this point I was consoling him as much as he was me.

"I know."

He shifted forward and planted his lips over mine, melting the rest of the world away. Maddox kissed me slowly, deeply, sending bolts of arousal through me that rejuvenated my tired body.

Damn...

Nothing had felt like this in a long time — maybe ever, really. Not a connection like this. Not someone I'd let this close to my heart... someone I was okay with opening myself up to, mind, body, and soul.

Much less three *someones.*

I sighed as my head hit the pillow. Maddox was over me in an instant, kissing me harder as my hands sifted through vast fields of luscious blond hair. His mouth parted mine, driving his tongue inside with deep, soulful kisses that had me gasping for more.

You have us now.

The words were amazing, even though I dared not fully believe them. And yet so far, these men had protected me. They'd dedicated the last year of their lives to watching over me, over nothing more than a deceased brother-in-arm's promise, and had already saved my life on more than one occasion.

And they were *solid.* As close and tight-knit as any three men could ever possibly be. In life, in war...

... in the bedroom...

I was still moaning into Maddox's mouth, my mind spinning off dizzily into blissful oblivion as I shoved him onto his back. Our eyes locked, and after a shared moment of understanding our hands moved quickly to our own bodies. Clothes flew everywhere, in a flurry of frenzied activity. They littered the bed. The floor...

Then I was on him, straddling his warm, muscular thighs.

"Are you really okay with it?" I asked, my lips brushing against his. I could feel his manhood, throbbing between my legs. Brushing against my entrance...

"Okay with what?"

"Sharing me," I said breathlessly. "With the others."

My hair hung down on both sides of us, locking us together. It swayed gently as he thrust upward, eliciting a strangled gasp as he pierced me the core.

Ohhhhhhh...

"Yes," Maddox said, when he was buried fully inside me. "Totally and completely."

I moaned loudly as his hands went to my breasts, shoving me backward to bear the full weight of my body. It drove him all the way in, bottoming me out as my palms went to his magnificent chest.

"Sharing is the one thing we do best," he said softly. "And having you with us has opened up all new doors in that regard."

Somewhere deep inside me his cock pulsed and twitched... as if he were already going to come. I could feel how incredibly rigid he was. How amazingly, beautifully hard.

"We *want* you, Dallas," he said, bouncing me gently. "All of us. Every part of us."

His hands slid down my body, dragging deliciously over my nipples before settling on my naked hips. From there he guided me up and down, taking over with his two impossibly strong arms.

"Every part of *you.*"

I cried out as he thrusted hard at the end of the statement, stretching me from within. He pulled down on my hips to maximize penetration, simultaneously rolling the rest of his body into me.

God...

"We're going to protect you, Dallas," he whispered huskily. "All three of us."

He was so deep! So achingly, wonderfully deep in my belly. Breathlessly, I could feel him throbbing. Pulsing. Twitching...

"And you'll *never* have to be alone..."

Twenty-Nine

MADDOX

Screwing her with the others had been nothing short of incredible. Seeing her writhe beneath us. Watching her expression of rapture as we took her together, the three of us, making love to her body from all sides, all angles.

But taking her alone...

Holy fuck.

Well, that was fun too.

It was all I could do to hold back, watching Dallas glide rhythmically up and down my hard shaft. Her body was warm and amazing, her breasts bouncing firmly and hypnotically with every upward thrust. It made me want to immediately consummate our union by exploding gloriously inside her. I wanted to fill her up... then watch as the remainder of my juices ran out the sides of her pretty pink pussy.

I could picture it in my mind's eye: the sweet, blinding ecstasy of my inevitable orgasm. My cry of victory that would rattle the walls of our shitty little motel room. Yet as incredible as it would be, it would be even more fun to wait. More fun to make *her* climax first, before going to town on what had to be the tightest, wettest lover I'd ever had the pleasure of taking pleasure in.

"Slow down..."

I grunted the words more than said them. Dallas only grinned, then shifted her weight so she could reach back and fondle my balls.

Jesus Christ!

It was a slow, arduous torment. Watching her beautiful hair, cascading down around her gorgeous face. The feel of her fingernails, tracing lightly over my most sensitive skin. I kept on screwing her, driving deeper and deeper into the warm, wet recesses of her lithe, feminine body...

Then her hand closed over me, giving my balls a gentle squeeze.

"Let it go," she winked.

My shocked expression was met by another smile, or more accurately, a devilish grin. I was seconds away from flooding her. Milliseconds...

Not. Yet.

I threw her off like a bucking bronco, then shoved her back down against the bed. A moment later I had her ankles in my hands, her legs spread high in a 'V'. I re-entered her with a grunt, pushing and pumping at angles where I knew I'd have all the control. Where I could fuck her *properly*, and watch her enjoy it.

Either we all have her or none of us do. There's no middle ground.

My own words, as spoken to the others. After what happened that first night, our little impromptu meeting had been necessary.

We'd all agreed that what happened had been spontaneous and blameless. Totally unplanned. And yes, maybe even a little screwed up. Especially when we factored Connor into the equation. I mean shit, after all—

"Fuck me..." Dallas moaned, pulling me further inside her. Her fingernails were digging into my ass now, and I didn't mind a single bit. "Go *harder*, honey. Please..."

I picked up the pace, matching her stroke for stroke until her head lolled back with a sigh. With her eyes closed and her full lips parted she looked like a goddess. She had the perfect features of a Greek statue come to life; pink flesh from sculpted stone.

We all need to be okay with this. Every one of us.

My words again, stern and commanding. Even though I was talking mostly to myself.

All of us or none of us.

Kane had agreed right away, with a grunt and a nod. He'd wanted her for so long there was no way he could ever go back. Austin had been a bit more reluctant, but only in that he was still shocked by what happened. Once we talked it out... discussed the rules and the reasons behind them...

It's more natural than it sounds, the inner voice in my head assured me. *For the three of you, anyway. Nothing more than an extension of a thousand other things you've shared together as soldiers. As brothers-in-arms...*

Yes, that might be true. But this was a *person*. A person with emotions, a person with feelings.

We go only as far as she's comfortable, and not an inch further, I remembered saying. *Hell, she could end it immediately. She could pretend it never even happened.*

It was a risk for sure. An obvious out. If Dallas wanted that, she'd have it — no hard feelings, no questions asked.

And if she does that, we have to respect it. It's over immediately... for all three of us.

Four actually, but who was counting? The important part was making Dallas comfortable. Chalking up our lewd little act to just that: a single night of one-time debauchery. A curiosity fulfilled. Perhaps even a fantasy, satisfied.

Except she enjoyed it. Faced and embraced it, even.

And she wanted to do it *again*.

"MmmmMMmMMMMMMM!"

I stared back into her eyes, at the penultimate moment of her climax. Dallas's legs quivered violently. Her back arched, her mouth opened, and suddenly she was coming.

Unfuckingbelievable.

It was, truly. She was so tight, so breathtakingly beautiful, I couldn't help but finish at the same time. Her pussy contracted around me, squeezing me like a vice as I drove myself home one final time. Then I was coming too — shooting and spurting, painting her from the inside out with jet after jet of my hot, runny seed.

Four pulses... five... six...

Every beat was pure white ecstasy. Every throb sent a new surge of pleasure rocketing through my endorphin-rattled brain.

I cried out, then began plunging in and out of her again. I kept fucking her... kissing her... crushing her beneath my hard chest while pushing her legs so wide I thought she might split in two.

Only she didn't. Dallas Winters took everything I gave her, crying and whimpering and clutching me back. She never stopped screwing for even a single second, squeezing me against her body until every last drop of me had been drained inside her.

Christ, I want this.

I knew it back then, the first time we'd been together. Hell, somehow I knew it even before that.

The others had better be on the same page, I thought to myself grimly. *Because... Well, because...*

"Holy fuck..." Dallas choked as we collapsed together. Our bodies remained wonderfully tangled. The whole room reeked of sex. "That... that was..."

"Life altering?"

A cute little laugh escaped her pretty throat. She nodded.

"I was going to say a religious experience."

I smiled and kissed her again. "Close enough."

Thirty

DALLAS

He took me again in the middle of the night, rolling me onto my back. Screwing me hotly in the semi-darkness, by the muted pink light of the motel's hideous neon sign.

Half asleep, still seeping from our previous lovemaking, I spread my legs for him. Maddox sank into me like a sexy torpedo, piercing me to my warm and welcoming — yet still very sore — depths.

And I *loved* it.

It was all too wonderful, being used like this. Being *pleased* like this. In all the years of being alone, I just wasn't accustomed to the closeness. The physical intimacy of sleeping naked with someone; the proximity of a warm boyfriend, or lover, or whatever the hell he was.

At the moment, I was too ecstatic to care. I was staring up dreamily into the mirrored ceiling, my head just visible above his massive shoulder. I watched the muscles of his broad back twisting in unison as he screwed me into the bed.

163

Remained hopelessly captivated by each movement of his perfect, bubble-shaped ass as it clenched and unclenched, drilling himself home between my outstretched thighs.

They want to share me. All three of them.

It was like a dream. A very wet, very dirty, very forbidden dream.

And yet...

Could you really do it?

Hell, I *was* doing it. The only question that remained was whether or not I could make it work. Or rather, whether or not *we* could make it work: my three sexy SEALs, plus me.

But could you really keep all three *of them satisfied?*

The jury was still out on that one, that much I was sure of.

But it sure as fuck would be fun to *try*.

They care *about you, Dallas.*

They really did. Of that I was absolutely positive. And even better, they cared about me in ways no one ever really had before. Not past boyfriends. Not friends with benefits. Not even Mark, the cute but funny neighbor who stopped by for dinner once a month last year, and who didn't often leave without ending up naked in my bed.

Mark, who'd moved away when he was offered a better job in a nicer city. Who'd been snatched away beyond my control... like everyone else in my life.

Yes but these guys are still here, Dallas.

It was like the voice in my head wanted to torment me.

Or at the very least, get my false hopes up.

And they've been *here for you, even when you didn't know it.*

The sun came up, and I found myself staring at Maddox for a very long time. I'd spent a good half-hour just watching his slow, rhythmic breathing. Recording every line and curve of his broad shoulders, his taut, muscular arms held high overhead as he lay face-down in his own pillow.

Could you be happy with them?

It was a fantasy to think that I could. Or rather, that they could be happy with me. All three of them. Sharing the same girlfriend.

I laughed into the fake Hawaiian sunset. I made for a pretty kickass girlfriend, that was for sure. Just... maybe not *that* kickass.

"Morning," Maddox said suddenly, his eyes still closed. He turned sideways, then stretched and grinned. "How was your sleep?"

"Interrupted," I smirked back at him.

"Ah yes," he said. "The snoring."

"Among other things, yeah."

He sat up quickly and easily, the muscles of his stomach rippling in a delectable wave. God, I wanted to drop my head into his lap. Stare at those muscles close up, studying them hard before reaching out to—

"You make coffee?"

I turned my head toward the Tiki bar and sneered. "In *that* contraption?"

Maddox grunted. "It's a coffee maker, isn't it?"

"Not by my definition, no."

My lover let out a long hiss of dissatisfaction. Then he rose, reached for his boxers, and began stepping into them.

"Damn shame," I said, screwing the cap off a bottle of lukewarm water.

"What is?"

"You covering up that ass."

He stopped with this thumbs still in his waistband. "Want me to stop?"

I considered it for a moment. The pleasant soreness between my legs spoke up for me.

"Not now," I said. "Later for sure though."

He nodded and continued dressing, twisting left and right to pull on the rest of his clothes. Goddammit, I couldn't find an ounce of fat on his entire body.

"They have an Emperor room here or something?" he asked casually. "We could play Caesar and Cleop—"

KNOCK. KNOCK-KNOCK-KNOCK.

I perked up instantly. Staring at the door, I went from a hazy half-sleep to wide awake.

"Relax," Maddox told me. "It's only Austin."

Relief flooded through me, then confusion. I hadn't seen him make any calls or check his text-messages. Hell, he hadn't even picked up his phone.

"Trust me."

I got up and opened the door. Austin strolled right in, followed by Kane. The two of them gave me a brief hug, then glanced around the disheveled room.

"Hawaii?"

"Yeah," grunted Maddox, as he laced up his boots. "It was that or the Moon Room."

"*Moon* room?" I laughed. "You mean we could've–"

"Yes."

"Well shit," I giggled, grabbing for my own clothes. "Next time we're taking a vote!"

I stood, letting the sheets fall away from my semi-naked body. I could feel the weight of their eyes upon me. Strangely enough, it didn't feel weird at all.

"Ain't gonna be a next time," said Kane, his voice sounding distracted.

"Oh no?"

"No," Kane shot back. "They've had us on the run for too long now. Been fucking us over at every turn; at your house, at our house...."

I wriggled into my pants, feeling no shame. It was actually kind of fun.

"But from this point on," Kane continued, "after what we found out last night?" His look was grim, but with the hint of a smile.

"*We* do the fucking."

Thirty-One

DALLAS

"Right here. This is as about as close as we get."

The truck rolled to a silent stop, three-quarters of a block from the house in question. It looked like every other house in the neighborhood. No bigger, no smaller.

I leaned forward from my spot in the back seat, straining to see.

"So what are we looking at?"

"That house belongs to Evan Miller," said Austin.

"And who's that?"

"Remember the Jeep you ran off the road two nights ago?" asked Maddox.

"You mean obliterated? Yeah."

"Well it was registered to him."

I stared on in silence, looking over Kane's big shoulder. The house was dark, the driveway empty. It was only nine o'clock, too early for bedtime.

"So where is he?"

"Probably a morgue," Kane grunted.

The thought was a little morbid, even for me.

"Maybe a hospital," Austin offered, "but based on our inquiries it would have to be somewhere under the radar."

"A third possibility also exists," said Maddox.

"And what's that?"

"He left town."

Maddox nudged me with his leg, from where he was seated next to me. "Dallas, think hard. Evan Miller." His eyes bored into mine. "Do you know the name?"

I shook my head slowly, thinking. I was drawing a complete blank.

"Did Connor mention him maybe? Talk about him in passing?"

"Not that I can remember. Sorry."

The two men in the front seat glanced at each other. I could tell they were holding something back.

"Come on now," I said. "Out with it."

"With what?"

"You *know* something. Something you're not telling me."

It was almost infuriating, that they'd keep anything from me at all. That even now, after all we'd been through — after all *I'd* been through — they could try leaving me in the

169

dark about something.

"Miller is a Navy SEAL, like us," said Maddox. "Special ops. Really covert shit."

"So?"

"So he's involved in things we wouldn't know about. Only maybe Connor knew." He looked uncomfortable. "Because..."

"Because he and Connor bunked together," Kane said coldly. "When they were stationed out in New Orleans."

My throat constricted a little. The thought of Connor being betrayed by a friend... much less a fellow soldier? It just wasn't something that had ever crossed my mind.

"Do you remember when Connor was in New Orleans?"

"Yes," I said numbly.

Austin scratched at his chin. "It was an unknown assignment, a few years ago. He was there six months I think."

"Eight," I corrected him.

"It was one of the few times he'd been stationed apart from us," Kane added. "Maybe the only time."

"I— I don't know what he was doing there," I offered. "If you're asking me what his duties were, he never told me." I paused. "And I never really asked."

I'd learned not to ask, actually. The one time Connor told me an operations story I'd been scared shitless of the things he'd done. Not scared of the people he'd hurt or killed either; I assumed they were all enemies, and the enemy naturally had it coming.

No. Instead I'd been scared of the *danger* he was in.

It drove me mad with worry, knowing how close I'd come to losing him. Knowing that my brother was a bullet or a grenade or one terrible move away from being taken from me forever, like everyone else. As a Navy SEAL, I was always aware of the *possibility* he could get hurt. But this was stark, detailed reality...

It had kept me up for nights on end, that single story. And even though he'd emerged victorious, I'd asked him not to tell me stuff like that again. True to his word, he hadn't.

And now it was going to bite me in the ass.

"FUCK."

Maddox's hand closed over mine. "What?"

"I don't know!" I exclaimed. "Shit, I don't *anything* about what he did, or where he went, or what the fuck happened to him!" I was growing angry now. I could feel a familiar resentment welling up from that empty place inside me. A resentment I hadn't felt since Connor's death.

"I'm useless," I growled. "He never told me anything. He never told me—"

I stopped cold, mid-sentence. My head cocked to one side.

"What?" asked Austin. "What is it?"

"I— I think I remember..."

Maddox opened his mouth to speak, but Kane's gaze halted him. He remained silent, while I searched my the big messy file drawer of my brain.

"Connor switched apartments twice," I said, "while he

was stationed out there. He said it was because he was following his roommate."

Austin squinted. "*Following?*"

"Yes."

"Is that the word he used?"

"I... I think so. I remember thinking it was weird at the time. But I just assumed he met a guy he got along with. Someone he liked enough to switch apartments with," I shrugged. "Maybe to grab a bigger place, or they had a landlord problem, or—"

"Yeah, but *twice?*" asked Maddox. "So he moved into three places within eight months?"

I was still nodding, still remembering. The guys were communicating with each other silently, the way soldiers who spent a lot of time around each other often did. By looks. By expressions.

"I never heard him mention the guy's name," I said. "But Connor talked about his roommate sometimes. He said they were on the same assignment. They were permitted to live off base, but they spent a lot of time doing the same kinds of things."

"He was onto him," said Kane.

"What?"

"This guy Miller. Your brother wasn't just in it for the shits and giggles, he was following this guy to keep an eye on him."

I looked past him, scowling out at the house again. The anger had drained away with recollection, but the resentment was still there.

"Do you think this guy... is the reason..." I tightened my jaw. Swallowed the growing lump in my throat. "That Connor is dead?"

No one said anything. Finally, Austin nodded.

"One of them, yeah."

It was all I needed. I popped open the car door and stepped outside.

"Then let's go fuck his world up."

Thirty-Two

DALLAS

I was halfway to the house when they finally caught up with me. I felt one hand on my wrist, and another on my shoulder.

I was surprised at how easy it was to wrench myself away.

"Dallas!"

It was a hiss and a scream at the same time. A command delivered sternly while trying to be silent.

"We can't just—"

"Can't just *what?*" I screamed, whirling around. All three three of them jumped back a little, in surprise. It was oddly satisfying.

"If this guy knows we're onto him, things will be even more difficult," pleaded Austin. "And if—"

"She's right."

Everyone turned to face Kane, including me.

"Either this guy is dead," said Kane, "or he's not home. Either way, let's go find something out."

"And what if he *is* home?" Austin demanded.

Kane's hands balled into two giant fists. "Even better."

My heart swelled with love. *Real* love. The love you feel when you've been around someone long enough to know you want to be around them a *hell* of a lot more.

"Fine," Maddox swore, scanning around. "Let's get out of the fucking street at least."

They moved again, this time past me, this time with purpose. And now they were moving like *soldiers*, too. It reminded me of the way they crept up in the alley.

Forgoing the front door, we made our way into the back yard. After examining every inch of a low window's frame, Maddox took off his camo and began wrapping it around one hand.

"No alarm," he said, with obvious distaste. "Either this guy is stupid or overconfident."

"Or both," Austin pointed out.

A minute later we were inside, weapons out, treading carefully past all the broken glass. The house was clean and well-kept. There wasn't a lot of furniture, or clutter, or really anything at all.

"Counters are clean," said Maddox, sweeping through the kitchen. "No mail. No anything."

Kane was already in the hallway, his pistol held high. We made our way down, past a bathroom, into a home office. The desk was clean — the drawers virtually empty. There wasn't even a computer.

"Someone's already been here," Austin said. He reached down and held up four or five wires. One of them was connected to a monitor, laying face-down on the floor. He tapped something else. A wireless modem.

"Bedroom," Maddox said, jerking his head.

My heart was pounding so hard I could feel it in my neck. In a way it was thrilling, being here with them. Seeing them work. Watching their movements and hand signals, the way they entered each room by drawing down and checking the corners.

They're amazing.

It was something I'd thought of numerous times over the last few weeks. And especially, over the past few days.

They're incredible men... just like Connor.

Oddly enough, I'd never dated a military guy before. I'd been around several, thanks to Connor, but I guessed they just always saw me as off-limits.

Still, these guys were different. They weren't just suitors, they were *protectors*. They didn't just like or admire me, they were devoted to me in ways that no other guy could ever be.

For that reason alone, I was in awe of them.

Yes... but do you love them?

I lusted after them, that was for sure. Their hard, lean bodies, strutting half-naked through the halls of the house we shared. The way they kissed me. Touched me. The way they *handled* me in the bedroom, passing me back and forth between them...

But what about love, Dallas?

I did, of course. Love them, that is. I loved each of them in the way I loved my brother, but now there was something beyond that too. Something foreign and intangible, scratching at the back of my mind. Something that set off alarm bells and whistles of warning... but something that registered other, more exciting emotions too.

"Closet's clean," Maddox said from his side of the bedroom.

"Bath too," Austin said, re-entering.

Kane reached down with one big arm and lifted the mattress. It went up easily, and his instant grin made my heart soar.

"Well I'll be dipped in shit."

We all glanced down. Resting on the box-spring was a laptop computer, all sleek and dark.

"Lazy motherfuckers," grunted Kane, picking it up. He handed it to Austin, then put the bed back the way it was.

Maddox shook his head. "I can't believe they missed this."

"*They?*" I asked.

"The other guys involved with Miller. Probably the same ones we chased in the alley."

Austin was already turning the computer over in his gloved hands. He opened and closed it, then nodded crisply.

"We happy?" Kane asked.

"Fucking ecstatic," Austin grinned.

Thirty-Three

DALLAS

It took Austin only an hour to break into the strange laptop. We spent another three looking over his shoulder, watching as he sifted through its contents, looking at files and photos and search history information.

In the end, there was very little to tie Evan Miller to Connor. Much less the Navy at all.

"It's a relatively new machine unfortunately," sighed Austin. "Couple months old."

"So... nothing?"

"Not yet, anyway." He rubbed at his temples. It was already past midnight. "Other than a few .gov logins, of which I'll need to reverse-engineer his password. If I get into the base system with *his* credentials I can tell you a shit-ton of stuff about what this guy's been doing. But as for the rest of what's on here..."

He clicked rapidly a few more times, then suddenly stopped. Austin's whole expression changed. His eyes

179

narrowed.

"What is it?"

"I..." He cleared his throat. "I thought I saw something, but no." He went to close the laptop. "It's nothin —"

My hand shot out so fast he jumped in his chair. I grabbed the machine by one rounded edge. Stopped him from closing it.

"Bullshit."

"No, really," he fake yawned. "It's just that—"

I tried pushing the laptop back open. Austin's other hand stopped me.

"Let go."

"Dallas, listen. You need to know something—"

I shifted my hand forward. The others were suddenly wide awake again.

"I said LET IT THE FUCK GO."

Austin looked to Kane for help, then Maddox. Maddox looked confused.

"What the hell is going on?"

"There's a... *file* on there," Austin said uncomfortably.

Maddox's brows came together. "What *sort* of file? Is it something we could—" He sucked in a quick breath and stopped. Whatever it was, he suddenly understood. He tried shifting mid-sentence.

"Oh yeah. O—Okay. Maybe it would be better if—"

"Show her."

Kane's voice was low and insistent. It left no room for argument.

"Yeah?" asked Austin. "You really think that's a good idea?"

"She deserves to see," Kane said with a shrug. Slowly, his brown eyes tracked over to me. "It's going to be hard though," he added. "Tough for you to get through."

A sinking feeling stole over my whole body. My stomach felt like I'd swallowed something sour.

"W–What is it?"

"It's a copy of the last thing your brother sent us," said Maddox gravely. "A message... from Connor."

I felt faint. Weak. Dizzy. The arm I was using to hold the laptop open was shaking.

"Is... it bad?"

"It's not good," Austin admitted.

I let go of the computer and sank back in my chair. My skin was prickled with goosebumps. Every hair on my arms stood on end.

A message. From Connor.

I tried to breathe but I couldn't. My chest felt like someone was sitting on it.

The very last message...

For a long time, no one spoke.

"Listen," said Kane, breaking the silence. "If you want,

we can *tell* you what's on it. Word for word, we can tell you what gets said."

"Said?" My voice cracked.

"Yes," said Maddox. There was genuine compassion in his eyes. "It's a video message. And it... well..." he swallowed dryly. "You'd just have to see."

The others were staring at me, as if trying to get me to understand. There weren't exactly trying to talk me out of it anymore. More like... prepare me.

Connor...

I thought about my brother, brave and strong. My brother, who'd faced death over and over without blinking. Who's delivered death himself, without hesitation, without compromise. Who'd even saved the lives of these very men who were now trying to protect me.

My brother the warrior, who was afraid of nothing.

"Alright," I said, inhaling a long, shivering breath. With the backs of my hands, I wiped away any tears that threatened to gather at the corners of my eyes.

"Show me."

Thirty-Four

DALLAS

I didn't expect the video to begin in darkness, but it did. That part was jarring. I was expecting to see Connor, prepping myself mentally for the image of my brother's face. The sound of his voice...

Calm down, Dallas.

I had to force myself to stop trembling. To keep my body from shivering all over.

That's not what Connor would've wanted.

As the camera adjusted its light, I could make out a small, nondescript room. There were no details, no distinguishing markings. It could've been any room, anywhere. But from the others' reactions, I knew differently.

This was going to be *the* room.

Holy shit.

The room where my brother died.

I felt a reassuring hand on my shoulder. Maddox's

fingers were warm, his grip firm. Austin sat to one side of me. Kane was pressed up against the other.

Are you sure you want to do this?

I shoved the thought away. Stared into the room, into the screen. Whoever had set up the camera must've done so from out of frame. I could hear noise now. The sound of doors, slamming.

Voices.

Gunshots.

I gasped as Connor entered the room. He swept in from the side, moving with the swift urgency of being chased, or hunted, or in big, big trouble.

He ran straight for the camera. Almost to the point where I expected him to grab it and shake it. Instead he stopped short, his hands on his knees, taking deep breaths. He looked winded. Covered in dirt, or grease, or something equally strange...

Connor!

The tears threatened to fall, but I choked them back. I concentrated on sitting upright, keeping my back straight, my legs together. Anything and everything but the emotions I was feeling right now.

"Listen..."

His head snapped up as he started talking, still gasping for breath. Suddenly he staring back at me with those big blue eyes.

My eyes.

"I don't have much time," Connor said. His voice was

tight and hurried. "By the time you get this..." he swallowed hard, "I'll already be gone. So don't act stupid. Don't think any of you can just rush out and sav—"

BANG!

Connor's head whipped to the right. Somewhere off screen, I could hear the unmistakable sound of a door being pounded...

Pounded by multiple people.

"If you loved me at all," Connor said quickly, "you'll find and protect my sister."

He was covered in blood. I could see that now. It didn't necessarily look like *his* blood, but it was blood just the same.

"My sister has—"

The voices were louder now. There was more banging, more shouting. Someone fired a pistol multiple times, making the rest of his sentence unintelligible.

"Find and protect Dallas," Connor was saying emphatically. "No matter what happens, you have to find her!" Now he did take the camera. He grabbed it and shook it.

"Go to her and keep her *safe*..."

BOOM!

The door bursts open. A shower of dust and debris flew past my brother in the background. There were more shouts. More screams...

I covered my face with my hands.

"I—"

At this point something broke into frame — a person maybe, or something more. It struck my brother hard enough to knock the camera — and him — straight to the floor.

CONNOR!

Everything spun dizzily as my brother disappeared from view. The noise stopped. The shouting stopped. The camera was face down, or powering down, or no longer working at all.

Then everything went black.

The 'pause' symbol appeared on-screen, signaling the end of the video. It was actually merciful. I was just seconds away from breaking out into tears.

Austin reached out and closed the viewing window. He took the laptop back and swung it shut, and this time I didn't stop him.

"I'm so sorry, Dallas."

Maddox squeezed me gently. He lowered his face to plant a kiss on my cheek... just as I flung myself into the combined embrace of all three of them.

Tears flowed now, and not just from me. I could see them streaking the face of Austin. Of Maddox. Even Kane's eyes had gone glassy.

It was unexpectedly comforting. Sharing my grief with the only other people on earth who could possibly relate to it.

"We're *all* sorry."

Thirty-Five

KANE

I was somewhere warm and wet, surrounded by heat and comfort. Floating. Spinning.

Happy.

There was no stress, no worry. These things were somehow foreign to me, although I knew I should feel them. Somehow they'd just dissolved away, in the wake of complacency and gratification. I was relaxed beyond all relaxation. Totally and utterly free.

And that's when I knew I was in a dream.

I woke slowly, aware of movement. Aware of warmth, and contentment.

Aware of the hot mouth, moving slowly up and down, between my legs...

Oh... shit...

I craned my neck to look down, and there she was. Dallas was blowing me, tip to base, her mouth wet and her lips

187

tight and her pretty blonde hair, brushing against my stomach.

Good morning to ME.

For a while I just watched her, totally transfixed. Enjoying the warmth of her talented mouth. The feel of her hot tongue sliding against the underside of my fully-erect shaft.

I shifted, and she glanced up at me. I saw her smile wickedly.

Then she lowered her mouth and went back to the task at hand.

Well this is a new one.

I let my hands go to her head, my fingers sifting into her silky hair. I didn't guide her at all, but rather followed her movements. Remained content to let her go at her own pace, slowly driving me crazy with every feverish push and pull.

Damn. A guy could definitely get used to this.

I could, of course. Only it wasn't just me. It was all three of us, and just one of her. And yet...

And yet you still love it. You're still okay with it, aren't you?

In truth I was. And not only was I okay with it, but I would've been wholly disappointed if it somehow came to an end. If, for some reason, we'd all decided to stop doing what we were doing. Or if Dallas...

If Dallas realized this wasn't for her.

I mean shit, right? It *was* crazy. Who actually does something like this? Three men falling for the same woman? Each of them willing to share her with the others, without feeling envy or jealousy or any of the other baser emotions that could rip such a delicate arrangement apart?

But then there was this other part of me. The part telling me it *wasn't* so crazy. That for us — Maddox, Austin and I — the rules were somehow different. That because of our training, our experiences, our long history of living and working and surviving together through some of the most hellacious shit imaginable, pulling off a relationship like this would actually be *easy.*

"Mmmmmm..." Dallas moaned, her mouth vibrating with me buried deep in her throat. I looked down at her again and she winked.

God!

Okay, maybe easy wasn't the word. Plausible. That was better. Maybe even *likely.* Hell, we'd shared everything else. We'd even chosen to live together after our service, when we could've just as easily gone our separate ways. Only we were better as a unit. Better as a team. In the Navy, in the civilian world...

And now, apparently, in a relationship too.

Is that what this is? A relationship?

Well it was certainly something. And I was willing to take it just as far as Dallas wanted to. Ultimately it would be up to her how long this went on, and when it ended. Or even *if* it ended at all.

I felt a sharp spike of anticipation at the thought. Just as quickly I pushed it down. No. I wasn't going to get my hopes up. Whatever happened, happened.

My body tensed. My legs locked straight as my arousal reached its peak, the feel of her wonderful mouth bringing me over the edge...

"*UNGHHH!*"

The cry was wrenched from my body, somewhere deep near my core. Then I was coming... filling her mouth over and over with what sure felt like *gallons* of my hot, sticky seed.

Jesus Christ!

Dallas's head stopped moving up near the tip, taking everything I gave her straight down her throat. She gripped me tightly as she swallowed once, then twice, and then finally a third time before lowering her lips back down again and cleaning the rest of me up.

My orgasm was apocalyptic. The purity of the pleasure was staggering.

Fuckkkkkk... I groaned inwardly, as she continued bobbing up and down on me. Dallas sucked me for another minute, as if too greedy to let go. When she finally did, I left her mouth with a satisfying 'pop'.

Our eyes met, through a tangle of disheveled blonde hair. Her lips were full and puffy now. They looked even more amazing than usual.

"Good morning sweetie," she smiled, pinning a lock back over one ear.

"It sure fucking is," I smirked back.

"You were dreaming," said Dallas. "At least, you were when I got here."

I nodded numbly. After the mind-erasing orgasm she'd just given me, fuck if I knew what any of my dreams were about.

"So... what exactly was this?" I asked, gesturing to my spent cock. "Not that I'm complaining, mind you."

Dallas chuckled softly. "A goodbye present?"

My brows crossed, but only for a moment. Then I remembered.

"Oh yeah," I said, kicking myself. "New Orleans."

"Uh huh."

She climbed up and planted a kiss on my chest. Then another. Then a third, and a forth. Her touch was as sweet as it was electric.

"The flight leaves in two hours," Dallas lamented, groaning into one nipple. "I should probably get showered."

She went to push herself up, but I had a hand on her naked ass now. I gave it a hard squeeze that made her eyes flare wide.

"So when do I get *this* present?" I asked.

Dallas moaned at my touch. She traced her tongue slowly around one nipple, causing me to relax my grip. Then she bit me playfully, and leapt nimbly to her feet.

"When you welcome me home," she winked, and bounced out of the room.

Thirty-Six

DALLAS

I was seated between Austin and Maddox, cruising along comfortably at thirty-five thousand feet. Contemplating how radically different my life was now than a month ago, and how I somehow wouldn't trade it for all the world.

Shit, if it meant getting to where I was now I would've burned the house down myself. Imminent danger of being killed aside, living with my three Navy SEALs had filled my life with action, excitement, and of course, near limitless amounts of dirty, filthy sex.

Only it wasn't just sex, and I'd be lying if I said it were. There were feelings now too; emotions and attachments that came hand in hand with being so close to them. The guys were fun and funny, lovable as well as gorgeous. And they were fiercely protective of me. Sweet and kind, but also alpha enough to give back every last ounce of sarcasm and trouble I dished their way.

And *God,* they were so fucking hot...

Going to New Orleans had been Maddox's idea, based on the intel they'd gathered so far. We needed to find out more about Evan Miller. And that meant diving into where he'd been stationed, and the commanders above him. Even the places he lived, which of course meant one thing:

I'd be walking in the footsteps of Connor.

There was a lot we could find out in New Orleans, and we hoped to make sense of my brother's last days. The recording of his apparent death had knocked me on my ass for a bit, but I'd gotten back up quickly. For Connor's sake as much as mine.

Protecting myself — and now my three incredible lovers — was something we all owed to Connor. We needed to find out who hurt him, and what they wanted. Most of all, I wanted to know why.

Clearing ourselves of this mess went hand in hand with avenging my brother's death; two birds, one stone. And if we dug deep enough to cause a little more trouble? Kicking the hornets nest was probably necessary to finding out exactly where to burn it all down.

"Another, miss?"

I smiled sweetly as the flight attendant handed me a fresh bottle of vodka. I still had enough cranberry juice left to mix myself happy for the next hour or so. Austin was staring out the window like a zombie, and Maddox was crashed out completely. His head rested so adorably on my shoulder, I didn't even mind the drool.

Leaving Kane had been a tough call, but there was still so much to be done back in Vegas. He had leads on who might be checking out the black SUV from Nellis, and he planned on following up with anyone associated with Miller, too. And though we were worried about leaving him a sitting duck and an easy target, he'd promised to sleep on base for however long we were gone.

Who was he really kidding, though? If I knew anything about Kane it was that he'd never back down. He wouldn't hide with his tail tucked between his legs — especially not with so much information still to be gleaned. More likely he'd stay up every night, staring at the outside camera feeds while cleaning his pistols, a fully loaded M4A1 rifle across his lap.

The image brought a smile to my face. So did the memory of this morning's farewell blowjob.

I sighed contentedly, settling into my seat as the third little bottle of vodka slid easily down my throat.

Yes, I was a happy girl.

Even with the shitstorm raging around us.

Thirty-Seven

DALLAS

New Orleans was even more fantastic, more breathtaking than I could've possibly imagined. And in my mind's eye, it was pretty damned beautiful to begin with.

We touched down mid-afternoon and checked straight into our hotel room, which was clean and nice and sported two queen sized beds. My stomach did a sexy backflip as I wondered if I'd end up in one or the other by the end of the night.

Or quite possibly, both.

"You guys sleep there," I laughed, pointing to the second mattress as I laid claim to the first. "He snores," I told Maddox, before moving my finger from Austin to him. "And *he* hogs the blankets."

The guys only looked at each other and shook their heads. Their plans were obviously different. I'd go along with whatever they wanted of course, but they didn't need to know that. Not right now at least.

I grunted, plopped my bag down, then fell heavily back into the softness of the bed.

New Orleans, I sighed to myself, staring at the ceiling. *Pretty fucking cool.*

It was, actually. The city was on my bucket list of places to visit before I kicked off the planet, and I wasn't even close to kicking off yet. So far, anyway.

"Get your pretty ass up," Austin ordered, offering his hand. I took it and let him pull me to my feet. "We've got work to do."

We freshened up quickly and headed back down to the lobby. Then, as a trio, we spent the rest of the day exploring the northern edge of the city. Our rental car was small and inconspicuous; despite my every attempt to get the guys to pick a convertible, we ended up with a small, four-door sedan.

"How boring," I whined, sticking my tongue out at Maddox. His mock grumpy face was kinda cute, but I especially liked Austin putting his hands on my hips... and practically shoving me into the car.

"Drive," Maddox said, totally shocking me as he handed over the keys. "And none of that race car shit you pulled back at home."

They worked their phones while I navigated, cruising my way around The Big Easy. Our first stop was a government contractor Connor had once done work for, and who Maddox had been talking with through text-messages. The contacts there guided us in another direction, and we ended up pretty far from our hotel by the time night fell.

The city looked even better at night. The mixture of

ancient architecture and modern uplighting lent everything a shadowy, spooky feel. Some parts of the city were darker than others, and you could always tell when you wandered into a very old area.

And it was *busy.* Lots of people, lots of cars. Tons of noise too, for such an old and historic place.

"Connor's first apartment is right up here," said Maddox, pointing through the windshield. "Three more blocks, then turn left."

I did, and we cruised to a halt before the blackened husk of a very large, very old, and very gutted three-story structure.

"Damn."

A fire had raged here, and not a particularly friendly one. It had consumed the entire complex we'd been guided to, and part of the next building as well.

"Dead end," sighed Maddox in disappointment. Though he sounded distracted, his eyes were still scanning shrewdly in every direction. "Okay, what's next?"

"East side," replied Austin, pointing. "Three miles that way."

He punched up a new address, then locked his phone into the dashboard holder. We'd all gotten new ones, immediately after our first run-in with the black SUV. And shit, I was just getting used to the old one.

"Your brother lived here and he never had you out?" Maddox was asking.

"Nope."

"Must've been in some shit then," he replied. "Connor *always* talked about you." He smiled cheerily. "And he always looked forward to coming home."

I returned the smile, wishing I could go back in time. Wishing I could make things different with a simple warning, something that could change the sad path that ended his life.

Choking back emotion, I followed the on-screen instructions directing us toward my brother's second apartment. I rolled intentionally slowly, so I could take in as much of the city as possible.

"Goddamit," Austin said abruptly from the back seat. "I *really* wish your brother had contacted one of us."

Maddox nodded. "Or *all* of us," he said. "Whatever he was up to, it was foolish of him to try and take it all on himself."

He seemed to regret the words immediately, glancing over at me with more than a little fear. But I only laughed.

"Did you even *meet* Connor?" I quipped. "Since when have you ever known him to ask for help with *anything?*"

Maddox grinned. Austin's head bobbed in agreement. "Your brother was always giving the help rather than asking for it," he said. "That's probably why it was so hard for him to reach out."

We continued on, and the conversation drifted fondly to Connor. The little things he did. The quirks and idiosyncrasies he had, like always leaving the television on, or not closing the bathroom door whenever he used it. It was heartwarming to learn I wasn't the only one who had to suffer these things. They'd lived through it too.

In a strange but distant way, it kept his memory alive.

"Did he jam all the condiments into random drawers of the refrigerator?" asked Austin.

"Always," I laughed. "I could never find anything."

"I think he did it on purpose," smirked Maddox. "He didn't even *use* ketchup but he was always stowing it somewhere. Hiding it away, and—"

His sentence stopped so abruptly I actually turned to face him. His expression had gone suddenly serious. Even worse, his eyes were locked on the rear view mirror.

"You see what I'm seeing?"

"Yup," Austin said from the back seat.

I heard the click of a safety being flipped off. The 'ka-chink' of a round being chambered.

Awww, shit.

I checked the mirror as well. There was another vehicle, maybe three car-lengths behind me, rolling along at the same slow speed. I gripped the wheel tightly for a moment, then remembered to relax. If I had to act fast, having my arms locked and my shoulders tight could be a big problem.

"What should I do?"

"Nothing yet," said Maddox. He'd abandoned the mirror and was looking over his shoulder now. "Hang a right, though. As soon as you can."

I did, and without signaling. Methodically, the other vehicle did the same.

"This road cuts through," Austin said, looking at his

phone's screen. "But it narrows first."

The two of them stared at each other, and a whole conversation passed between them. Austin smirked. Maddox nodded.

I jumped a little as a third sidearm was tucked carefully into my lap. I could tell it was already cocked and loaded.

"Pump the brakes hard when we tell you to," said Maddox, "and come to a quick stop."

I was nervous. Scared. A little bit confused.

But also thrilled.

"It's time for some goddamn answers."

Thirty-Eight

DALLAS

We waited until we'd passed the choke point, until the sidestreet had finished narrowing off and was about to open up again. That's when Maddox double-tapped my knee, and I jerked the car to a stop.

A split-second later, everything happened at once.

The guys left the car from either side, doors flying open while they drew down on the vehicle behind us. Shots rang out — two quick ones fired into the air rather than at a target.

I exited my own side, hunched behind the door and clutching my weapon. Moving rapidly, Maddox and Austin advanced on the car we'd all but trapped in the alley. There was nowhere for it to go but back. Barely enough room on either side of the vehicle to open the doors without hitting brick.

"Easy, easy!"

The vehicle stopped and two men got out, immediately

holding their hands high in the air. My SEALs took each at gunpoint, patting them down, making sure they weren't armed before shoving them face-down on the hood of what looked to be an old Ford Bronco.

"Why are you stalking us?" Maddox demanded, grabbing one guy by the collar. "What are you trying—"

"Orders."

Slowly I lowered my weapon. My two lovers looked at each other.

"We're only following orders, sir," said the shorter of the now prisoners. "CPO Woodward sent us to warn you. To deliver a message, and—"

Maddox twisted his grip and bore down. The driver of the other vehicle cried out in pain.

"A *warning?*" he spat angrily. "Who the hell is Woodward to—"

"Not from us, sir! From... from..."

"Bro, ease up."

Austin's words caused Maddox to look up. He gave him a firm nod.

"I know Woodward," said Austin. "Partially, anyway. He's good people. If he sent these guys, they're legit."

Slowly we all relaxed. Half a minute later everyone was standing upright, the guy driving the Bronco still rubbing at his neck.

"Sorry if we spooked you," the passenger said. He was taller than the driver and clean shaven, head and everything. Both men wore casual fatigues. "Woodward said you'd be coming. Told us to track you down, arrange a meeting with him."

Maddox still looked confused. "Who's Woodward?" he asked, more to Austin then to the others.

"One of the officers running a few things over here," Austin replied. "Special programs. Biodynamics, I think." He looked at the passenger. "Am I right?"

"Yes sir," the man said. "The Naval Biodynamics Lab is mostly shut down, but there's a lot of residual. CPO Woodward's been in charge of sewing things up. He's not here now, though. Not for a couple days."

"That's why they sent us," the other soldier added. "We're supposed to find you. Give you this."

He reached into a shirt pocket and pulled out a phone. It wasn't a smartphone. It was one of those pre-loaded flip-open models, without any features. Exactly what the police and drug-dealers in movies were always calling 'burner phones'.

"CPO Woodward needs to meet with you," said the driver. "He'll call you when its right. Until then, he's told us to instruct you to lay low. You're being watched already..."

At that, all four of them scanned the shadowy little alley. Everything was quiet but the sound of ambient city noise, way off in the distance.

"Watched?" Austin asked skeptically. "We just fucking got here."

"We know. You checked into the Sierra a couple hours ago."

Maddox swore mightily, a whole stream of curses that

ended in him shaking his head at the ground.

"The car's no good either," one of the soldiers said. "We've been ordered to switch."

He tossed Austin a set of keys, and he caught them deftly. The two SEALs glanced at me, then each other.

"So what now?" asked Maddox. "We sit on our hands until Woodward calls?"

"That's about the size of it," the bald man said apologetically. "CPO says you should switch digs. Move into the French Quarter, where the crowds make it easy to blend in. We grabbed you a spot where you can disappear for the next 36 to 48 hours, until that phone rings."

"Relax a bit," said the other guy. He even smiled. "Enjoy Mardi Gras."

My mouth dropped open. "*Mardi Gras?*"

Suddenly it made sense. The noise. The traffic. The sheer number of people. We'd stuck to the upper part of the city, so we hadn't really been around the bigger party areas. But now...

"Mardi Gras..." I repeated in amazement.

All four guys were staring at me now. Maddox's mouth twisted into a smirk.

"What, you *really* didn't realize what month it was?"

Thirty-Nine

DALLAS

Once we reached the heart of the city, it was like being immersed in splendor. For one, it was Friday night. The weekend before Fat Tuesday. The BIG weekend, or so I'd read, or so I'd seen in dozens of spectacular videos online.

None of them however, did this party any *true* justice.

The French Quarter was a stunning array of 18th century Spanish-style architecture, splashed with a modern flair. Walking its three-hundred year old streets was awe-inspiring enough, without bumping elbows with dragons and zombies and beautiful young men and women in painted masks. Everything I saw took my breath away; the fun and excitement of carefree carousal, the explosion of sights and smells and sounds that made up the weeks-long party of Mardi Gras.

It was all so fucking awesome.

The best part was the anonymity. We blended seamlessly into a crowd of *thousands*, and we could wear disguises to boot. After grabbing a round of drinks and some street-food we wound our way up Bourbon Street. We walked hand in hand to avoid getting separated, with me happily in the middle.

"Masks?" asked Austin, approaching a vendor. "Just to be safer?"

Maddox shrugged. "Why not?"

A few minutes later both my lovers were sporting elaborately-made half-masks that covered both eyes and nose. Austin's was some kind of black and red demon, which looked as fiercesome as it did cool. Maddox's mask was painted to look like metal, all bolts and rivets and interlocking plates of steel, frozen in a warrior's grimace.

"Now you," one of them said.

"Already a step ahead of you."

I pulled them over to a second vendor, who was painting faces. I sat while she layered color after color over me, all around my eyes and cheeks. When she finally handed me a mirror and I was staring back at a blue and gold peacock mask, all wispy and feathery and beautiful.

"Alright," said Maddox, slipping his hand back into mine. His grip was strong, his smile warm. "*Now* we can have some fun."

We walked some more, threading our way through merry, happy crowds. It would've been hard for me, dodging the drunker people ready to stomp all over my feet... if not for Maddox and Austin at the end of each arm. With the two of them standing six-foot-plus and imposing as hell, I was given plenty of room. Even in the Central Square, where the sheer number of undulating bodies mashed together would've given even the staunchest Fire Marshal a heart-attack.

It was all good though, and all part of the scene. We saw three different parades, each more beautiful and wondrous than the last. They rolled slowly by the cheering, drunken throngs, flinging beads in every direction like silly-string.

I caught more than my fair share, and didn't even have to lift my shirt. Not that I wouldn't have. After dipping into a few different bars for drinks and shots, I was certainly feeling no pain.

"You happy yet?" Austin grinned, kissing me as the crowd cheered another float going by.

"Cloud fucking nine," I practically shouted into his ear, before biting it playfully.

They were both kissing me constantly. Both grabbing me, holding me, pulling me against their hard, lean bodies. In any other circumstance, it would've been totally outrageous — two strong men sharing the same woman between them, making out with her publicly, walking with one hand on each globe of her ass.

But here at Carnivale... no one even batted an eye.

Shit, I wanted to *live* here.

We drank some more, but the guys were disciplined enough to always remain in control. I myself was smart enough to keep hydrated, too. I carried a water bottle with me everywhere we went, and filled it whenever I could. It also helped when we finally grabbed a very late 'dinner', sitting down for finger-foods at some cute outdoors cafe that was about to close up for the night.

The night wore on. The streets thinned out. It was

well past midnight, but I wasn't even tired! My heart was racing, my skin flush with the blood pumping through my veins. I never wanted it to stop. Never wanted it to end. It was all too perfect.

"Our hotel," Maddox pointed with his chin, trying not to spill his latest beer, "is right over there."

I turned to look at the ancient, twisted building. Centuries old, it was absolutely gorgeous. Wrought-iron balconies interlaced the multi-level structure, which stood halfway down a side-street, right off the main thoroughfare.

Austin's arm slid around me from behind, pulling me into him. He put his lips right up against my ear.

"Take the party inside?" he growled suggestively.

By now I was absolutely randy. The alcohol had loosened me up, as well as all the kissing and touching. My early morning tryst with Kane had made me horny as hell. If our plane hadn't been leaving I'd have turned around and made him hard again... jumped on him and rode him until we both saw stars.

God, was that really *this morning?* This was the longest, most glorious day of my life.

In answer I spun around, throwing my arms around them both. I kissed them in turn, with heat and passion, sliding my tongue into each of their mouths. Four hands went to my body. Twenty fingers explored downward, sliding over my ribs, my hips, the flat of my stomach...

Oh my God.

... and even lower.

"Yes..." I breathed, my voice swallowed up by the noise of the crowd.

Austin pulled me tighter against him. A hand pierced my waistband, two fingers gliding down to hover over my button. My panties were already soaked through.

"We didn't hear you."

"Oh fuck..." I groaned, writhing in his arms. Then, more loudly, "I said *YES*."

"Did you hear her, man?" Austin teased. "I think she said something."

Maddox took my face in his hands. He lowered his lips to mine and gave me the hottest, wettest open-mouthed kiss of my life.

Holy fuck.

A finger slipped inside me. It went in so easily I could feel the wetness gathering along the insides of my thighs.

If I didn't do something soon they were going to fuck me on the street.

"Take me back to our room," I barked at the both of them. "NOW."

Austin raised an eyebrow. Maddox outright laughed.

"Take you back and *what?*"

I put one hand between each of their legs. Both of them were already hard.

"Take me back to our room," I growled, giving them each a squeeze. "And fuck me *senseless.*"

Forty

DALLAS

Our secondary hotel was smaller and cozier than the first. Provided by Woodward's men — who'd also sent for our things — it was also older and much more historic. Tighter in terms of space, it did have one major advantage: a single, king-sized bed.

"You guys *better* not have clothes on," I called out from the tiny bathroom.

Maddox's voice floated in on a laugh. "Come out and see."

I adjusted my thigh-high fishnet stockings. They ended in lace trim, attached to a red and black garter by snap-on garter belts. A cherry red satin bra and matching G-string panties completed my outfit, along with my Mardi Gras beads.

Lots of beads.

"Get in here or we're coming in after you!"

"Yeah," I heard Austin agree. "Until you get here we're

210

just two guys laying uncomfortably in bed together!"

That last part made me giggle. I killed the light and strutted forward, pausing in the doorway. Shifting my hips left and right, I did a slow spin so they could get the full effect.

'God *DAMN*..."

Austin swore. Maddox whistled. The two of them were lying on either side of the bed, naked except for their boxers. Their *bulging* boxers. That part I could barely take my eyes from.

"You switched masks?" I smirked, approaching the bed. Maddox was the demon now, Austin the warrior. "Did you think I wouldn't notice?"

Either they'd done it for fun or they were actually trying to trick me. Which was ridiculous of course, because I already knew every delectable inch of their bodies.

"Can't get anything past you," said Maddox.

"Nope."

My knees hit the bed, and now I was crawling toward them. Crawling *between* them. My lovers looked amazing in the twinkling half-light — all muscle and sinew and warm, delicious man-flesh. The thinnest sheen of sweat brought out every magnificent ripple of their flat stomachs, each ripped with its own quivering six-pack.

Holy shit, Dallas! my mind swore.

Austin tugged his own boxers down, and his cock sprang free. He closed his hand over it and began stroking it slowly up and down... a visual that made me instantly wet.

What on earth did you do to deserve this?

Out beyond our quaint little balcony, the sounds of laughter and distant partying were still winding down. The guys reached for me together, each closing a hand against my face. Maddox's palm was warm, gently caressing my cheek. I closed my eyes and tilted contentedly into it, just as Austin slipped his thumb slowly, sensuously, into my mouth.

Wow...

Already I felt my breath going shallow. The last twenty-four hours had been the pinnacle of my existence; my best day ever. And it was about to get better...

They pulled me forward between them, down into the softness of the bed. Then they began kissing me. Over and over they did it, their hands freely exploring my body, my skin, the satin and silk of my lingerie. They kissed me back and forth until until I was dizzy; until my head was swimming with lust, and need, and desire.

And there was something else there too. Something that made me warm and tingly. Almost even queasy inside.

You're falling in lov–

A hand slid between my legs and my thighs automatically parted. I was on my back, looking up. Staring at two of the most handsome, chiseled faces I'd ever known. Austin was dragging his tongue over my neck. Planting kisses on all the most sensitive spots, while his hot breath sent shivers across my skin.

And Maddox...

Oh God.

Maddox was nibbling his way down my stomach. Kissing lower and lower, until he reached the thin strip of skin between my garter and my panties, which were already so damp they were two shades darker than when I'd put them on.

His mouth closed over my mound. Then my back arched, my hands clawing the sheets beneath me as he blew a steady stream of hot air right through my G-string and directly onto my pussy.

"*Unnnnghhhhhhh!*"

It came out as a groan — raw and loud and totally pure. There was no need for discretion. No need to be quiet. I could scream if I wanted to; I could let them pound me and jackhammer me and crush me beneath their bodies. I could yell out loud as they pinned me between them, utterly destroying me from both ends...

And no one in the entire world would know but *us*.

My bra came down, and a hot mouth closed over one nipple. Austin was kissing one breast while kneading the other. Rolling one hard nub firmly between his fingers, while tracing circles around my areola with the tip of his hot tongue.

But down below...

"MmmmMMmmmMmmm..."

Maddox was driving me out of my fucking mind. He was still blowing, but now he was humming too. Eating me through my panties, licking and kissing and sucking my pussy with nothing but the tiniest, wettest strip of fabric separating his eager mouth from my aching, throbbing slit.

How the hell *did I get here?*

It was a fair question. If I'd met these men a year and a half ago it would've been as Connor's brothers-in-arms.

213

There would've been polite handshakes and warm smiles, maybe a few drinks and some storytelling. But that would've been it. That would've been the full extent of our relationship because these were my brother's friends... and my brother's friends had always been off-limits.

But *now...*

I gasped as Maddox's tongue slid inside me. He'd finally pulled my panties to one side, then dove forward to devour me properly. His hands went to my stocking-covered legs, spreading them even wider.

I swallowed hard, past the throbbing of my own frantic heartbeat. No, now things were different. Now I was as close to these men as Connor had been, if not through combat, at least mentally and emotionally. And physically...

Well, physically I had him beat.

This is crazy this is crazy this is crazy...

My head thrashed side to side as I rolled my fists into Maddox's hair. I was grinding him now. Rolling my hips into him like some greedy, needy whore. I glanced down, and saw I was being eaten by a demon. The image was so uniquely hot I wanted to sear it into my brain...

My beads slid noisily as Austin shifted them out the way. He was teasing my nipples, alternating between licking one and pulling on the other. The way he was cupping and rubbing my tits felt wonderful. His hands and fingers looked perfect on me, so strong, so masculine.

God, I could really live my life like this...

The thought floated in randomly, through my haze of euphoria. For the first time I actually considered it. It could *be* like this, if the guys wanted me the way I wanted them. The four of us could make it work... maybe. At least for a little while.

Could you, though?

I sighed, biting my lip, as all new levels of arousal surged up from within. Without warning I was writhing, grinding, coming all over my lover's face. Showering his lips and tongue with a stream of hot juice, as I squirted for the first time since my failed attempts at going away to college.

"GODDDDDD!"

I went *literally* out of my mind. My head smashed backward into the pillow as my body twisted, my hands squeezing uncontrollably around thick fistfuls of Maddox's beautiful blond hair. Still clutching him I screamed into an imaginary sky, still coming, still squirting. Only vaguely aware of the warmth and wetness, somewhere beyond the pure white elation of my earth-shattering climax.

When I came to, my chest heaved. My stomach fluttered in and out with every ragged breath. I looked down apprehensively, and everything was *soaked*. Maddox included.

"Sorry for the mess," I smiled apologetically. "I—"

"Don't be."

My thighs swung wide for him as he slid between them. The erection Maddox held in his fist was massively hard, the head swollen and huge. It felt like a small apple as he guided it against my throbbing, glistening sex... while Austin cradled my head in his warm, naked lap.

"This doesn't even *begin* to describe the mess we're about to make of you..."

215

Protecting Dallas - Krista Wolf

Forty-One

DALLAS

I was already delirious when he began fucking me. My whimpers of pleasure turned straight into gasps as Maddox drove his cock deep, the throbbing head dragging wonderfully against my inner walls.

I looked up at him and saw all new hunger in his eyes, an unstoppable need to *have* me. He was all business now. Totally devoted to the task at hand, which at the moment included pounding himself in and out of my tender body, fast and hard.

Mmmmm...

Absently I wondered if his expression looked like this on the battlefield. Fun-loving Maddox... suddenly intensely focused, devoid of humor. He was drilling me now with strong, powerful strokes, unaware that his fingers were turning into talons as he pinned my knees back to either side of my head. I was bouncing beautifully against his rock-hard body. Staring up at him in awe and wonder, in happiness and lust and yes... even love.

Love.

Damn, there was that word again.

A warm, tingly feeling stole over me, sending all new butterflies fluttering through my stomach. I decided to table those emotions for now. Put them to the side, and focus on the task at hand.

"Damn bro," Austin chuckled. "You're gonna *break* her."

The pleasant ache deep inside me would've told me this was true, even if I wasn't watching Maddox currently fuck the shit out of me. A finger — no, a thumb — entered my mouth, and I turned my head to suck it. Austin was holding either side of my face. He pinned my hair back over my ears as I sucked his thick digit into my hungry, eager mouth.

It went on and on, Maddox screwing me deeper and deeper until I could feel tears of joy gathering at the corners of my eyes. Somewhere in the back of my mind, my legs ached. His fingers were no doubt leaving bruises on the undersides of my thighs, and my leg muscles would be sore tomorrow from being stretched past all normal limits.

Holy... holy shit...

Jesus Christ, I was going to come again. If he kept fucking me like this...

"You gonna give that up anytime soon?" Austin jeered, "Or am I gonna have to take it from you?"

Maddox pumped me a good two dozen more times before reacting to his friend's statement. He actually looked frustrated as he withdrew.

"Turn her over," said Austin. "I've got an idea."

They flipped me together, as easily as they were tossing a pillow. Austin took me by the wrists, pulling my arms over my head. Then he dragged me downward, to one corner of the bed.

"Put your head down."

I did was I was told. I was face down, ass up in my own wetness. On my knees with my pussy still throbbing, ready for anything.

Suddenly I felt a tug. A moment later Austin was taking my beads and pulling them over my head. There had to be a few dozen of them; cheap plastic Mardi Gras necklaces painted in every conceivable style and color.

He bunched a few together and began wrapping them around my wrists...

Oh wow.

Alone they were thin and fragile. Together, they made a strong sort of braided rope. Austin looped some together, binding my left and right wrists until they were tight against each other. Then he looped more necklaces through those, and tied the whole thing off to the corner bedpost.

"There. Now she's ready."

I twisted a little, testing my bindings. They held firm. Much firmer than I thought they would for a bunch of plastic beads.

"Go on," he said. "Try to get out of it."

I pulled harder, but the result was the same. I was hopelessly tied to the bed, face down, my arms high overhead.

One calloused hand went to my ass. It rubbed my skin slowly, in tantalizing circles. The touch felt wonderful... until the hand left me and came down hard with a loud SLAP.

"OHHH!"

"Dig in," growled Austin, as he slid into position behind me. "You're about to have fun."

Not as much fun as you, I wanted to say but didn't. I was already breathless. Totally turned on by what was about to happen to me.

His hand came down a second time, then a third. Each time I flinched, but now I was clenching my jaw through the wonderfully exquisite pain. I hadn't been spanked in ages. And never like this... Never like—

"*FUUUUCK.*"

Austin spat the word out as a curse as he sank into me. It felt like being split in half. He was bigger and harder than ever, and the downward angle made my pussy so tight he could barely complete the stroke. If I weren't so hot, so juicy fucking wet...

He shoved himself snugly against me, until I could feel the hard ripple of his abdominals tight against my ass. I was trying to swallow, but there was a baseball in my throat.

"You like getting filled like this, don't you?"

His voice was tight and jagged, like gravel. His two hot lips were pressed against my ear.

"Yes."

It came out a little too faint, too meek for him. He brought his hand down again, slapping my ass, and I yelped in pain and delight.

"YES!" I repeated, this time nodding and biting my lip.

Austin accepted my response this time, and went straight into fucking me. Every push was pure pleasure. Every return stroke stretched me tight against my bonds. The beads clacked against each other, in steady rhythm with our lovemaking. Only this *wasn't* lovemaking. I was being thoroughly and completely *fucked.*

This is what you wanted, wasn't it?

Shit yeah it was. I'd even asked for it.

Be careful what you wish for...

I was suddenly aware of my other lover, standing before me at the foot of the bed. I reached out for him, and had just enough slack to pull him in by the root. My mouth opened. I waited until the timing was perfect, then slipped him between my lips.

"There we go," Austin grunted. He gave me another slap, but this one was more encouragement than admonishment. "Goddamn, taking you together like this..." He rolled into me hard, driving his friend deep into my throat. "It's such a fucking turn-on."

I kept going like that, blowing one lover, screwing back against the other. Both of them plunging into my body, again and again, from in front as well as behind. I was pinned marvelously between them. Living out every girl's deepest, darkest fantasy.

So good...

The whole thing was blisteringly hot. So far beyond

the scope of reality, I could barely keep my senses. I was screaming into Maddox's thigh while Austin fucked me. Holding onto the base of his cock, more for leverage than actual pleasure.

So fucking good!

My skin was flushed, my eyes wild. Maddox suddenly stepped back and grabbed me by the hair, yanking my head up to face him. His too-blue eyes bored into mine.

"Look."

He took my chin and guided my head. There was a full-length dressing mirror in the room, and only now did I realize they'd moved it. From the angle I was at, I could see the three of us centered perfectly.

"Classy," I smirked, nodding that way.

Maddox chuckled malevolently. "We *thought* you might like that."

He kissed me wetly, then plunged back into my mouth. My eyes were still on the mirror though, watching myself as I was spit-roasted between them. I sighed, reveling in the filthiness of letting go, of prostrating myself before these two strong, powerful men. Allowing them to take me in any way they wanted. I would've said anything for them. Done anything...

You're such a slut!

The word held no negative connotation here. It was the most incredible feeling in the world, being shared freely like this. Total liberation; pleasure without judgment, or expectations, or—

"I'm getting close..."

Austin's voice came floating in from behind me, where he still drilling away. His pace was the same, but his breathing had changed. For some reason it made me proud. Proud that I could tire someone like him out. A Navy SEAL, in prime physical condition...

You're going to... come again...

Out in front I was doing the best I could. Keeping my lips wrapped firmly around Maddox while his friend, his brother-in-arms, stretched me beautifully from behind.

"I can't... Can't keep..."

"Then don't," I said, whipping my head around to face Austin. I smiled at him wickedly. "Finish, baby. Shoot it in me."

Austin's hands crushed my hips and there it was — his grunt of pleasure, of triumph, of penultimate release. He thrust forward one last time and then went completely and utterly motionless, buried all the way to the hilt in my pussy.

"NNNNGHHH!"

I could feel him throbbing and pulsing, blasting off inside me. Filling me with his liquid fire. It triggered my own climax, which surged through my body. It took me over. Obliterated, for a few brief shining seconds, everything else in the universe... the bed, the room, Maddox's cock, still gripped tightly in one hand. It all just faded away, like dust in the hurricane of my own violent orgasm.

And then, in the middle of everything, it was raining. Raining down thick, warm droplets everywhere, as Maddox's come splashed hotly all over my cheeks, my chin, my neck and forehead.

Ohhhhh...

Through it all I kept one hand between my own legs, two fingers plunging into the depths of my messy pussy. Extending my orgasm as Austin continued fucking me, his cock sliding against my fingers.

We collapsed at the same time, in a heap of sweat and sex and come. Each of us spent. Each of us smiling.

"Well..." Maddox grunted when he could breathe again. He tilted his head in my direction and grinned weakly. "You *did* say senseless."

Forty-Two

DALLAS

They shared me again, and again after that. Time passed and the outside noise grew dim, but inside our little hotel room things were just heating up.

In a way, it was almost like a competition. It seemed as if each of my lovers was trying to prove something to the other: how hard or deep they could go, how fast they could recover.

Either that, or they just couldn't get enough of me.

I lost track of how many times they took me. I was fucked on the bed, on the floor, even standing up against the wall. Austin clapped his hand over my mouth while Maddox screwed me over the arm of some vintage loveseat... only to have them switch places, and start all over again.

Out of everything we did however, the balcony was my favorite.

It was late — *very* late — by the time they dragged me outside and bent me over the wrought-iron railing. The air was

225

cool, the sights and smells of the city finally died down. The crowds of the main square had all but dispersed, except for a few drunken stragglers wandering down sidestreets like ours.

It was as daring as it was fun, screwing outside in plain sight. Standing there with my face-paint all smeared, my tattered fishnets hanging down my legs as they took turns stuffing me from behind.

God, Dallas! Look at you!

My body was shaking from all the adrenaline. My garters and panties were long since gone. My hands had been bound to the railing with beads again, only by now most of them were snapped or broken.

Just imagine this, I thought to myself.

Every. Single. Day.

Yes, every day... just like this. Only even more, because Kane would be there too. Satisfying the physical and emotional needs of three strapping Navy specialists seemed like a dream come true. Only it *wasn't* a dream, and it *might* come true, and understanding these things all at once made me suddenly frightened.

The gushing orgasm I had on the balcony was much like the first, only this one drained me completely. I moaned like a whore, causing a trio of onlookers to glance up from the alley. What we were doing was unmistakable, but our audience was too inebriated to care. Plus it was Mardi Gras. And also, three or four in the morning.

One by one my lovers finished inside me, thrusting so hard I thought I might finally go over. Instead I gripped the twisted iron railing and held on for dear life, my grip so tight I was *sure* I'd bend the bars.

Then we were crashing against the bed. Falling exhaustedly into the blankets and soft down comforter.

Sleep took me before my cheek could even find the pillow.

I woke up face-down in the semi-darkness of impending dawn, to the sensation of a hard cock pushing its way slowly inside me. From this angle I didn't know if it was Maddox or Austin. Not that it mattered. I spread my legs willingly, letting out a groggy, satisfied groan as I was filled easily from behind.

"MMMMmmmm..."

Everything was so *wet.* So warm and snug and comfy. The lover behind me was pressed tightly against my back, skin to skin, crushing me hard into the softness of the bed. I could feel my pussy gushing around him. Dripping with sex.

I still want it.

It was more than obvious by the way my body reacted. As dog-tired as I was, everything still tingled. My nipples went hard.

God, I still need *it.*

"Spread for me," a voice growled. "Wider."

I still couldn't tell who it was, and that part was most exciting of all. The anonymity of getting fucked like this... of pretending it could even be a total stranger. Someone I didn't even know, ravaging me, just taking advantage of my warm, sleep-deprived body.

A pair of lips nibbled my ear. An arm slipped around

my belly, arcing my ass upward, adjusting the angle of penetration. My lover drove himself home, all the way in, all the way out. It was slow. Lazy. Beautiful.

I whimpered softly, my head lolled to one side. My eyes had adjusted enough to make out the smooth, dusk-colored skin of the man next to me. Austin slumbered in peace, blissfully unaware of what was going on just inches away from his half-covered body.

So it's Maddox then. He's the one inside me.

I wriggled my ass playfully, screwing it back into him. It felt so good I was practically purring. He kept grinding away, rolling whenever his hard body bottomed out against my soft, supple ass. He was close to coming. Close to adding yet another load inside me, mixing in with the others. Mixing with my own hot juices, and even—

Suddenly he left me. I waited for him to thrust back in, or in lieu of that, the warm feel of his come shooting all over my naked back. Instead, I was treated to a much different shock:

He was pressing the very tip of his cock against my slick, puckered asshole.

I gasped, my eyes going wide in surprise. It was *just* the tip. Just enough to penetrate me the tiniest bit. My mouth opened halfway...

... and then suddenly he was coming.

Oh my GOD!

All the breath was sucked from my lungs as I felt him go off, shooting long, heavy jets of hot semen directly into my ass. It was warm and sticky. Totally nasty, dirty and forbidden.

And somehow I *loved* it.

It was incredibly filthy, being filled up like this. Laying there pushed face-first into the pillow, as my lover held his cock pressed against me... filling my ass with his boiling hot seed.

What. The. Fuck.

Maddox continued stroking himself, draining his balls completely. Pumping until he was finished, at which point he broke the seal between my ass and the tip of his cock.

He grunted in satisfaction before rolling over, leaving me used and trembling. I was in the same position I'd been in when he woke me up... only now, a steady stream of warm come was leaking from my asshole.

I drifted off, staring into the budding dawn. Wondering how we'd ever get up to face the day, or whether we could draw the curtains and sleep through it all warm and cocooned and nestled together.

The wetness continued dribbling out from behind, running down my warm, aching pussy. I closed my eyes, relishing in the moment.

It was by far the hottest thing anyone had ever done to me.

Forty-Three

AUSTIN

We walked through a light rain, past what could've been offices, or barracks or anything else. The base was hodgepodge of old and new. Of modern, more recent structures as well as existing brick and cement buildings.

"There's a gazebo up here," said the man we were following. "We can talk there."

Chief Petty Officer Woodward was a short, squat man, with the underlying frame of someone more powerfully built in youth. He wore his thinning hair proudly, in a style he wasn't trying to hide. He also walked faster than most men I knew with legs twice as long.

Maddox was dragging his ass, which was funny to me. I would've laughed at him, but I was dragging ass too. We were both exhausted, both totally worn out from our activities of the past two nights. We'd also grown used to sleeping through the first half of the day and partying all night long.

But hey, it was Mardi Gras.

"Okay," said Woodward, finally arriving at our destination. "We can talk freely here."

The US Naval Biodynamics Laboratory had been around since the early 1970's, mostly as a medical research facility. It was partially converted in the 90's to accommodate other Naval offices, including the ones where Woodward was in charge.

Right now were in an old gazebo, standing defiantly upright even if at a slightly crooked angle. Once, a long time ago, it was would've very pretty. At the moment however, it was sorely neglected. More paint than wood by this point.

"If you're going to tell us your office is bugged..." started Maddox.

"Want me to be honest?" asked Woodward. "Who the fuck knows? These days I don't trust anyone. I'm just putting in the rest of my time, finishing out my thirty-five."

He shrugged, leaning back against one of the old wooden railings. But not before testing it out with his hand first.

"There's a lot of creepy shit going on," Woodward said. "People in places they shouldn't be. Sudden promotions, even faster demotions. People pulling rank out of the clear blue sky."

He scanned around, glancing over both shoulders. It wasn't exactly a nervous look, but it wasn't a good one either.

"Long story short, I wouldn't even be doing this, except in person. And I wouldn't be doing it with *anyone* except people I knew were good."

Maddox scratched his head. "And, uh... how do you

know we're good?"

"Because Winters vouched for you," Woodward said firmly. "And Winters was as solid as they fucking come."

A long moment of silence and respect passed between us. An unspoken pause between soldiers.

Eventually the old veteran pulled something from his pocket and thumped it hard several times against his thumb. He opened the green container and took out a pinch of rich, black tobacco.

"Your friend Connor stumbled onto something," he mumbled, jamming the small wad between his cheek and gums. "Something he shouldn't have."

"We knew this part already," I said impatiently.

"And where most people would've backed slowly away," Woodward continued, ignoring me. "He pressed on harder than ever."

Maddox shot me a sideways glance. From how tight his mouth had gone, he was thinking the same thing I was.

"Are you saying you turned a blind eye?" I challenged. "That you let him do this alone?"

"I'm saying he went too deep, too quickly," the man spat. "And that by the time he brought it to me, it was already too late."

I stood there in the cold, clenching and unclenching my fingers, attempting to keep calm by staring out into the rain. I tried imagining what the base looked like in its heyday, back when it was filled with people. How green the trees and lawns might've been. How smooth the cracked sidewalks were, alive with people. The vast empty parking lots, filled with vehicles.

"I tried to help him," said Woodward. "Actually I *did* help him, but he kept coming back. Kept digging even after I covered his tracks, kept pushing his way through the layers of muck." He shook his head slowly. "I've got a family. A wife, kids — some of them in college. There's no way I could—"

"We get it," I snarled. "You left him out there, all on his own. You hung him out to—"

"I TRIED, goddamn it!" The CPO spat again, and this time his spittle was a gob of greasy black liquid. "I went to bat for him! When I figured out they were watching him, I got him a new place. When he came to me with what he had, I even brought it to my superiors."

I inched forward expectantly. "And?"

"And they squashed it," the man said helplessly. "Just as fast as he compiled it, they... they..."

Maddox nudged me as the man dropped his head into his hands. He was almost in tears. Almost.

For me, it wasn't good enough.

"Tell us what happened," I growled. "And tell us *everything*. Leave nothing out."

Woodward stepped closer to the middle of the gazebo, urging us forward. A breeze wafted in and his voice went lower.

"There's a lot of old hardware around here," he said confidentially. "High-level technology, resting in old places, sitting on old drives. Buried in the backs of decommissioned buildings," he continued, "information that's been copied and forgotten... just not by everyone."

"So... secrets?" Maddox asked.

"Yes."

"Someone's stealing secrets," I repeated.

The man nodded. "Stealing and selling them off, although I never knew everything. Winters kept most parts to himself. When he realized how dangerous it was, he didn't want me involved anymore. Even when I went after him, tried to get him to talk to me, he basically blew me off."

As much as I wanted to be angry, it sounded like Connor. It would've been something he'd do; put the needs of others first, well before himself. He'd done it on the battlefield for sure. And it seemed he was doing it here, with Woodward, right up until he died.

"What kind of information can you give us?" I asked.

"Even better," Maddox interjected, "who's watching us?"

"That part I don't know," said Woodward, glancing around again. "But whoever was after Winters followed him back to Nevada. And they're Air Force, not Navy. Stationed at Nellis. Connor told me that much at least."

I jerked my head toward Maddox. He took his phone out of his pocket and pulled up a photo.

"Know this guy?"

The CPO answered immediately. "Of course. That's Evan Miller."

"He wrapped up in this?"

I watched carefully as the man shrugged. The gesture seemed genuine.

"I– I can't imagine he would be. He was Connor's friend. His roommate too, if I remember."

"He ever say anything bad about him?"

"Who?"

"Connor."

"Not that I recall." He thought for a moment, then put a finger to his chin. "But..."

"But what?"

"But I remember Miller being kinda angry when Connor left. He put in for a transfer almost immediately. I always assumed they had some sort of falling out, but then the transfer was to Fallon, so..."

Maddox took a slow step back. Fallon was an air station out in Churchill County, back in Nevada. Combat Search and Rescue training took place there, SEALs only.

A transfer like that made sense. Only it put him within six or seven hours access of Connor.

"Listen to me," Woodward said, his voice going so low it was barely audible. "Whatever these guys wanted, Connor already *had* it. And it was important to them. They were looking for it, shaking him down trying to find it."

I squinted hard. "And how do you know that?"

"Because they tossed his place twice trying to find it."

And because they stationed Miller with him to look for it as well, I thought silently.

A gust of wind picked up, surging through the old gazebo. It whistled eerily through the broken teeth of the fancy upper cornices.

"Now that Connor's dead," said Maddox. "Think they're still looking for it?"

The Chief Petty Officer spat again. He looked past us, at something on the invisible horizon, then nodded slowly.

"You can bet that until they've found it, they're not going to stop."

Forty-Four

DALLAS

The guys showed up not long after I'd ordered room service. It was a bitch not eating until they got there, but somehow I managed.

"How'd it go?"

"Tell you in a bit," said Austin. He rubbed his stomach. "While we eat, of course."

We were all famished. And tired. Exhausted actually, but who was keeping track anymore.

Maddox walked in behind him, sniffing the air. I had the balcony doors wide open. The sounds and smells of the growing crowd wafted in from outside.

"New sheets," smiled Maddox, glancing around approvingly. "New blankets too."

"We needed them," I chuckled.

"Sure did."

"You guys *defiled* me last night," I said with a smirk.

237

"The night before too, come to think of it."

Austin cracked his knuckles before grabbing a spoon. He sat down at the little table before a big bowl of Jambalaya.

"If I remember correctly, you did quite a bit of defiling yourself."

"Maybe," I shrugged.

"*Definitely,*" insisted Maddox. "Not that we're complaining, of course."

He began lifting the metal tops and peeking into every dish. After fifteen minutes of agonizing over the menu, I'd ordered just about one of everything.

For the first few minutes I said nothing, I only let them eat. Maddox inhaled two hamburgers, while pushing the accompanying onion rings away. Austin picked at a little bit of everything, eating a bit from this plate, a bit from that one.

"No beer?"

I nodded to a stainless steel bucket down near the floor. It was filled with frosty cold bottles, surrounded by a whole sea of melting ice.

"You're the bees knees, you know that?"

"I know."

Austin twisted the cap off three bottles. He handed one to me and one to Maddox. I tilted my head back, letting the cool liquid slide down my throat. My mind wandered back to the previous nights events, which were somehow even dirtier and more carnal than the first evening we'd arrived.

My beer was half-finished by the time I slammed the bottle back against our little table. The carbonation still burned in my throat.

"So... about Connor..."

Maddox took a deep breath and briefed me on the day's events. He talked about Woodward, their meeting, their ride back from the Naval base. About how Connor had been in imminent danger, and no one had done anything to help him.

It made me upset, then angry, then sad. I tried to keep things together, to understand why my brother had done what he did. To be angry, not at Connor, or even Woodward for not being able to help him; but at the people who'd taken away the last person who loved me, from my life.

"It's not his fault," said Maddox, echoing my own thoughts. "Woodward, that is. From what we could tell, he did what he could. He tried protecting Connor. We're sure of that."

Glumly I nodded. The whole thing was fucked, soup to nuts, front to back. I didn't need to know the specifics of what Connor had been doing, only that he valued it enough to risk his life for it. The only real question I needed answered was who was responsible.

"We're getting there Dallas," Austin was saying. "It's just gonna take a little time."

I shoveled some scrambled eggs onto a piece of toast and popped the whole thing in my mouth. Though it was well past noon, I was still in the mood for breakfast. Hell, I'd only been up a little over an hour.

Last night had been... well, busy.

"What now?" I asked.

"We have a few things to tie up," said Maddox. There was a double entendre in there somewhere. He gestured at our not-so-little banquet. "Right after this."

"Like what?"

He shot Austin a quick glance. "Like checking out Connor's last apartment again," he said. "We didn't get to see it all yet. Might be something we missed."

I crunched down on some bacon and stood up. "Good. Let me shower, and—"

"Shower, yes," Maddox interrupted. "Come with? No. You stay here."

"The fuck I—"

"Dallas," said Austin, "you can't come *everywhere* with us. Besides, we need you to pack us up. We'll be quick, less than an hour."

My eyebrows went up. "We're leaving?"

"Probably, yeah," Maddox confirmed. "There's nothing else for us here. We should get home, see what Kane's managed to dig up."

Home. Suddenly it was a good word again. A warm word. The thought of seeing Kane again excited me too.

I still wanted to come with them though.

I opened my mouth, a protest already cocked and loaded in my mind. But I was just too tired. Too exhausted to even argue.

"Fine," I sighed, falling back onto the bed. "I'll stay and pack up."

Austin smiled. "Like I said, you're the—"

"Bees knees," I groaned, my mouth betraying the slightest hint of a grin. "Got it. Whatever the fuck that is."

I rolled back into the softness of our latest comforter, the fresh scent of commercial laundry detergent still lingering across the surface. Stretching my arms and legs in four different direction, I groaned contentedly.

"When you guys get back..."

They both stopped eating at once. Very abruptly, I had their full attention.

"Defile me again?"

Austin casually dabbed his chin with a napkin. Maddox smirked.

"After all," I purred. "We can't let these fresh sheets go to waste."

Forty-Five

DALLAS

The shower was baptismal; a near-scalding stream of blessedly hot water that cleansed me, mind, body, and soul. Too bad it couldn't wash away my sins. Not with *that* water pressure, that's for sure.

What sins, Dallas?

I laughed as I killed the water, then bent over to shake out my hair. Surely I'd done something wrong. Then again, I must've done something right too. As bad as I was, a girl didn't end up in the position I was in without making a few *good* choices along the way as well.

It was a funny thing, having choices again. Finally being able to call my own shots, rather than roll the dice of fate. Since I'd lost Connor, things just sort of happened to me. My brother's death, the loss of my home, my job, my life... the illusion of free will was gone, replaced instead by a series of terrible events beyond my control.

And now...

Now I had Maddox, and Austin, and Kane. Three men who I dared say loved me, or at the very least, were in love with the idea of keeping me safe from harm.

And I loved them as well.

The full realization had come to me last night, staring up at the ceiling. Nestled between them, feeling the slow rhythm of their breathing on either side of me... the whole ordeal had sparked some very deep thinking.

Was it okay to love them? Connor sure had. He'd loved them as friends, as comrades, as brothers.

And yet, for the four of us that ship had sailed. We were already way too far gone to go back. Too deeply entwined in the physical and emotional sense to ever pretend we hadn't connected on the deepest of levels... or screwed each other's brains out on a balcony overlooking an alleyway, deep in the French Quarter.

But yes, I loved them for who they were, and for what we'd *shared*. I suspected it was this way with Connor too, I only wished I could've gotten to see my brother around them.

I thought about all these things as I stepped through our quaint little room, wearing the scratchy old bathrobe the hotel had provided us. I had a towel wrapped around my hair as well, as I stepped out onto the balcony and looked toward the Central Square.

Even now, the crowds were enormous. It was Sunday, the day of the Orpheus parade. The day before Lundi Gras. *Two* days before Fat Tuesday, when everything including the alley below me would go absolutely fucking berserk.

Damn. I sorta wished we'd be here to see it.

I leaned happily against the balcony, giving myself a few final minutes of relaxation before getting ready to pack up.

I wanted to remember this place. Hell, I wanted to remember this *balcony*. This railing. This...

My thought process trailed off as I spied someone deep in the heart of the crowd. It was man. A very tall and lanky man, wearing what appeared to be some strange animal mask. He looked like every one of the other hundred people surrounding him in every direction.

Only this man was looking directly at *me*.

No, he can't possibly be looking at—

I was sure of it.

I gulped and stepped back, still not taking my eyes off the masked stranger. He stood there staring back, completely immobilized. Totally unmoving and out of place, while the crowd surged and writhed and undulated around him.

Then he began walking toward me, and my heart skipped a few beats.

He doesn't see you, the little voice in my head admonished. *That's impossible.*

It sure didn't *seem* impossible. Especially in that he was picking up speed. And he was still walking pointedly in my direction. Making a beeline for my exact alleyway, when he probably had a dozen others to choose from.

Dallas...

The man kept coming, and I realized my body was frozen in terror. My feet were glued to the balcony floor. All the muscles in my legs suddenly stopped working at once.

Dallas!

The masked man reached the edge of the square, then

burst into the alleyway. *My* alleyway. He was practically running now, still coming up the sidestreet. Still headed with grim determination directly toward the door of our hotel.

He swiped at his face, and his mask flew off. My breath caught in my throat.

It was *him*.

By the time I recognized him he was already inside, already disappeared through the hotel's main entrance. I could picture him sprinting, bounding his way through the lobby. Bursting into the stairwell, his long legs taking the steps three at a time.

Coming for me...

It was too late to stand there cursing my inaction. Our hotel was small, the corridors tight. Even worse, the elevator was slow and ancient. There was a chance I could make the stairs... but an equal chance he'd be coming up them, ready to take me.

Instead I locked the door, then engaged the slide-bolt. It was a flimsy piece of steel chain, but it was better than nothing. My hands betrayed me, dropping the chain three times before I finally slid it in. By the time I did, my heart was thundering out of my chest.

I had less than a minute to prepare for him.

With trembling fingers I fumbled at the nighttable drawer. Knowing, with ninety-nine percent certainty, I'd left my sidearm in the Bronco's glovebox.

It slid open... totally empty.

SHIT!

I could hear footsteps now, pounding up the hall. I had only seconds. I ran to the bathroom, then frantically back into the main room again. My weapon of choice was pretty fucking ridiculous, but then again, it was better than nothing.

I stood behind the door, watching the doorknob, waiting for it to move. A good part of me was paralyzed by fear. But another part — the part that was growing increasingly pissed off at always having to run or hide — was just getting warmed up.

The vintage glass knob jiggled hard, but only for a moment. Then, after two seconds of silence, the door exploded inward in a shower of paint chips and splintering wood.

Forty-Six

DALLAS

The man with the stark white hair burst through the doorway leg-first, the momentum from his kick carrying him through. The noise was loud. Violent. In his haste he tripped on a few shattered pieces of the centuries old door, which threw him off balance, just for a moment.

But a moment was all I needed.

I screamed like a banshee as I brought the toilet tank cover down against the back of the intruder's skull. It connected solidly, with a sickening, satisfying crunch. The strike practically brained him before he could recover, causing him to pinwheel across the room and slam head-first into the opposite wall.

Then he collapsed in a heap of blood and dust.

I looked down, and I was holding a jagged piece of porcelain. The top two-thirds of the toilet tank cover was gone now — shattered into a million pieces.

I dropped my makeshift weapon. The man was motionless. Lifeless. I sank back against the wall for support, wondering if maybe I'd killed yet another person who'd been trying to kill me.

God I hoped so.

I closed my eyes for a moment, reveling in a strange new feeling of superiority. The vainglorious triumph of having bested an enemy, in a contest at the highest of all possible levels: life or death.

Adrenaline surged through me, causing my limbs to shake. I wondered if it was like this for my Navy SEALs, too. If Maddox and Austin and Kane had experienced the same sort of feelings on the battlefield. The same euphoria and relief and exultation over an adversary, even sharing those feelings with my brother.

Dammit, Connor. Now you've got me killing people, too?

I swept my hair back with one hand, my fingers spread. No matter what I did, it kept flopping back over my face.

You should've stayed with us.

As time went on, I realized I missed my brother more and more. Perhaps that had something to do with the guys. They were keeping his memory alive for me, constantly talking about him, bringing him up. Not allowing me forget about him. Not letting the memories — or the pain that came with them — fade.

And just maybe that wasn't such a bad thing either.

I reached for my brother's pendant, to derive some measure of comfort and reassurance. It felt warm in my palm.

Connor, I wish—

A hand closed over mine! My eyes flew open, and

what I saw was terrifying. The man was *on* me! He'd somehow crawled over, his eyes wild, his hair plastered to his head by a helmet of congealing blood.

"OHHH!"

I tried pushing him off, but he was too strong. Tried slipping out from under him, but he was too big. I pounded my fists against his back. Then his hands went for my neck, fingers splayed, trembling... reaching...

I kicked, and managed to pull away just enough that he missed. But his eyes, unfocused as they were, were gaining in strength and coherence.

Then he stood up.

"DALLAS!"

I whirled, and there was a blur of motion. Someone flew over me, crashing into the man head-first. They went sprawling across the room, in the direction of the balcony.

What the—

I saw Austin, off to my side. He had his pistol out, but he wasn't aiming it. Instead he was turning it over in his hand, butt-first. He stepped forward, intending to use it as a club...

Whoosh!

The intruder slipped from Maddox's grasp. Without looking back he vaulted over the railing and fell two stories into the street, landing with a hollow-sounding THUD!

A car alarm blared. We ran to the edge of the balcony, just in time to see the man getting up. Somehow, incredibly, a car had broken his fall. Or he'd broken the car, or they'd broken each other, or—

"No!"

Maddox's hand shot out, just as Austin was about to fire. He closed it over his arm and shoved downward, diverting the sidearm's barrel at the balcony floor.

"Can't do it man," he gasped. "Too many people."

Austin roared in frustration, screaming at the sky. Still, he knew Maddox was right. Together we watched the white-haired man flee through the alley, trailing droplets of bright red blood behind him. He headed immediately for the nearest group of party-goers. He reached the edge of the street and limped into the crowd, just another strange face melting into the chaos.

"FUCK!"

Austin was still pissed. He turned toward Maddox, his expression full of wrath.

"Couldn't hold him," Maddox said by way of apology. He held up a pair of blood-smeared hands. "Too slippery."

A few people were staring up at us. Some of them had even cheered, probably drunkenly, no doubt thinking our struggle was all part of some little act.

Eventually we closed the balcony doors. It took another minute or two to calm down, and then the guys were on me immediately.

"Are you hurt?"

"No," I said, shaking my head. "No, I'm okay. He— He came in, I mean he broke in, and we struggled, and—"

"What *happened* to him?" Maddox asked, looking

around.

"I hit him."

The guys were still incredulous. There was debris everywhere. Splinters of wood, pieces of door frame. Hundreds of jagged slivers of pure white porcelain...

"What the hell'd you hit him with?" Austin asked.

"Toilet tank cover."

"Jesus Christ," he swore in admiration. His smile finally returned. "Good one!"

"Thanks," I breathed. "I saw it in a movie once."

A young couple walked by in the hallway. They took one look through the broken door — at me still in my bathrobe, at the guys standing in the middle of the debris field — and kept on walking.

"We need to get out of here," Maddox said. "And fast."

I nodded, staring down at my blood-splattered robe. I turned in the direction of the bathroom, when I got hit in the chest with a small pile of clothes.

"You should probably put something on," smirked Austin.

Forty-Seven

DALLAS

We left New Orleans in haste, taxiing directly to the terminal and grabbing the first available flight back to Vegas. We made the gate just as the plane was about to detach from the boarding ramp, and settled into our seats right as the aircraft began taxiing for takeoff.

Not twenty minutes after that, both guys were sound asleep on each of my shoulders.

I squirmed back in my seat, accepting a water from the flight attendant this time around, rather than alcohol. It had been a crazy fucking weekend. A whirlwind of sex and debauchery and weaving through crowds, of running around and laughing and fleeing, of fighting and bloodletting.

Exactly as I always pictured Mardi Gras might be.

"You should've been here Connor," I sighed, raising my plastic cup and toasting my invisible brother. Then, after looking left and right at my two slumbering lovers: "Umm... then again maybe not."

The flight was smooth, and over quickly. After grabbing our bags we made our way home, the cool desert air rejuvenating our tired bodies as we pulled down our block and into the driveway.

Kane was there to greet us, resting comfortably in one of the chairs on the front porch. A rifle rested casually across his lap, his hand stroking it absently like he was petting a cat. It made me wonder if he'd sat like this the whole time we'd been away.

He stood only when I reached the door, scooping me into his big strong arms. Squeezing me tightly but gently against his beautiful chest, before picking up my bags and carrying them inside.

"Coffee's up," he said, sliding out one of the kitchen chairs. I could see he'd already poured himself a cup.

"You first?" Maddox asked him.

Kane scratched at his chin, which was covered with about three days' worth of stubble. "Sure," he grunted eventually. "Why not?"

We sat down and listened as he went over his weekend, which included equal time spent at home and at the base. Apparently he was 'through running', and that anyone and everyone wanting a piece of him could 'come right up and get it'. Austin laughed. Maddox snickered. Yet the three of us knew, all humor aside, that he meant everything he said with deadly seriousness.

"It was dead here," he said, jerking his head at the nearest wall. "All weekend long. Not a peep, not a poke, not anything at all."

"Even during the times you were away?" asked Austin. "On base?"

Kane nodded from his corner of the kitchen. "I checked the cameras and they all came up empty. Every feed, every angle." He crossed his arms and leaned back in his chair. "Unless they tunneled their way over, no one came to the house."

The guys looked at each other. Maddox raised an eyebrow. "You know what that means."

Kane nodded again. But now I was confused.

"What?" I demanded. "What does that mean?"

"It means whoever came here," said Austin, "lost all interest after you were gone."

My eyebrows came together. I still didn't get it.

"Why would they lose—"

"Because they're after *you*, Dallas," said Maddox. "You're their primary goal. They followed us to New Orleans, and they're sure to follow us back."

Confusion turned to realization. I felt suddenly sick.

You're endangering them.

The words were chilling, but they were also the truth. These men who I suddenly cared about so much... I was putting their lives at risk.

Whatever these people want, it has to do with you.

"What do they want from me?" I pleaded. "They already got Connor. Why would they keep coming after me, even after my brother was dead?"

"Revenge?" Austin offered. But Kane shook his head.

"It's not revenge."

"How do you know?"

"Trust me," said my biggest protector. "I just do."

Austin didn't seem convinced. He wrinkled his nose in disbelief. But it was Maddox who slid his chair over in my direction.

"Think, Dallas," he said, and not for the first time. "They want you... or they want something *from* you."

I was fighting hard to maintain control, to prevent the stronger feelings from taking over on either end of my emotional spectrum. I wanted to laugh. I wanted to cry. I wanted to punch a hole in every wall of the house.

"What could you have that they might want?" Austin jumped in. "Something. Anything..."

"I have absolutely nothing!" I shouted, breaking into tears. "Or don't you remember?"

The three of them went silent now, looking back at me with pity. I didn't want their pity. I wanted to crumple their pity into a ball and shove it right back down their throats.

"You were there, all three of you. You saw me lose everything! My house, my things, every last possession I owned!" I sniffed hard, trying to breathe. "There's nothing left," I went on. "I lost my phone, my computer... even my family's photo albums."

That last part was like an ice pick to the heart. A searing stab of pain, reminding me of something I'd tried so hard to forget.

"I... I don't even have *pictures* of them anymore," I cried. "My mother, my father — they've been gone so long they're fading in my head. Fading in my *heart*." I swallowed hard. "I don't want that to happen with Connor! I *need* to remember my brother. And you guys need to help me. But I... I guess..."

All the helplessness left abruptly. Anger flooded in. I was absolutely infuriated about everything, all at once. I stood up so fast I knocked down my chair.

"Dallas—"

"Don't 'DALLAS' me!" I shouted at whichever one of them had said it. "You have each other, at least. You'll *always* have each other. But Connor... Connor's gone. Gone forever from my life, just like everyone else."

I stared back at them accusingly, their pity only magnifying my rage.

"Dallas, listen..."

"No, *you* listen!" I screamed. "You can't even imagine what it's like. You can't possibly—"

"DALLAS!" someone boomed.

I stopped in the middle of my rant, my whole body shaking, tears streaming down both my cheeks. Two fell simultaneously from either side of my face, racing each other to the floor.

"Dallas," Kane said again, his voice only slightly lower this time. "You said you came here with nothing but the clothes on your back?"

It wasn't a statement, it was a question... and one that made little sense. I cocked my head and stared back at him icily. There was challenge in my eyes.

"Yes," I practically spat. "What's your point?"

Slowly Kane raised his arm. He extended one thick finger and pointed it directly at me.

"So then what's that around your *neck?*"

Forty-Eight

DALLAS

I reached up without thinking, my hand closing reflexively over the tiny diamond-shaped pendant. My *brother's* pendant.

"Connor gave it to me," I said defensively.

"When?"

I had to think for a moment. "For my birthday," I said, remembering. "H—He sent it to me for my birthday."

"*Sent* it to you?"

"Yes," I said, lowering my head. The sorrow was threatening to take over again. "It... it was..."

"The last thing he sent you before he died," Kane finished for me.

I nodded glumly. A few moments of silence went by, and Maddox picked up my chair. The only noise in the whole kitchen was the ticking of the cheap plastic wall clock. I really should've bought a better one.

"Was there a note when he sent it?" asked Kane. "A card or something?"

I sniffed again. The tears were still coming. "No."

"Bro," Maddox stepped in. "Enough with the Connor questions, huh? She's upset. She's—"

Kane halted his friend's sentence with a hard, scary look. Reluctantly but definitively, Maddox backed off.

"No note, no card," I answered, thinking back. "Just the pendant."

Come to think of it, it was something I'd thought was weird at the time. Connor *always* sent me birthday cards. He liked to write notes too, hinting at where he was, or what he might be doing.

"A pendant..." Kane asked, squinting. "or a *locket?*"

It took me a moment to react to what he was saying. When I realized what he was driving at, I blinked.

"Can I see it?"

Slowly I reached up and unclasped the thin silver chain. The pendant gleamed, dangling heavily in my hand. For the first time since I put it on, I really *looked* at it.

It was never particularly pretty, but it wasn't ugly either. It was thicker than it appeared, with edges that were sleek and rounded. And maybe it wasn't a diamond-shape after all. Maybe it was a square on edge.

My arm shook a little as I handed it to Kane. Everyone crept in a bit closer as he turned it over and over in his palm.

"Look. It's got hinges."

He tried prying it open, gently at first, then adding more pressure. But his fingers were just too big, too thick and calloused.

"Here," said Austin. "Let me try."

We stood there in the kitchen, waiting in silence as Austin slipped two thumbnails into an almost invisible crease opposite the concealed hinges. He pushed hard for a few seconds...

CLICK.

The pendant — now locket — swung open. The four of us nearly bumped heads trying to see inside.

He shook the locket gently against his palm. On the third hit, something popped out.

"Holy shit," Austin swore. "It's a chip!"

Maddox squinted. "A what?"

"A memory chip!" he exclaimed.

"You mean like a SIM card?"

"No, not at all," said Austin. He held the chip up so that everyone could see it. "This is NOR flash memory. Military grade."

Kane took the pendant from him and closed it. With a gentle smile, he pressed it back into my hand.

"What do you think is on it?"

"Who the hell knows?" said Austin. "Something good though. Something *big.*"

I cleared my throat. "Something my brother died for..."

The kitchen went deathly silent again. I wasn't trying

to be dramatic, it just came out that way.

"Just sayin'."

Everyone watched as I clasped the locket back around my neck. When they were sure I was okay, they went back to looking down at the tiny black chip.

"Wait a minute!" Maddox cried suddenly. "That's it!"

My brows knitted together in confusion. "What is?"

"That's what Connor meant on the recording!" he blurted. "The part that gets cut out. The part where he says '*my sister has*'..."

We all glanced at each other. One by one, our expressions crossed with the same grim realization.

"So you've had it all along," Austin swore. "All this time. *That's* what your brother was trying to tell us."

I rubbed hard at my eyes. Everything was happening so fast.

"Let's put it in the computer," said Maddox excitedly. "See what's on it."

But Austin shook his head. "It doesn't work that way."

"Why?" I asked, alarmed. "Can't we see what's on it?"

"Not with the setup I currently have," he said. "This is older tech. Late 80's." He rolled his eyes toward the ceiling. It was something he always did, whenever he was thinking. "I know a guy though..."

"A guy?"

"Yes. He's old school. An ex-hacker, back from the

days of modems and BBS systems and—"

"Where is this guy?" Kane interjected. "Call him. Get him over here."

Austin laughed. "Oh, trust me. He doesn't leave the house much."

Maddox shrugged. "Then we'll go to him. Right now, if he's still up."

"He probably is," said Austin. "Except that he's in Los Angeles."

Everyone's shoulders slumped.

"I'll go tomorrow," said Austin. "First thing in the morning."

"Good," I said. "We'll all go."

Austin made a face. It wasn't a good face. It was the kind of face that always preceded bad news.

"What?" I demanded. "Are you telling me I have to stay here?"

"No, not just you," he said. "Everyone."

"Why?" asked Maddox. "This is pretty fucking important. Now that we know what those assholes are looking for we should *all* go. Together we could—"

"This guy," Austin cut him off. "He's easily spooked. He trusts me, but he'll balk if I bring someone. He's not exactly... well..."

"Sane?" I asked.

"That," Austin allowed. "Plus a few other things too."

I let out a long, exasperated sigh. "So he's the quintessential paranoid hacker who lives in his mom's basement and will only talk to *you*, and you alone?" I asked smartly.

"All of that except the mom's basement part," said Austin. "This guy has *money*. Lots of money." He shook his head. "And it's not exactly legit money either, which is why he's so careful."

Maddox rubbed at his neck. "Alright, fine."

"Also," Austin added, "he has a long list of reasons to be paranoid. Legitimate reasons."

"Enough already," Kane said. "We get it. You go alone."

Austin palmed the chip and nodded. "It's a six-hour ride. I'll leave early, and be back by nightfall." He shook the hand holding the chip. "Maybe the next day, depending on whether or not the data is encrypted."

All of this was Greek to me. And if you asked me, it would've been Greek to Connor too.

Then again, there were a lot of things about my brother I still didn't know about.

"What if it *is* encrypted?" I asked.

Austin grinned broadly. The excitement in his eyes was kind of cute.

"Then my guy knows a guy..."

Forty-Nine

DALLAS

It was just past midnight when I left my room, padding silently out into the hall. I was hopelessly restless. Not even tired. Mostly because we'd stayed up so late the last few nights, and I was getting used to a nocturnal schedule.

But it was more than that, too.

I wanted to see Kane.

I was shocked to find him at the end of the hall, once again staring out through the same big window. The light was eerie tonight. More purple than blue, with less moonlight than before.

Approaching him slowly, I wondered if I should speak out. He was shirtless again. And he seemed to be in a trance, almost even sleeping as he leaned against the old frame. But then I saw him shift, and his head turned back in my direction. I laughed silently at myself for ever thinking I could sneak up on a Navy SEAL.

"Anything good out there tonight?"

I stepped into him, and he slipped his arm around me. The movement was familiar, like we'd been doing it for years.

"Dust. Dirt. Desert."

I looked outside with him. "Kinda boring."

"Yeah."

I wondered what it was, that kept him up at night. What kinds of demons he might be battling in his head. It could've been simple insomnia, of course. But it could've been worse.

Either way, I wasn't about to ask. He'd tell me if he wanted to. Instead I sighed softly, and switched gears.

"Think we'll get them before they get us?"

The hulking soldier barely registered the question, other than his mouth stretching into a tight half-grin. "Oh yeah."

The way he said it was reassuring. With confidence, not bravado.

"The trick is getting *all* of them," said Kane. The muscles in his shoulder's flinched a little, even as I admired them. "One way or the other."

I opened my mouth and then closed it, realizing that my next question was foolish. I already knew exactly what he meant.

"You alright with that?" he asked.

I squeezed my body against his. "More than alright."

"Good girl."

God, he felt so amazing! So big and strong and self-assured. Physically he was a warrior. Emotionally, he and I made silent connections I couldn't ever hope to understand.

I felt so safe with him. Safe being *around* him. And he was wise, too. He talked so infrequently it made every word he *did* say carry that much more weight.

You love him.

I really did! Just as I loved the others too, but in a different way. With Kane, our bond wasn't something that needed to be ratified or constantly reassured.

Inside and out, he was the perfect man.

"I'll never forgive myself," he said abruptly, still staring out the window. "For what happened to Connor."

My heart dropped into my feet. I wanted to hold him! To slide my arms tightly around him and make him realize I was there, and that nobody blamed him, and that Connor had made his own shitty choices all on his own.

"Kane," I said. "You can't—"

"I know," he said quickly. "And I get that. Still..."

His whole body tensed at once, every muscle drawing into itself in an frightening display of strength and power. Even his jaw went tight. The next words out of his mouth were terse and unflinching.

"I'm going to get everyone involved in betraying him," he growled ominously. "Every. Single. Fucking. Person."

I nodded into his chest, indicating I understood. That was I was behind him. Beside him. No matter what.

I'm not sure how long we stood there. Whether it was another five minutes, or fifteen, or fifty. The important part was holding each other. Of staring out into that dark horizon of nothingness, while our souls spoke at length with each other.

"I talked to Maddox and Austin," he said at last. "Seems you guys had... fun this weekend."

I glanced up and saw his knowing grin. I could only smirk right back at him.

"Yeah," I said with a little laugh. "I guess you and I have some catching up to do."

"Some welcoming home actually," Kane nodded. "Unless you forgot?"

I chuckled again. "Forget? Please." I stood on my tiptoes and pressed into him. "It's why I left my room tonight to begin with."

Kane's eyes caught mine, then he lifted me into the air like I was nothing. My arms went over his shoulders, my legs sliding around his warm, naked torso.

Then we were kissing, with hunger and intensity. Over and over again, in the silent sanctity of our shadowed little hall.

"Take me back to your room," I whispered, when I finally broke free of his lips.

My lover shook his head and smiled.

"Your room this time," he said, walking us in that direction. "It smells like you, and it's a lot softer and nicer in there."

Fifty

KANE

It was so fucking *warm* inside her. Warm and wet and spectacularly good. She felt absolutely incredible with her body spooned into mine, my arm firmly around her waist, pinning her tightly against me as I chewed on her shoulder.

There was a lot comfort in screwing her on her side. For one I could kiss her as much as I wanted to. Kiss her while thrusting myself deep inside her, tilting her chin back in my direction as I kept sawing and plowing away.

"Baby..."

Her moans were soft. Mere whispers of words. Each time a hot breath left her lungs, I could feel it on my own lips.

"Oh honey..."

We'd been screwing for a long time. Doing it slowly, lazily, my arms wrapped around her as I penetrated her from behind. My hands were free to roam her perfect breasts. They made their way up to her neck, where I applied just enough pressure to leave her gasping with pleasure, even as she sucked, one by one, the fingers of my free hand into her wet, desperate mouth.

"Oh fuck, Kane," she gasped greedily. "*Fuck me...*"

God, I'd missed her. So much more than I wanted to. So much more than I *thought* I would, even though she'd only been gone for a couple of days.

Part of me kept telling myself that was a problem. That I was getting in too deep, too fast. Becoming too attached to someone who could, at any moment, literally be torn from my life.

Just like Connor.

I growled and thrust harder, taking out all my frustrations and worries and fear. Dallas responded by groaning even more loudly, and calling for me to fuck her even more deeply than I was.

After what happened to her brother, nothing would keep me from protecting her. I'd trusted Maddox and Austin enough to take care of her while I stayed behind. And yet from the stories they told me, she'd almost been... almost been...

"Unnhhhnnnhhhnnnhhh..."

I flexed my arm as she came, pulling her into me so hard I drove the air from her lungs. I could feel her soft, supple ass, grinding back against me. The rhythmic contractions of her pussy milking me, over and over, through an unforgettable series of orgasmic throbs and pulses.

Don't. Come. Yet.

Damn, that was easier said than done! Every nerve ending in my body was standing on end, telling me to erupt. Giving me full permission to blast off inside her, filling her with three agonizing days' worth of my hot, juicy come.

269

Somehow, through some miracle, I didn't. And that was solely because I was enjoying myself too much. Savoring the feel of being *inside* her while I was holding her, of letting my throbbing cock just marinate itself happily, deep in her womb.

"Baby..." Dallas breathed. She craned her head around to face me again, all jasmine-scented skin and soft blonde hair. "You can *let go...*"

Her lips were plump and full, and just slightly wet from where she'd bitten the lower one into her mouth. I leaned in and kissed her, and my whole body exploded with warmth and love.

Go on. Do it.

I wanted so badly to come inside her. I'd done it once already and it wasn't nearly enough. Last time had been a sort of free-for-all, a breakout orgy of want and lust and raw sexual need. But this... right now...

Right now I wanted to consummate our union. I wanted to fill her with myself, yes, but I wanted to kiss her while I did.

I wanted her to know how I truly felt. I needed her to realize the full extent of my feelings.

Tell her.

My mind was screaming at me to stop being ridiculous. That it couldn't possibly be like that. But my heart was telling my mind to shut the fuck up.

Just tell her.

I couldn't hold back any longer. The come was boiling

up from my balls. In seconds it would surge forward, rushing out of me. It would splash into her in a glorious moment of pure ecstasy, filling her to overflowing.

SAY it!

Our mouths were locked, our tongues still dancing hotly. But at the last moment I pulled my head back. In those very last seconds, as my cock jumped in that first euphoric pulse, the words I couldn't bring myself to say out loud still formed themselves with my lips and tongue.

I lov—

I froze... and there was Dallas, her eyes locked against mine. Her face was bright. Her expression soulful, grinning.

"I love you too," she smiled, then kissed me. "Now *come in me...*"

I didn't just explode, I detonated.

She grabbed my head as I shoved myself forward, drilling her to the core. Every twitch was an all new exhilaration, every throb bringing me agonizingly closer to heaven. Our tongues danced again and we kissed hard, my swollen cock flooding her pussy, devouring each other in a storm of heat and passion. I kept shooting and convulsing, firing myself so deep, so fully inside her, that if the universe ended at that exact moment neither one of us would've had a care in the whole fucking world.

It seemed like it would never end. Like I would keep pouring myself into her through the intimacy of our connection, and Dallas would hold me fast, kissing me while the world spun around us.

When it was finally over we didn't move an inch. I

kept her pinned tightly against me, curling my body around hers without breaking our connection.

I could feel the warmth of her womanhood, throbbing around me. Holding me inside her as our heartbeats slowed and our breathing became regular and we fell fast asleep, together, with her wrapped in my arms.

Fifty-One

DALLAS

The light streaming in through the kitchen windows was bright as hell, sending my arm up over my eyes like a vampire. Maddox laughed as he slid me a cup of coffee. Kane slid me something else: a plain white paper bag.

"What's this?" I grunted.

"Lunch."

I noticed he was reading a newspaper, while chowing down on a thick, juicy cheeseburger. It was a good one too, from one of the better fast-food restaurants. I wrinkled my nose.

"What the hell *time* is it?"

"Afternoon time," said Maddox. He pointed upward as he sank back into his chair.

The plastic wall clock read one-thirty.

Holy shit!

"You gonna eat those?" Kane asked, indicating the rest of Maddox's fries.

273

"Nah."

"More for me then."

It was incredible, that I'd slept this late. That I'd slept this *well*, because I already felt alive and awake and refreshed. Even with only a few sips of coffee.

You've got Kane to thank for that.

That part was undoubtedly true. After what we'd shared together, both at the window and in my bed, I'd slept like a baby wrapped in his arms.

"So... you kids have fun last night?" Maddox chuckled, kicking his feet up.

I poked my tongue out at him and worked on my coffee. I had no interest in whatever was in the white bag. Yet.

A thought suddenly occurred to me. "Austin check in?"

"Not yet," said Maddox. "He was out by O-five hundred. Should be there by now. Then again, LA traffic." He shook his head disgustedly. "The freeway's gotta be one of the seven levels of hell. I can't fucking imagine how anyone could ever live there."

"Nine levels," said Kane.

"Nine?" Maddox squinted. "You sure about that?"

Kane kept chewing without looking up from his newspaper. "Yup."

"Circles," I said eventually, adding to the meaningless conversation.

"What?"

"They're circles of hell, not levels. According to Dante at least."

Maddox looked at me strangely. "Who the hell is Dant—"

"You guys wanna go out to the desert tonight?"

It was the strangest question, especially coming from Kane. Maddox and I glanced at each other quizzically, then back at him.

"The desert? Why?"

"Because I did some digging around while the three of you were gone," he said. "And I found out some stuff."

"You *did?*" asked Maddox incredulously.

Kane nodded, stuffing fries into his mouth.

"Well why didn't you say anything?"

He shrugged. "No one asked."

Maddox stared back at me, his mouth open. He looked so funny I actually giggled.

"So... are you going to *enlighten* us?" I asked.

Kane dabbed at his mouth with the napkin and pushed the remains of his meal away. "Sure."

For the next few minutes he talked more about his weekend. About how he'd spent time at Nellis, getting all the information he could. Kane's contacts were impressive; even on the Air Force base, he had plenty of people who owed him favors. He explained there were people even higher than that who owed *them* favors, and in turn, everything got cashed at once.

It reminded me of something Connor once said, about how saving someone's life could change protocol. When you realize your very existence on the planet earth is owed to someone else, you tended to take care of that person's needs no matter what they might be. Even it meant breaking the rules.

Especially if it meant breaking the rules.

"I wormed my way into the motor pool," he said. "The SUV Connor's been tracking — the one we chased off? The device is gone now. They found it."

"Figures," said Maddox.

"I was going to plant another," said Kane. "In fact, I was going to put one on every goddamn vehicle in that garage. But then a buddy of mine came up with something better. Something much more useful."

He reached down and pulled out a tablet in a flat black case. After tapping a few buttons, he turned it around so that it faced us.

"I had this loaded with the past three years of GVT data," said Kane "And then I made a fuck-ton of coffee, and I went over it."

I tilted my head. "GVT?"

"Government Vehicle Tracking," Kane replied. "Keeps a running log of every government vehicle equipped with a GPS system, which by now, is pretty much all of them."

Maddox let out a low whistle. "Well, shit."

"Yeah."

The screen he was holding out to us looked like something straight out of *The Matrix* — a whole bunch of

276

letters and numbers arranged in seemingly endless vertical columns.

"Well that's all very nice," I laughed, "but what are we looking at?"

"Here," Kane said, tapping the screen.

I saw more numbers, more letters. I was still confused.

"This vehicle," he said, "has gone out to the same spot in the desert as the SUV we chased." He shifted his finger a bit. "The coordinates match exactly."

"How many tim—"

"Once every two weeks," said Kane. "Going back over two years. Always on the same day of the week — this day — and always at the same time of night."

Maddox shifted closer to the table. He reached out and pointed with his own finger.

"These are service identification numbers."

"Yup."

Maddox's eyes went wide with excitement. "So we can look up who this guy is!"

Kane swung his head slowly up and down. Somehow however, he didn't seem as excited as his comrade.

"Already have."

Slowly Maddox sank back into his chair. "Holy shit."

"I'm thinking something along those lines, yeah."

My heart was beating fast again, my blood pumping. I could actually feel the progress now, like we were finally getting closer to the truth about Connor.

"So... who is this guy?" I asked hesitantly.

I saw Kane's eyes shift downward, in the direction of the floor. I knew something was wrong right away. Kane *never* looked down.

But I wasn't the only person in the room who sensed it.

"It's someone we know," Maddox said solemnly. "Isn't it?"

Kane cleared his throat uncomfortably. His arms were crossed over his chest now.

"Someone we served with..." Maddox went on.

Very slowly, almost painfully, Kane nodded.

"Tell me," demanded Maddox. His expression was twisted with fury and anger now. "Tell me which rat fuck son of a—"

"It's Dietz."

Fifty-Two

DALLAS

The ride out to the desert was sullen and strange. I sat alone in the back seat, silent for the most part, listening to the conversation between Maddox and Kane.

They talked at length about a man named Dietz.

Dietz... Dietz...

For some reason, the name rang a bell. Either Connor had mentioned him directly, or I'd heard my brother talk about him in passing. Whatever the case, the man was a soldier they all knew, and apparently loved.

Worse, it was a person they all trusted.

"How in the fucking world could Dietz have gone bad?" Maddox was saying. He sat in the passenger seat, sounding as hurt as he was confused. "And how could he have *ever* gone against Connor?"

Kane didn't say much of anything, but he did a lot of jaw-clenching, and flexing of his fists. Before the end of the trip I was sure he'd squeeze the 10 and 2 points of the steering wheel into dust.

We left early, hours before the times usually indicated on the GPS logs. There was no real-time tracking of our target, and no way to be certain they were coming at all. But if they followed the already-established pattern, and the previously-visited coordinates? We'd get there well before they would.

Kane had already entered the spot into his phone's own tracker. It was a blip on a digital map — a place that grew infinitesimally closer with each rock and pebble that whizzed by. We'd left the road half an hour ago. The hills and ridges beneath our tires were hard-packed sand, almost like concrete as we wound our way downward into what looked like a tiny, stone-faced valley.

"There," said Maddox, as we approached the end of our journey. "That ridge looks good."

"Not good," muttered Kane. "It's perfect."

We rolled upward, as they talked more about the apparent betrayal of their former brother-in-arms. I could tell they were holding back a little. Sometimes the conversation would dip low for a phrase or two, as if they were saying something they didn't want me to hear.

Normally it would've made me angry. Right now though, I was pretty numb.

Connor came here.

It was all I could think about as I glanced around. All I could really see. Whatever had gotten my brother killed, it all started right here, in this little stretch of desert. This stupid fucking strip of nothing, where he'd stuck his nose where it didn't belong.

Don't be like that, an inner voice admonished me

sternly. *Your brother was a goddamn hero.*

Up in the front seat, the guys' conversation went low again. Though I knew they were mostly just trying to protect my feelings, it might be time to remind them again about how we'd all agreed to keep everything transparent.

Eventually we crested the final rise, and Kane rolled us to a dusty stop. He parked back a ways from the lip of our cliff face, a good thirty or so paces from the edge.

"Let's check it out," said Maddox.

I walked with them wordlessly, listening to the dull silence of the desert. The dying sun felt good on my face. The wind had a faint vanilla scent to it as it swept through my hair. Both men pulled out very expensive-looking military binoculars, making minor adjustments as they pointed them down into the valley below.

"There," said Kane. "Right near the overhang."

I squinted hard, straining to see.

"You could've brought *three* sets of binoculars, you know."

Kane ignored me completely. Maddox spun one of the dials with his index finger. "Yeah," he said distantly. "Sorry."

I started thinking about Connor. Wondering if my brother had stood at this exact vantage point, looking down over the same section of valley. I decided he probably had. They'd all had the same training, shared the same basic tactics and knowledge.

He might've been my brother by blood... but he was also their brother in every other sense of the word.

I felt a tap, and Kane was handing me his binoculars. They were three times heavier than they actually looked. I peered through them, trying to see the same things they did.

"See that spot," he murmured into my ear. "Where the sand is a little bit darker?"

I saw. I nodded.

"What else do you see?"

I focused. Scanned. Concentrated.

"Tire tracks."

"Yup."

I sighed and handed the equipment back to Kane. "What now?"

Maddox lowered his own optics and rubbed at the bridge of his nose. "Now... we wait."

Fifty-Three

DALLAS

The first set of headlights showed up well after dark. In the clear desert night we could see them coming for miles away, bouncing their way along into the valley below.

"Chevy pickup," said Maddox, peering through the view-piece. He'd already changed over to a night-vision setting. "Brown. Maybe blue."

Kane and I huddled on the cold ridge, just next to him and slightly behind. The truck drew slowly closer. When it got beneath the rock outcropping it stopped, and the doors opened.

"Three men," said Maddox. "All of them armed." His voice went lower. "They're scanning around. Stay absolutely still."

Seconds passed, with only the slow click of the binoculars to mark the passing of time. And then:

"They're unloading something," Maddox went on. "Four packages. Now six..."

I was trying not to shiver. At first I thought my body was coming alive with the thrill of danger, the rush of adrenaline, but I quickly came to realize something entirely different:

It was fucking *freezing* outside.

"Get in the truck," Kane urged me.

"No, I'm good."

"At least you'll be out of the wind."

"I said I'm *good.*"

He could argue all he wanted. I wasn't missing this for anything.

"You're shaking like a dog shitting razor blades."

I squeezed my jaw tight to keep my teeth from chattering. "Fuck you."

Kane flashed me a rare, half-smile. "Later," the big SEAL huffed.

Maddox kept watching, kept counting. He reached thirty eight packages and stopped.

"Alright, here comes someone else."

We all watched together as a second vehicle arrived, this time from the north. Either it was the same SUV as before, or a very similar model. It was the same color. It was bound to be from the motor pool.

"They're all together now," confirmed Maddox. "They're talking."

Shutting up became a team effort, as we all held our breath and strained to hear. Voices drifted up from the little canyon. Even a peal of deep, menacing laughter.

Eventually the SUV's back door opened and a man got out. He looked significantly larger than the rest. He also carried himself very differently.

Kane, who was looking through his own set of binoculars, suddenly stiffened.

"That him?"

Maddox held up one hand. He used it to make the 'affirmative' symbol.

"Good enough."

Kane twisted at the waist... and suddenly came back with a long, beige sniper rifle. It was sleek and corrugated, with a sinister-looking scope mounted along the entire top length.

"Wait, no!"

Maddox whirled at the sound of my voice. His hand shot out and grabbed the barrel just as Kane was setting up his aim.

"Bro, wait!" he hissed. "What are you doing?"

"Exactly what needs to be done."

Maddox slid down, until he and his comrade were face to face. He shook his head, but Kane's lips curled back in a snarl.

"Let. Go."

"What about Austin?"

"Austin's a big boy," Kane seethed. "He can take care of himself."

"But we promised not to make any moves without him."

Kane slid the bolt back then jammed it forward, chambering a round.

"Kane!" Maddox hissed. "C'mon man, this is crazy! You can't kill Dietz, we haven't even—"

"As far as I'm concerned, he's already dead."

Things were going bad, and very quickly too. Kane's eyes were murderous. They told me that if Maddox didn't let go of the rifle soon, he was going to snap his fingers off the barrel one by one.

"What about *her?*" Maddox pleaded.

Kane froze for a moment, then his gaze shifted reluctantly toward me.

"We can't do this now," said Maddox. "Not with her here, and not without Austin."

"There are only five of them," growled Kane. "I'm pretty sure can get them all."

"Six," said Maddox. "One more just got out of that SUV." Slowly he took his hand from the weapon's barrel. "And yeah, maybe you *can* get them all. Or maybe you can't. Maybe one of those vehicles gets away." He shrugged. "Even if you drill them all dead, we learn absolutely nothing."

Something in the back of Kane's eyes shifted. I could see it reflected in the moonlight.

"We'll *get* Dietz," Maddox assured him, "just not right now. It's too big a risk."

I let out a long, relieved breath as the tension went out of Kane's shoulders. He slid the bolt backward. Popped the round out.

By the time he'd the folded the rifle away, the business in the canyon had finished. The vehicles drove off in different directions, the rumble of tires on gravel fading slowly away.

"It was the right call," said Maddox, patting his shoulder. "We'll get a better opportunity."

But Kane didn't seem all that convinced.

"I wonder if Connor waited too long," the big man said ominously. "Hoping for a better opportunity himself."

Fifty-Four

DALLAS

We waited five minutes after the last sign of their taillights. Ten minutes after that, we'd made our way down the hill and were standing beneath the rocky outcropping.

"This is the spot," pointed Maddox.

The tire-tracks were faint; so much so that you had to *know* they were there to even see them. The ground all around the entire area was packed hard, like cement.

"Look around," I said. "Maybe they left something behind."

"Probably not," said Kane.

"Why?"

"That was a simple exchange," he said. "They met out here for anonymity, so they wouldn't be seen."

"Then why were they unloading stuff?"

Kane looked back at me and shrugged. "Product for money?" he guessed. "They buyer had to count it. Had to see what they were getting."

"Yeah, but their truck had a bed," I said. "And a tailgate."

"So?"

"So why would they unload everything onto the *ground?*"

We all looked down at the same time. That part *was* weird, I could tell by the fact neither of them had an actual answer.

"And that first truck," I said. "We saw its *reverse* lights. It actually backed up to something."

Kane and Maddox gave each other a 'holy shit' look. I felt another swell of pride.

All those episodes of Columbo... finally paying off.

"Where was the first truck parked?" Maddox demanded.

The three of us shuffled around, sweeping our flashlights. It took some doing, but eventually we found one set of tracks that was deeper than the others, like it was doubled over. It also ended abruptly.

"Here."

Kane knelt and began poking the ground. So did Maddox. So did I.

Five minutes passed. Ten. We were on our hands and knees, smoothing through the hard-packed gravel. Knocking on the desert earth with our bare fists, which were starting to get chewed up.

"I was looking more at their faces," said Maddox. "Trying to recognize someone. I wasn't really looking down at

_"

He stopped talking as his whole body froze. Then he looked up.

"What?"

Maddox lifted his hand from the dirt. Clenched in his fist was a short length of sand-colored rope.

"Damn."

Kane came over, and the two of them grabbed it. The pulled together, hard, and suddenly the entire desert floor shifted.

Or at least, a five-by-five foot section of it.

Holy fucking shit!

It was a hole. Carved into the sandstone, chipped into the clay, it was about three feet deep with squared off corners.

"You gotta be fucking kidding me."

Maddox was holding his hair back from falling over his eyes. Down in the hole were a few dozen packages, all wrapped in brown paper. They were stacked neatly, like bricks, all tied off with butcher's twine.

"What is it?" I asked, knowing the answer.

"Drugs."

"You sure? Maybe it's money."

Kane huffed disgustedly. "It's never money," he spat. "It's *always* drugs."

"I can't believe this," Maddox was saying. "What do we do now?"

"We leave it."

Kane and I muttered the same sentence at the same time. We looked up at each other in acknowledgment.

"For now, anyway," he added.

A scratching noise floated in from off in the distance — a critter maybe, or an echo from further away. It lent a sudden urgency to the overall mood.

"I can't believe we found this," said Maddox.

"*We* didn't find shit," said Kane. He nodded my way. "She found it."

"Whatever." Maddox turned to face me. "Shit Dallas," he swore. "I could kiss you right now."

"Later," I shot back, and Kane nodded his agreement.

"After we bury this back up *exactly* the way we found it."

Fifty-Five

DALLAS

The television played, but none of us were really watching it anymore. It was some obscure drama whose plot required total attention, not the restless wanderings of three tired minds.

"Another beer?" asked Maddox.

Kane and I shook our heads. We'd already had a couple, but it didn't seem to dull the edge. We were still too wired, too strung out. The adrenaline still hadn't made its way out of our bodies.

So we sat there in the wee hours of the morning, stretched out on the couch together. Austin wasn't coming home. He'd called to establish that even before we'd left for the desert; apparently his 'guy' still needed more time.

I was, as usual, thinking about Connor. But Maddox and Kane...

They were thinking about Dietz.

I'd tried getting them to talk about it, to tell me more about this guy who possibly betrayed my brother. Yet every story, every tale — it only seemed to make them more tense, more wound-up and angry. And not just at Dietz, but at themselves too.

It was something I was unfortunately familiar with: survivor's guilt. The constant wracking of your brain, thinking about what you could've done differently. How if you could only go back to *this* day, or *that* day, you could somehow make everything right again.

The whole thing was a rabbit hole without a bottom.

Maddox returned, sinking heavily into his end of the sofa. Seated between them, I stretched myself out... and laid my body across both of theirs.

"C'mere."

My arm went up, my hand sifting through Maddox's hair. I pulled him down to me and kissed him, driving my tongue into mouth, demonstrating an emotional need to be close, to be *with* him, even in this one, small way.

Then he kissed me back... and I knew what I had to do.

I sat up and placed my hand on his wonderful chest. Then I pushed him back against the couch, and slid to the floor.

"Relax," I smiled, unbuckling his belt while Kane looked on. I put a hand on each of them. "The both of you."

In the slow, flickering darkness, I massaged two growing bulges from my position on the floor. It was hot, just seeing them slumped there. Watching the tension go out of their big strong bodies, as the restlessness shifted over to curiosity and then flat-out arousal. They were both hard by the time I got Maddox's pants down around his ankles. I pulled his cock free through the hole in his boxers... then leaned forward to swallow him whole.

Mmmmmm...

He was a mixture of musk, and salt, and sweat. Manly but not unpleasant. I bobbed up and down on him, enjoying my second favorite part of any blowjob: the feeling of a man growing stiff and hard in my mouth.

My eyes wandered over to Kane. I shot my gaze down to his crotch, which I was still touching and rubbing. He took the hint and unbuckled his own belt.

Through clenched teeth, Maddox let out a long, heated sigh. His thighs parted. His hand went to my head, rubbing me gently as I sucked him off.

Then I switched to Kane, who already had his cock out.

Jesus, Dallas.

It was pretty amazing, how powerful I could feel from my knees. How I was in total control over these two unstoppable men; the immovable object trapped between the irresistible force of their hard, shredded bodies. I blew one while stroking the other, switching back and forth whenever I wanted.

Then I got nasty, too.

I'd wink at Maddox while blowing Kane. Look up into Kane's eyes while sticking my tongue out and licking up and down the length of his friend's cock. Back and forth, back and forth, stroking and sucking them until each of their already considerable erections were hard enough to pound nails.

Or preferably, pound *me*.

As wonderful as that sounded, I didn't want to be pounded. It was a late, lazy hour. And hey, I wanted to be the one calling the shots. I wanted to make them *come*.

Kane moved to rise first, and I anticipated the movement. Before he could leave the couch I was already pressing my hand against his chest, fingers splayed, pushing him back against the cushions.

Then I stood up, slipped out of my bottoms, and sat right down... on Maddox's glistening, rock-hard dick.

He slid all the way inside me with a grateful sigh.

Two sexy SEAL hands went to my hips. I pushed them away, placing them back on either side of the couch. I could've put them on my aching, heaving breasts. Could've enjoyed the feel of his fingers rolling my nipples as I glided up and down on him, fucking him deep, rolling into his body on every downstroke.

Instead I threw my arms over his shoulders and fucked him like a needy, greedy whore.

Kane sat there and watched. His eyes traveled hungrily over my body as I screwed his friend, watching my every movement, listening to every whimper and sigh. His hand traveled up and down his own member, the head so swollen and engorged it looked ready to burst.

God...

I couldn't wait to sit on it. Couldn't wait to climb in his lap and fuck him next. But not until I had Maddox. Not until I'd done what I set out to achieve.

"FUCK, Dallas..."

It turned out it didn't take long. Maddox's ass left the couch as he flooded me with his come, surging upward and into me in the most delicious way. Deep down, I could still feel the pain of Mardi Gras. The soreness of two days of non-stop satisfaction, followed by last night's amazing tryst in my own bed.

I finally allowed his hands on my body as my first lover finished, his fingers clenching and unclenching against my naked ass as he rode out his last euphoric contractions. Then, still leaking his come, I climbed into Kane's lap...

... and sank all the way down to the balls on his steel rod of an erection.

Ohhh... ohhh FUCK...

I hadn't planned on coming myself. I'd been only interested in *their* pleasure, enjoying the feel of them dragging around inside me.

All of a sudden however, things had changed.

"God, you're such a fucking mess..."

Kane was kissing my neck, chewing my shoulder. Holding me against him while I rode up and down. I didn't stop him. Shit, I couldn't if I wanted to.

Dallas...

My orgasm was gathering like a coming storm. Picking up steam as my lover drilled me from beneath, fucking upwards and into me every bit as much as I was screwing down into him. I had my head lolled back, my face thrown at the ceiling. A mouth closed over mine and then Maddox was kissing me... kissing me even as Kane's tongue trailed down my neck, as his cock was buried deep in my come-soaked pussy, all warm and wet and dirty and—

"OHHHHHHHHH!"

I screamed the word out loud. Or rather, it was torn from the depths of my throat.

"*FUCKKKKK!*"

It happened right in the *middle* of my climax: Kane's hands screwed into fists, and he unloaded into me. His cock jumped and thumped and pulsed, shooting me full of his seed. Adding his load to Maddox's, filling me with so much come I could feel it running down my thighs, his thighs, the couch... everywhere, all at once.

I rolled and thrashed on his cock, swinging my hair back and forth. Somehow still kissing Maddox, who had his arms around me.

My God...

Someone was cupping my breasts beneath my shirt, dragging his calloused hands over my nipples. It could've been either of them. It could've been both. I was so lost in ecstasy I didn't care if it was the devil himself... and based on my behavior lately, that was a possibility I wasn't ruling out.

Delirium and euphoria gave way to pleasure, which gave way to reality. I slid from Kane's lap, flopping between them. Squeezing my thighs tightly together as they both ran out of me, while my chest heaved with the exertion of fucking them both.

"Tension breaker," I breathed, smiling as I quoted one of my favorite movies. "Had to be done."

Fifty-Six

MADDOX

The perimeter alarm chirped sometime around noon.

It was strange, because we hadn't picked up signs of motion. There was no one outside, nothing to be seen anywhere on the property. After checking the feeds, none of the monitors showed activity on the block either.

KNOCK KNOCK KNOCK.

Kane was already at the door, pistol drawn. I had the safety off on my MP5, just past the south window. In perfect position to back him up.

For a few long seconds we did nothing. Then, just after the second knock came, Kane snuck a peek through the peephole.

"Unfuckingreal."

He grabbed the handle and flung the door open. Before I even knew what was happening, he'd grabbed the person on our doorstep and heaved him into the house, slamming him against the nearest wall.

"EASY! EASY!"

299

The man stood on his tiptoes, hands held high over his head. He was big. Big like us. Blond hair, squared shoulders. I couldn't see his face yet, but Kane's pistol was jammed so far under his chin his tongue was practically forced out of his mouth.

"Fuckin' RELAX!" the man snarled.

That voice...

I'd already drawn down on him. Now I stepped in and jabbed my barrel violently into his ribs. He doubled over in pain, and in a flash Kane both kicked the door closed and slammed the man in the jaw with the butt of his Sig Sauer.

"I've seen a lot of shit," Kane growled, dropping his knee onto the man's back. He grabbed his arms. Pinned them behind his torso. "But never a straight-up deathwish like this!"

"Motherfucker," the man growled from the floor. All the air had been knocked from his lungs. He was wheezing hard, trying to regain his breath. "Shut the fuck up already... and *listen.*"

Holy shit.

Dietz.

"Listen to what?" Kane growled. "To how you betrayed us? To how you got Winters *killed?*"

"I didn't—"

"To the sinister shit you've been doing out in the desert with your *friends?* " I added. I produced a pair of thick white zip-ties. Kane had the man bound in seconds, hands and feet, still coughing as he lay on his side.

"Pat him down."

We did it together. The whole thing happened quickly, surgically. Like we'd done it a thousand times.

Which of course we had.

"He's clean. Not even a blade."

Dietz coughed again, and this time there was blood on his lips. Kane slid a chair over, and together we lifted him up and planted him upright.

"You assholes," Dietz spat, and a tooth came out. It skittered noisily across the tile floor. "This is how you answer the door?"

"It is when a traitor shows up."

Karl Dietz looked like shit warmed over. Part of it was his scraggly patch of stubble, which was halfway between clean-shaven and a respectable beard. The other part was his dirt-streaked face. His dust-caked hair. The pink froth of blood, dribbling from his split bottom lip...

Well, I guess that last part was on us.

"How the *fuck* do you even have the nerve to show your face here?" I demanded. I still had a lot of anger. A good part of me wanted to swing my rifle butt straight into his jaw, claim another tooth for myself.

Dietz spat again. On our kitchen floor, mind you.

Holy shit he was making me angry.

"I came to *warn* you," he growled. "Why the hell do you think I'm here?"

"Who the fuck knows?" asked Kane. "Lots of people have been coming here, including some of your friends. You haven't been keeping very good company lately."

"I came alone," Dietz said. "Unarmed. In the middle of the fucking day."

"So?"

"So use your head!" he practically yelled.

"Fuck you."

He shook his head and laughed. "Unreal." His eyes found Kane's. "You never were the smart one, were yo—"

The second shot came from Kane's fist, rather than his pistol. Dietz's head whipped to the side so fast it left his hair standing exactly where it was. I could tell Kane was holding back only because our captor's neck wasn't broken.

"GodDAMMIT!" Dietz shouted in pain. "Shit, STOP already!" He winced hard, but some of the defiance was gone now. "And one of you get me a fucking aspirin!"

Neither of us moved. Neither of us said anything.

"What do you mean by *warn* us?"

Kane and I turned at the sound of Dallas's voice. She was standing half in the hallway, her hair still wet from the shower.

And she was staring daggers at the man tied up in our kitchen.

"They're coming soon," said Dietz ominously. "All of them. At once."

Kane shot me a concerned look. "Now?" I asked.

"No. Not now. But maybe tonight, maybe tomorrow. I'm not sure, and—" He paused and winced again. "Can I get a glass of water at least?"

To my surprise, Dallas fetched him one. She moved barefoot across the kitchen, still in her bathrobe. She even took the towel from her head and used it to wipe the blood from his lips before tipping the glass back so he could drink.

"Thank you," Dietz grunted. "Shit, at least someone here's got some sense."

"You're lucky she doesn't pour Drano down your throat," I warned. "That's Dallas *Winters*. Connor's sister."

Dietz chuckled through his missing tooth. "I *know* who she is."

"You're the reason her brother's dead!" Kane shouted. He was a half-second away from hitting the man for laughing. "You and your frien—"

"No!" Dietz jumped in angrily. "NOT me! I'd never hurt Winters." His eyes shifted briefly to Dallas, then back to us again. "You've got it all backwards."

"Oh?" I laughed. "So that wasn't you out in the desert last night?"

"Of course it was me. And shit, you guys ought to be ashamed. A high school band could've made less noise up on that ridge."

I closed my eyes. *Damn.*

"What, you think no one noticed?"

Kane hissed through clenched teeth and shifted uncomfortably. The movement was subtle, but there.

"*I* noticed," Dietz went on. "Not them, though. Just me." He shrugged. "It's the only reason you're still alive. The only reason I even came here. In fact—"

"Did you hurt my brother?"

Dallas's words came out deadly calm. But there was an underlying tension though, a sense that at any point her resolve could break.

"No."

"Do you know who did?"

Karl Dietz lowered his chin to his chest. His expression softened. He looked troubled.

Dallas edged closer. She knelt down, squatting until her face was mere inches from his. The arm still holding the glass of water was trembling.

"I *said*," she growled, "do you know who—"

"HOLD HOLD HOLD..."

Austin flew into the kitchen, surprising us all. He had both hands held outward, looking rushed, hurried. He didn't even bother to close the door behind him.

"Stop," he said. "Everyone just *stop*."

He pulled out his knife. I watched as he approached our captive, sitting in his chair...

With one swift movement he sawed through the zip-ties, cutting them off. The man in the middle of our kitchen began rubbing his wrists.

"Trust me," said Austin, as he sheathed his blade. "Dietz is okay."

Fifty-Seven

DALLAS

I wasn't sure what was going on, where Austin had come from, or how things had gotten to this point. There was only one thing I *was* sure of, however.

The man in our kitchen looked *pissed*.

"Got anything other than water?" he grunted, still holding my towel against his mouth. Maddox went to the fridge and returned with a beer. Dietz took it without thanking him, twisting the cap off in one big hand.

Everyone else remained standing, while the others greeted Austin in turn. When he reached me, I gave him the biggest hug I could manage.

"Everything alright?"

He nodded and smiled. "Yeah. Better than alright."

My body relaxed just the tiniest bit. That was good news at least.

"Who's talking first?" Kane asked, arms folded. "Seems we don't have much time."

"You don't," Dietz confirmed. "So... me."

305

He lowered his bottle to the table. Half the beer was gone already. He sucked in a long breath, then launched into his story right away.

"It all started about two years ago..."

The stranger in our kitchen talked, and the four of us listened. Most of what he said at first was military jargon; stuff I could only marginally understand. The gist of it was he'd fallen in with some bad people. Or rather, fallen in was a bad word. He'd *inserted* himself into something in order to gain trust and intelligence, at the behest of one of his commanding officers.

And then halfway through it... that commanding officer had been killed.

"By then I was deep," said Dietz. "Too deep to get out. At least not immediately. Not without attracting attention."

"What kind of attention?" asked Kane.

"The kind that got my commander killed."

The murdered man was Wesp. His death was officially ruled an accident. Dietz almost brought the whole dirty thing to the man above *him*, but then that man showed up in the circle of bad people as well.

"They were trading secrets," said Dietz. "Failed bio-weapon projects. High level intelligence from the old New Orleans lab that people had forgotten about. Only not these guys. There was an old timer from the lab — a guy by the name of Cameron — who turned everyone on to what they had. He thought it could be useful. But I don't think this guy realized what they'd be doing with it.

"You're talking about him in the past tense," said

Maddox.

"Yeah," Dietz nodded grimly. "Good catch on that."

He went on, talking in detail about how things progressed. The story only got worse from there.

"With Cameron out of the picture, no one knew what they were doing. They had free reign over the old database. Two guys started picking it apart, while a third went and started looking for buyers. They cut a deal with someone over the border. Started drip-feeding the database to some very bad characters, in exchange for—"

"Drugs," Kane finished.

Dietz nodded in confirmation. "They've got one big dealer from Vegas who buys everything in bulk. He picks it up from out in the desert, and his network deals it to the tourists." His lip curled into a snarl. "If I told you how much money they're raking in, it would make you—"

"I don't care about that," Kane growled. "I care only about the guys harvesting and selling bio-weapon secrets."

"The guys who had Connor killed," Austin added.

Dietz nodded his acknowledgment. He motioned for another beer, and Maddox brought him one.

"So how are you involved?" asked Maddox. "Why were you even down there last night?"

"Because I have full security clearance," Dietz said, "for the lab and otherwise. This makes me invaluable to them."

Kane sneered at him. "And when the *fuck* were you gonna stop trading military secrets for drugs?"

"He already stopped," Austin cut in. He held up a

small, grey thumb-drive. "According to Connor."

Everyone turned Austin's way. Dietz tipped his bottle toward him gratefully.

"The chip from Dallas's necklace contains a complete report of everything that went on," said Austin. "The whole undercover operation, including Wesp's files up to and including his death."

The room went silent for a moment. Details were coming fast, and there were some questions I wasn't sure I wanted the answers to. I stepped forward anyway and let out a shuddering breath.

"So where does my brother come in?"

Dietz took one look at me and his expression completely changed. He looked genuinely sad.

"I brought Connor in," he lamented. "He'd already figured out some stuff for himself, and was getting in way over his head. The others were noticing. They were talking about... about..."

"We know what they were talking about," I said calmly. "Go on."

Dietz nodded appreciatively. "I got to him before they could," he said. "That's when I told him everything. I *gave* him everything, all of it, and told him to take it to someone far enough up the chain that it would actually matter."

Maddox nodded. "He tried that. Only it didn't work."

"Woodward," Dietz confirmed. "Yes."

"So then what happened?"

Dietz rubbed at his overgrown crewcut. He'd been tough the whole time he'd been here, but this part was difficult. I could tell he was grieving.

"Connor came back with an idea," he said. "We'd keep going, and he'd keep feeding me data from the lab. He had the same clearance I did. He could get the same things I could, so he got himself transferred to New Orleans."

Kane shook his head gravely. "No way you're gonna convince me Connor gave up secrets."

"He didn't," said Dietz. "He mocked up the data. Took what was there and screwed with it enough that it was useless." He smiled a little at the recollection. "Shit, it was genius. They never knew. Even now, they *still* don't know."

"But they're going to find out," said Austin. It was a statement, not a question.

"Yes. Fairly soon, too."

"Which is why you're looking to get out."

Dietz dropped his head into his hands. "I've been looking to get out the whole time," he said. "Don't you realize that? Once Wesp was gone I was fucked. Connor and I tried to blow it all open, but with Woodward failing to come through and then... and then they got to Connor..."

"Hey."

The voice somehow didn't seem my own. Dietz looked down, and realized I'd laid my hand over his. The physical contact seemed to relax him, even if just a tiny bit.

"Who killed my brother?"

The man looked up at me, his eyes laden with sorrow.

"Tall guy. White hair. Almost albino, I think."

My eyes closed. A chill ran through my body.

"Guy by the name of Alacard."

Fifty-Eight

DALLAS

It turned out to be the strangest day.

I spent most of it up on the roof, watching over the neighborhood with Austin. Talking about the things on my brother's memory chip — a whole digital array of secrets that got him killed. I wasn't sure which was more ironic: that I had the answer to my brother's death the whole time, or that I'd somehow worn it unknowingly around my neck.

"You sure you're okay?"

I nodded for the fifth and final time. "Trust me," I said, pulling the blanket around my shoulders. "After the shit I've been through, it's nice to finally have answers."

It was cold up on the roof. I was tired. Aching. Even hungry. Plus, to top it all off, my ass was falling asleep.

"When do you think the others will be back?"

Austin shifted the rifle that rested in his lap, just long enough for a quick glance down at the phone's screen. Then he went back to being vigilant.

"Maddox and Dietz are almost back already," he said.

"Kane... I don't know."

I turned and put my back against his. Stared out over the remains of the once-nice homes of our once-busy block.

"What's going to happen when all this is through?"

Time passed. The wind whipped my hair back against my face. Austin remained silent, until finally:

"Dunno."

It was a question he wasn't expecting. Or maybe he was just thinking of a thoughtful answer. Either way, it was all coming to a head. Their surveillance of me had turned into protection, which had turned into a full-blown investigation that had led us here, to this moment. And now...

Now we were on the verge of settling things, one way or another. Either the people involved in Connor's death would be brought to the mother of all reckonings...

Or *we* would.

"Want half?"

He passed me a foil-wrapped Hershey bar. Or rather, part of one.

"Half? You ate three quarters of it."

"Sue me."

For some reason it made me laugh, and Austin started chuckling right along with me. It felt good, laughing into the wind, his broad back shifting up and down against mine. Hell, it was fucking cathartic.

"You think we got this one?" I asked, going suddenly serious.

Austin paused. "Maybe."

"Gimmie the odds."

"Sixty-forty."

"Us or them?"

I felt him shift to glance back at me. "Do you really wanna know?"

I sighed without turning around. "No, actually."

"There you go."

The sky was a rich purple now, the sun almost level with the horizon. Out in the desert things got cold quickly. Warming up sometimes took a while, but the cold...

"Dallas."

I shifted again, this time so I could see him. Austin was facing me now. Completely ignoring the half of the neighborhood he'd been tasked to watch over.

"I love you."

I blinked, dumbstruck. Not because of the admission, but because it came at the strangest of all possible moments.

"I love you too," I told him.

We were almost face to face now. Cheek against cheek. The wind sent a blast of cold over me, causing me to shiver.

"When did you know?" he asked.

I thought for a few seconds. "When you told me how much you loved my brother."

Silence reigned. A moment passed between us... of shared feelings, emotions, love.

"That time out on the balcony didn't hurt either," I smirked.

He kissed me, and suddenly it wasn't so cold anymore. It was just the two of us, sitting on top of the world. Looking out over oblivion and holding each other, while the rest of the universe went to complete shit all around us.

You do *love him, Dallas.*

It was fantastic, even just for a minute, to forget about everything else. To press my lips against his, to feel the fire and heat of his body against mine.

You love them all.

I came to groggily, wondering how it suddenly got so dark. Wondering if we'd somehow fucked up, or if ninjas had dropped from the desert trees and were right now climbing the walls to get us from all sides.

Headlights appeared, and we were back to back again. Austin's grip on the rifle tightened... then relaxed in the span of a single heartbeat.

"C'mon," he said, standing up. He offered his hand and I took it. "Maddox is home."

Fifty-Nine

DALLAS

"So did you reach anyone on the list?" Austin was asking.

Maddox shook his head from his end of the table, where he was cleaning a variety of weapons. It wasn't a good sign. Or a good start.

"What about Flynn?"

"Out of town."

"Sully?"

"Nope."

Dietz was in the fridge again, rummaging through our meager pickings. I figured he was looking for another beer, but he came out with a container of milk instead.

"We set up what you told us to, though," he told Austin. "What did you call it again?"

"A dead man's switch."

"Yeah," he nodded. "That."

I winced as Dietz drank our milk straight from the

carton. It was almost as terrible as the idea of us getting wiped out, and having to rely on a computer to release the information my brother compiled.

"So how are we doing this?" he asked.

"By ambush preferably," said Austin.

"Obviously."

"We're not going to sit around, waiting for them to come," Maddox went on. "We strike first. We strike hard."

Dietz wiped his mouth with the back of one arm and put the milk back. I winced again.

"Yes, but—"

"We lure them back out into the desert again," said Austin. "The buyers, the sellers, the dealers... *all* of them."

Dietz laughed. "With what? Cheese?"

"Better than cheese," said Maddox. "*You'll* get them out there."

"Don't think so," said Dietz. "I don't have nearly the pull you think I do. They won't come."

The door swung open, and Kane lumbered into the kitchen. He already wearing his desert camos. On top of that he was strapped with weapons and Kevlar, armed and armored to the teeth.

"They will if you tell them," Kane said.

Dietz shook his head again, as if he were trying to explain something simple to a small child. A child that just wasn't getting it.

"And what in the fucking world would make you

think that?"

Kane's arm swung up, and two big bricks thudded to the table. A cloud of dust preceded them, all tied off and wrapped in brown paper.

"Because you're gonna tell them their drugs are missing," said Kane. He jerked a dirt-caked thumb over his shoulder. "And that's something they're probably gonna want to check out for themselves."

Karl Dietz complexion was already fair. But now he went as white as a ghost.

"Holy shit," he croaked. "We're all dead."

Maddox laughed from where he was reattaching the stock of his rifle. Austin patted him consolingly on the shoulder.

"Did you really want to live forever?"

Their former comrade was still glaring sightlessly down at the table, looking like he was in shock.

"Well... I kinda wanted a *little* more time."

"Then follow the plan," said Austin. "Don't deviate. Don't waver. And whatever you do, don't blink or panic."

The camera on Kane's phone clicked as he took a close-up shot of the two dusty bricks. He pressed a few buttons, and another beep sounded from Dietz's hip.

"There. I just sent you that photo."

"A—And?" Dietz's voice was still broken.

"In about an hour, you'll send that to *them*. Tell them it came from an unknown number."

I watched the man's Adam's apple bob hard as he swallowed. Dietz was scared. Legitimately frightened.

"And then what?"

"And then we wait," said Maddox. "In position, of course."

"They're going to come pick me up immediately," said Dietz. "They're going to drag me out to the desert with them."

"That's fine. You'll send the message from your place."

Dietz's eyes went ridiculously wide. "*FINE*? How the fuck is that fine?"

"Because you're gonna play it cool," said Kane. "*Real* cool."

"Your best poker face cool," said Austin.

"Life or death cool," Maddox added, putting down his barrel brush.

By now Dietz looked like a deer in headlights. Through it all, he kept shaking his head.

"This isn't right," he said. "Even if they don't kill me outright, they'll shoot me like a dog when we get out there and the drugs are missing."

"Not if you play it right," growled Kane.

"No," Dietz sneered. "You don't get it! You don't *understand* these people—"

The sharp clack of a weapon being racked turned everyone's head in Maddox's direction. He stood his fully-assembled Barrett up on the table. It was so long, the muzzle nearly scraped the ceiling.

"We're not looking to *understand* them," said Maddox.

Sixty

DALLAS

The desert was somehow warmer this time around, or maybe it was because I'd prepared myself for it. The night sky was crystal clear. Looking up from our position on the ridge, it was like being trapped under a bowl of a million stars.

"You remember what we told you?" said Maddox. It was more an order than a question.

"Yes."

"You are to *hang back,* no matter what. Stay completely out of the line of fire."

"I know."

"You don't engage unless it's bad." His voice went ominously low. "*Really* bad. As in the rest of us are already—"

"Stop, already. I *get* it."

He stared at me hard, the wind blowing his blond hair over one stubbled cheek. I wanted to kiss that cheek. I wanted to feel it warm against my lips, while it was still safe, still mine...

"Alright," said Maddox. "With that in mind, come

with me."

He walked back to the truck, and I solemnly followed. It was just the two of us on the ridge. The lump was still in my throat from saying goodbye to the others.

Dallas... don't.

It was hard not to think that way, not to imagine what could happen. But if I was going to be of any use at all, I had to put it out of my mind.

Maddox pulled a flat black case from the back of the vehicle. He unlocked it with two sharp clicks, and swung it open.

"You know what this is?"

I stared down at the weapon. Like a ghost from the past, it stared back at me.

"It's a SCAR."

He nodded slowly, looking impressed. "That's right. It's a SCAR-H, Mark 17 battle rifle. Ever shoot one?"

Now it was my turn to nod. "Yes, a bunch of times. I used to shoot Connor's."

"This *is* Connor's."

The skin all along my arms prickled with goosebumps. For a split-second I tried to convince myself it was the wind. It wasn't.

"I... I didn't realize..."

Maddox lifted the weapon with practiced ease and put it into my arms. For some reason it felt warm. The grip fit perfectly into my palm, like it was made for my hand.

"Your brother saved my life with that rifle," said Maddox gravely. "Kane's and Austin's too."

Connor's rifle...

I stared down at the weapon with all new eyes. I was holding a piece of my brother. An extension of his life, an artifact that had outlived his body but not his legend.

"There were others too," Maddox went on. "Names you would've know. Brothers of ours that Connor was willing to sacrifice himself for, and—"

BRZZZ!

A crackle of static burst from the radio at Maddox's hip. He plucked it from his belt, just as Austin's voice came through.

"HEADLIGHTS. THREE KLICKS OUT."

Maddox looked back at me. Our eyes locked.

"Only if it comes to it," he said sternly. "Promise?"

I nodded slowly as I checked the magazine on my brother's weapon.

My lover swore under his breath. "Not good enough. *Say* it, Dallas."

"I promise."

He swept me in and kissed me, pulling me tightly against him. He smelled like war — like iron and leather and fire.

"You're not just Connor's sister," he murmured. "You're much more than that to us."

My forehead was pressed against his. Maddox's gaze

was piercing, his irises bright and alive as they bored into mine.

"We're *in love* with you Dallas."

The lump in my throat was back. This time it was the size of a softball. I wanted to speak, but I could barely breathe. There were so many things to say...

"TWO CLICKS," the radio spat.

He was staring at me like no one had ever stared at me in my life. Looking at me not only as Dallas Winters, but as a woman. A lover.

"We'll get through this," Maddox assured me. "All of us."

Somehow I swallowed past the ball in my throat. "For Connor," I managed to squeak.

We were lost together in a sea of wind and stars and crisp night air. Pointing our weapons downward with one arm, holding each other with the other.

"For Connor," Maddox agreed.

Sixty-One

AUSTIN

The column stretched backwards into the night; three trucks, then four, then five. More vehicles than we initially realized.

A *lot* more.

I watched from my belly, peering over the ridge with my night-owl optics. The vehicles joined the ones already there, the ones that came in from the west. The ones that came from the north too, although that 'column' consisted of a single Escalade that arrived before anyone else.

It was funny, how dark everything was. Every car, every truck, every SUV — all of them were painted in black or midnight blue. Like they were telegraphing their own evil, beneath the cover of night.

They can't possibly think they blend in better.

I laughed at that part. Odds are they probably did. Yet beneath the desert moonlight, each of them stood out like dark ants on a sand-colored hill.

"I HAVE EYES ON DIETZ."

Maddox's voice called back to me from the other hill, on the opposite side of the canyon. We'd switched to earpieces now. Everything else was silent, save for the chatter in the valley below.

God, there have to be twenty of them.

I picked through the growing crowd. At least a dozen men had rifles slung. A few others were strapped with sidearms, too. They'd already uncovered the hidden compartment, and were in the process of sliding it open.

"I HAVE DIETZ ALSO," I murmured back, although there wasn't that great a need to keep my voice low. With all the talking and arguing going on down there, I could start whistling if I wanted to.

I watched the last of the vehicles roll to a dusty halt. The smoke cleared, leaving them in a rough semi-circle. I picked Dietz from the crowd again, zooming out a bit to follow him.

"KANE'S IN POSITION."

That part I had to rely on Maddox for. Kane was positioned three-hundred feet directly beneath me, tucked into the terrain. From the original ridge, Maddox could see him. I couldn't.

I hope this works...

It certainly wasn't ideal. 'Hoping' for something wasn't in our playbook — planning was. Hope was for the weak, the lazy, the ill-prepared. Of course we always did have prayer, but was the last page, the final resort. And it generally didn't do any better than hope when it came to determining outcomes.

Person by person I scanned the crowd, thumbing the 'save' button on my optics for each. I was taking pictures of the bad guys. Digital images that would become records proving their involvement tonight... provided someone were to ever download the scans.

That of course, would all depend on who won and who lost. What was the old adage? History is always written by the victors?

My eyes fell back on Dietz. He looked stiff. Nervous. Jumpy...

Dammit Dietz, stay chill.

Mentally I projected the words. If he heard them, it didn't show in his body language. I was happy to see he was still carrying his weapon. If they hadn't taken it yet, they couldn't suspect *too* much on his end.

Then... next to Dietz...

"I HAVE ALACARD."

I said the words low, as if trying to keep them from Dallas. But of course that was silly. Dallas had an earpiece too.

It was strange, how calm she'd gone after learning who killed Connor. As if the knowledge had alleviated the anger, instead of releasing all the pent up rage, sorrow, and other emotions.

I knew better though. If anything, she was bottling it up even *more*. It was something she'd eventually have to talk about, or at the very least let out. And the longer she went in silence...

"DIETZ IS MOVING."

Maddox's last phrase caused me to drop my binoculars. I grabbed my weapon and looked through the scope, where everything seemed smaller and further away, yet just as clear. Finally having a target reticle on these assholes felt pretty damned good. I switched from target to target, assigning each of them a value. Assessing each in terms of threat level.

Basically figuring out which of them I'd do first.

"BE READY..."

I'd been ready for months. For just over a year, to be precise.

"WAIT FOR THE SIGNAL..."

I couldn't be *more* ready.

"DIETZ IS—"

BOOM!

An explosion rattled the rough stone valley, sending up a thick plume of dust. It was followed by another, more familiar sound:

BBBRRRRAAAAPPP!

Gunshots! Fully automatic fire.

The restless milling in the canyon suddenly became frantic, as half the men dropped instantly to their bellies. The other half scrambled for cover.

"FUCK!" I heard Maddox swear over our channel.

More dust swirled upwards, whipping into the air. *Too* much dust. Someone had set something off — a concussion grenade, or maybe a small explosive device. In the confusion I lost everyone; Dietz, Alacard, the guy with the Kord 12.7mm I wanted to nail first. No, scratch that. The guy I *needed* to nail first, because if I didn't get him the Russian heavy machine gun would tear us all to shreds.

FUCK!

My sentiment echoed Maddox's exactly. I could only hope he still had Kane. That he had much better sights than I did, and somehow, through all the chaos, he had our friend covered.

Down below, it was total bedlam. The swarm of people were scattering, with no one actually sure which direction to run. The smart ones fled back to their vehicles for cover. The dumb ones...

I swept the area with my scope. It panned over just in time to see Dietz putting someone down with the butt of his rifle. I couldn't tell who, but the man was wearing a suit. A *suit.* Out in the middle of the desert.

CRACK! CRACK!

The sharp report of Maddox's .50 caliber rang out from above. I glanced up, peering to the other of the canyon. Muttering under my breath that no matter what he did, no matter what happened, he'd *better* keep her safe.

Then I saw what was happening over there... and a spike of terror bolted straight through me.

Sixty-Two

DALLAS

I made the truck in seconds. With a quick turn of the key it roared to life, billowing dust all around me as I slammed it into gear.

My heart nearly exploded in terror as it lurched *forward*... straight toward the edge of the cliff.

Oh SHIIIIIIT!

I stomped down on the brake with both feet. The tires screamed to a halt, but the momentum kept me moving, sliding, skidding inexorably forward. Pushing me to the very lip of the terrifying, three-hundred foot drop...

"DALLAS!"

Austin's scream nearly tore out my eardrum. I reached up reflexively to pull out the earpiece, but my hand clamped right back over the steering wheel.

This is it...

At the very last second, the truck skidded to a halt. I could see Maddox through the passenger window, lying on his belly, clutching his rifle. He turned his head, a look of total incredulity frozen across his face.

"DALLAS, WHAT THE–"

I didn't hear anything else. I was already in reverse, tires spinning backwards, skidding down the embankment while looking wildly over my shoulder. I couldn't believe I was doing this! But even more unbelievable, I'd nearly driven over a fucking *cliff* in the process.

"–GET BACK HERE! DON'T EVEN THINK ABOUT–"

Now I *did* yank out the earpiece, tossing it over my shoulder. It was loud, it was distracting, and nothing they could say would stop me anyway. After witnessing the pandemonium below, my only thoughts were with Kane. He was still down there, all by himself, with only Dietz as a potential ally.

And the last thing I'd seen before the explosion... a half dozen men, weapons drawn, closing in on his position.

Hurry up!

The truck roared down the hill, picking up speed. The vehicle was already shaking, every bump magnified by a factor of ten. I was clenching the wheel. Shaking left and right, up and down...

Go faster!

"OWW!"

I cried out as my head bumped the roof. I was already pushing the limits. Every pebble was a boulder at this speed. Every piece of debris was—

THUMP!

I didn't even see the first guy I plowed into. All I saw was his rifle, lying across the windshield as he went straight over the roof.

Holy shit holy shit holy shit!

Another thump, this time off to the side. I saw two very surprised bad guys literally bounce off my fender. The looks of utter shock frozen upon their faces actually made me laugh out loud.

What the fuck are you laughing at?

My heart was hammering out of my chest. My whole body was flooded with fear and adrenaline and a whole host of other emotions I couldn't even stop to consider.

How are you going to find him?

I really had no idea. Right now it was like driving through a dust-storm, steering blindly left and right. I pointed the nose of the truck in the direction I *imagined* I saw Kane last. But whether or not I was right...

BBBRRRRAAAAPPP!

Something loud and obnoxious erupted somewhere off to my left. I steered away from it, only vaguely aware I was now probably skirting the face of the cliff.

I had to slow down. Only I *couldn't* slow down because there were people everywhere. I couldn't see them but I could hear them; shouting, crying out, somehow even firing, although I couldn't imagine they weren't just as blind as I was. And then all of a sudden...

WHOOSH!

I was out of the dust cloud. Into the open. I saw three

men react immediately, raising their weapons until they were level with my truck.

SHIT!

I ducked, jerking the wheel hard. Loud pings and ricochets echoed across one side of my vehicle. Following that, I heard two sharp cracks, from far away. When I looked up again, two of them men had fallen.

Whoa.

The third one was sprinting like hell in the opposite direction.

"UMMPH!"

I whirled, and suddenly there was Kane. He was flat on his back, covered in dirt. Writhing around... with someone else pinned against his body.

I flung open the door and ran for him, without even thinking. As I got closer I could see what was going on. He had one man in a headlock, while two others stood there kicking him in the ribs. A third stood poised over my lover, with the butt of his rifle raised high. Ready at any moment to bring it down on his skull...

"KANE!"

They whirled, and it occurred to me instantly that shouting probably wasn't the best option. I hadn't even flipped the safety on my weapon yet.

"Dallas?"

I saw Kane's broad back twist viciously, and the guy he'd been wrestling with suddenly stopped moving. Half the men facing me turned back around. The others raised their rifles.

CRACK!

A bullet tore though an enemy's shoulder. This time it came from the side, instead of above. Another man was advancing forward calmly, his teeth stark white against the dusky gloom of his face.

It was Dietz.

Thank God!

The other man scrambled sideways, firing as he ran. As he and Dietz traded shots, I advanced forward... just as Kane grabbed the leg of his nearest opponent and yanked him to the ground.

That left the man with rifle butt, who turned to face me. His gaze caught mine and there was an instant of shock... then recognition.

ALACARD.

His face was still bruised, his forehead scabbed over from our scuffle in New Orleans. He didn't seem phased by it. In fact, his mouth curled into the most wicked of grins.

Dallas...

He moved slowly now, like a snake. No... like a snake *charmer*, keeping me locked in his trance-like gaze. Holding me prisoner with his beady black eyes, unable to move or do anything or—

DALLAS!

In a fraction of an instant, he snapped his weapon downward and leveled it at me. It happened robotically, like his arm was hydraulic...

CRACK!

The rifle came alive in my hands. Shit, it was like it shot itself.

Alacard looked down, at the blossoming red hole in his chest. A dark stain was spreading outward, looking black in the moonlight.

Best of all, his face was contorted in a mask of complete surprise.

CRACK! CRACK! CRACK!

He jerked a few times, stumbling backwards. Then he crumpled, just as Kane sprang to his feet.

"Dallas!"

CRACK CRACK CRACK CRACK CRACK!

"DALLAS!"

Somehow I stopped before my clip was empty. But only just barely.

"Holy shit, Dallas." Kane's hand closed over the barrel, pushing it downward. "I've never seen you move that fast," he swore.

You've never seen me deal blackjack.

The thought only barely registered in the furthest recesses of my mind. I was still numb. Speechless. Tingling all over.

My lover's arm slid around my waist, pulling me in the direction of the cliff face. "C'mon."

"B—But the truck..." I managed to say. "It's that way."

Kane said something, but I could barely hear now. I thought maybe I'd gone deaf from the sound of gunshots, but then I realized the deafening sound was above me. And it was getting louder and louder.

"Forget the truck," Kane was practically shouting into my ear. "Come this way, we need cover."

"What's happening?" I yelled. The dust was swirling again, only this time there *was* a storm. Or at least it seemed that way as I looked up, trying to find recognizable patches of the clear night sky.

My whole body was shaking. Even my ear drums were vibrating.

"What the hell is going on?" I shouted.

Kane's breath was hot against my ear. His voice was loud but calm.

"Helicopters."

Sixty-Three

KANE

It was beautiful, seeing the way it all unfolded. Watching the entire platoon repel from the two Sikorskys, inserting themselves smoothly and effortlessly into the fight.

My only regret was that it was over too soon.

Less than five minutes after the first chopper arrived, it touched down safely on the hard-packed clay. Thirteen SEALs and two officers stood over a line of fanned-out prisoners, all disarmed and zip-tied and face down in the dust.

"Medina, right?"

The man addressing me by my last name was as grizzled as they came. He stomped over confidently, the dark hair peeking out beneath his hat all streaked with grey.

"Yes Chief," I saluted.

He extended his hand. I shook it, while he measured me with his eyes.

"Chief Rogan. Team Four, third platoon."

"I know who you are, sir."

"Good. Now why the fuck are you grinning?"

I wasn't even aware I had been. As the man stood waiting for an answer, I couldn't do anything but shrug.

"I really didn't think you were coming."

The Chief scowled and removed his hat. "You shitting me son? After what *you* told us?"

I wanted to laugh. Not at the man, but at the situation. It was all so absurd, so totally insane. It would take a whole day to explain it, and another week to—

"Of course we came! Woodward was pretty goddamn insistent. Between him and what I read of your service record, we couldn't *not* come." He paused for a moment. "Although there *was* some pushback..."

For a few seconds he looked thoughtful, as if considering something unpleasant. Then he shook his head.

"This is a right fucking mess, son," the Chief spat, looking around. "You know that?"

"Oh I know it, sir."

"Quit all that 'sir' shit and tell me what the *hell* is going on."

As the choppers' engines wound down, I went over the basics. The details could come later. It took me a minute to identify the parties involved, pointing out men, bosses, vehicles...

"Two trucks slipped away," I said abruptly. "I think they headed east, while we were in the middle of..."

"The shitstorm?" he finished finished for me. "Don't worry, we know all about it. We've already got intercepts. Hell, this is a joint operation, between the Army and Nellis and—"

"SIR!"

We both turned our heads at the same time. Two men had pulled back the hidden dust-cover and were standing over a whole pit of perfectly-stacked brown paper bricks. The Chief raised one wild eyebrow.

"Cocaine?"

"We assumed as much, yes."

"This about drugs, then?"

I shook my head. "Much more than that."

The man paused, putting his hands on his hips. He let out a long, deep breath.

"So..." he squinted up at me. "That stuff Woodward was telling us..."

"All true, Chief. Every bit of it."

He scanned around again, looking at everyone, everything. His eyes swept over the men on their bellies. His face contorted into a grimace.

"Jesus Christ," he swore loudly.

"And Mary and Joseph," I added.

Sixty-Four

MADDOX

It was several hours before it was all over. Before every last suspect left in the back of a police car, or worse, chained hand-and-foot and dragged off by the Military Police. The LVMPD wanted us to follow them back for statements of course, but the Chief got us out of there by claiming we were 'his people'.

Eventually, only one of the choppers was left.

"Full debriefing," Rogan barked, as he walked back to the transport. "My office, all of you. When I'm good and ready."

Kane replied with a curt nod. It seemed to satisfy the man.

"For now," the Chief said, "get some rest."

He disappeared into the transport, two men shifting quickly aside for him. I marveled at how he seemed almost totally surreal. Like a character out of a movie.

"So this was your doing, huh?" I poked Kane. It was the first actual conversation we'd had since the chaos started.

"Yup."

"Alright, then. How'd you pull it off?"

Austin and Dietz inched forward. They were both pretty interested themselves. Dallas was already by my side, hanging off one shoulder. Probably already trying to make amends for the truck incident.

"Well I touched base with Woodward first," Kane said. "Told him the shit was about to hit the fan, and he was standing way too close not to be splattered."

The analogy made me laugh. "So why didn't he just move?"

"I didn't give him the option," Kane replied. "I told him if we went down, he was next. Without question."

"And he believed you?"

"He had to. Especially when I told him Dietz was hearing things. *Bad* things. Namely, that he was flapping his gums to us back in New Orleans."

Austin rubbed at his jaw. "God, that's dirty."

"Dirty times," Kane acknowledged.

"So then what happened?" asked Dallas.

"Woodward got in touch with all new superiors. Between the both of us, not to mention Dietz on the inside, we rattled the tree hard enough to shake a platoon loose."

"And we ended up with Rogan."

"Yup," Kane said again.

"We got lucky," said Dietz. "Lucky that he's good people."

"We sure did," Kane agreed. "Because this almost didn't happen. There are officers involved who aren't even here right now. People that were trying to squash this every inch of the way."

"If not for Rogan," Dallas theorized.

Kane nodded slowly. "Yeah. If not for Rogan."

The whole thing was a can of worms. A filthy, shit-stained can of *rotten* worms, that nobody really wanted to touch.

But the can was open now. And there was no closing it.

"Ever think of telling us?" I needled Kane.

"Telling you what?"

"Oh I don't know..." I sneered. "That maybe you had *SEAL Team Four* showing up?"

"Nah."

"Why the fuck not?"

"Didn't wanna get your hopes up."

I still couldn't believe it. Still couldn't comprehend how everything could get this messy, this fast.

"There's enough on Connor's data chip to take down some *very* high-level operators," Austin vowed. "And way too many people here tonight, for it to get swept under the rug."

Thank fucking God, I thought to myself.

"So shit's about to get hairy?"

Dallas jerked her thumb over her shoulder. "*That*

341

wasn't hairy?" she exclaimed.

"Hell no," I teased. "We had the whole thing under control... that is, until you took the wheel again."

Austin couldn't suppress a chuckle. Even Kane smiled.

"Yeah, somebody take her keys away already?"

While the laughter died down I studied Dallas's expression. Even now she was still flush with heat and adrenaline. But she wasn't sad. She wasn't upset, or shell-shocked, or distressed, or anything like that at all.

Considering what she'd been through, and what she'd just done, it was almost a miracle.

And that's exactly why you love her.

I realized that it was. Dallas had brains, courage, and strength. A rare and wonderful combination in *any* person, much less a soulmate. And that wasn't even taking into account the rest of her assets.

"So that's it?" Dietz asked finally. "We're all done?"

We stared at each other for a moment, all five of us in a circle. The only sound was the low hum of the Sikorsky going through its pre-flight.

"Seems like it," Austin shrugged.

Kane spat a gob of blood through a split lip. "Better be," he added.

Dallas was kicking at the ground. Not saying much of anything.

"I can go *home*," Dietz said. His voice was different now. Softer. "I'm finally out."

I reached out and laid a hand on his shoulder. "Gonna be some loose ends," I offered. "A lot of them, probably. But nothing that can't be tied up."

Out on the horizon, the first hint of pink was cracking the sky. Dawn was coming. My stomach rumbled.

It was Austin who spoke up at the end.

"Anyone for pancakes?"

Sixty-Five

DALLAS

Two weeks. That's how long it took to sift through the ashes. Two weeks of meetings and debriefs and borderline interrogations.

The police wanted answers, of course. But with the LVMPD getting credit for one of the biggest drug seizures in Nevada's history, their interviews were all good coffee and even better smiles.

When it came to the MP's however, things were a lot more complicated.

We didn't hear from Rogan until after a sweeping series of arrests had been made. It was all internal stuff. Very nasty. The kind of high-level shit the Navy and Air Force both wanted to keep tightly under wraps. When we were finally called in, the whole process took several long days. But between Woodward and Dietz and the files my brother had squirreled away, the last pieces of a really fucked up puzzle finally started coming together.

Alacard, thankfully, was gone. So was Evan Miller, although I was never really told if that happened by my hand or a result of someone else's. Either way, three Captains and two Chief Warrant Officers were literally hauled off in chains. There would be more than just court-martials - there would be military tribunals. And these, I was assured, would take place behind *very* closed doors.

April was just a few days away by the time it was all finished. Dietz had finally gone home to Norfolk, even taking his tooth with him. My insurance checks arrived; structure and content money from the fire. Numbers and commas on two tiny slips of paper... all that was left of my childhood home.

One evening I was looking at the guys, watching them mill around the house. They looked restless now. As if struggling to find something to do.

They've been protecting you for so long, the little voice in my head told me. *They don't know what comes next.*

It was a stark realization. One I hadn't even considered, or prepared for.

So what does *come next, Dallas?*

I supposed I needed to move on, maybe get a fresh start. I could probably get my job back, but for some reason dealing cards just didn't seem all that appealing anymore.

Neither did Vegas.

There were just too many memories here. Too many ghosts. Too much in the way of bittersweet—

"Dallas?"

I glanced up and Maddox was leaning into my doorway, looking more amazing than usual. His arms were all pumped up. Probably from just working out.

Damn.

I let my eyes crawl over him for a few happy seconds. Time had been short lately. Over the past couple of weeks, there really hadn't been much room for—

"Can you come with me for a minute?"

I smiled as I followed him down the hall. He extended his hand, and I took it happily as he led me into the kitchen.

The others were there too. Neither one of them were seated. Austin stood to one side of the table, arms folded. Kane was on the other, leaning back into his usual spot against the counter.

"Another family meeting?" I joked.

"Something like that."

I looked down, and noticed there was a box on the table. A gift box in red and white, tied off with a ribbon.

"Well it's not my birthday," I said.

"We know."

The box *did* look like a cake box, only fancier. I was blushing a little as I stepped up. Austin pulled out a chair for me.

"Oh, so I'm gonna to need to sit down for this?"

The guys looked at each other, all three of them.

"Probably," Kane offered. "Yeah."

I sat down. Pulled on the ribbon. It fell away, and I lifted the lid, wondering what in the world they were collectively giving me.

Inside the box was a beautiful, leather-bound book. I took it out, surprised at its weight. How heavy and warm it felt in my hands.

"Open it."

I flipped the cover, and there he was: Connor. Staring back at me through time. Flashing me the most beautiful, wonderful smile... a smile I almost forgot he had. Almost, but not quite.

I think I gasped. Covered my mouth with my hands. But then I was flipping through the book, page after page, picture after wonderful picture of my brother in the prime of his life.

Tears welled up instantly, then began to fall. They streamed down my cheeks so quickly I had to lean back to avoid them dropping onto the beautifully embossed pages.

"Here."

One of them handed me a tissue, but it wasn't nearly enough. I might need a hundred.

"I..."

The sentence failed. Words were absolutely meaningless. I kept flipping and sobbing, over the most amazing set of photographs I'd ever laid eyes on. Connor, in various uniforms, camos, and fatigues. Standing or kneeling in the most exotic locales. Grinning back at me, first from a ship, then from a desert, then from some tropical beach with a bright blue sky.

There were dozens of photos. *Hundreds.* Lots of pictures had the guys in them as well. Photos of Connor and Maddox holding their rifles, shoulder to shoulder. Photos of my brother with Kane and Austin, playing cards in a quonset hut.

"Keep going," Maddox said.

I flipped some more, and suddenly I saw myself. It was a picture taken while we teenagers, or at least while I was. Connor and I stood together, embracing and laughing, as if the photographer had done something funny. Or as if the two of us were sharing some secret, silent joke.

I reached out blindly for more tissues. They were handing them to me as fast as I could grab them.

"There's more."

In the last few pages of the book, the photographs were much older. I was young in them. Connor too. And also...

"Oh my God..."

My parents stood there now, smiling back at me. My mother and father looked heartbreakingly young, the way I remembered them. There were twenty or thirty photos like this. Family photos. Images of birthday parties and picnics and holidays. Of barbecues outdoors, of camping and hiking and rollerskating.

I paused at an especially precious one, of Connor and I tearing open presents on Christmas morning. I choked back even more tears, remembering that particular day.

"These were among your brother's things," said Maddox, "that somehow never made it back to you. They were on base with him. He kept them in a special envelope, and took it wherever he went."

I was smiling now. Even laughing. Laughing through

my tears.

"You should've gotten these a long time ago obviously," Austin said. "But after what happened... it's a blessing that you didn't."

I thought about the fire. About how these things would've be utterly and completely gone. I felt a stab of panic at the thought, but they were here now. Here where they belonged, safe in my hands.

"I... I don't know what to..."

"Say?" Kane offered, finishing the thought.

He'd left the counter and was kneeling beside me now. I dabbed at my eyes and sniffed.

"Say you'll make even *more* memories with us," Kane said gently. "Add pages to this book. That you'll add *another* book's worth of photographs, and then another."

I looked at him, then Austin, then Maddox. My beautiful blond SEAL smiled down at me and nodded.

"Say that you'll stay... and help us preserve the memory of Connor *together.*"

Sixty-Six

DALLAS

I sat there in a daze, trying desperately to understand. Attempting to comprehend what they were saying... what they actually *meant* by the words coming out of their mouths.

"Y—You want me to stay?"

They nodded collectively.

"With *all* of you?"

"Of course," said Austin.

They were looking back at me casually, like they'd just suggested something simple like going to the movies. Like they hadn't just dropped some incredible, life-altering proposal in my lap, with all the nonchalance of asking what I might want on my pizza.

"*Stay* with you," I said again. "As in... as a..."

"Girlfriend," Austin answered. "Yes."

"More than that though," Kane grunted. "Much more."

My mouth was dry. My head was spinning.

"What's so hard about this to understand?" said Maddox, smiling. "We love you. We *need* you." He shrugged. "We want to be with you."

Now the whole kitchen was spinning. I put my hand on the table to stop it.

"But... it's not fair to you," I replied, kicking myself as I said it. "You all have lives. Or rather, you *had* lives before all this, and you gave those lives up for me."

The kitchen was silent again, except for the ticking of the clock. That damned clock. I wanted to break it.

"You've been protecting me for so long, you don't have anything else," I said. "Maybe you don't want me. Maybe you're just *used* to me. You know, having me around. On your monitors at first, and then in your home." I swallowed dryly. "And then... well..."

"Do you love us?" Kane asked suddenly. The question seemed even more abrupt, coming from him.

"With all my heart," I said immediately.

"Then that's all that matters."

I felt warm, but it was a good warm. An enveloping warmth that brought with it peace and comfort.

"Dallas listen," said Maddox. "We could all go our separate ways. Maybe meet other people, eventually even fall in love. We'd marry different women. Raise families..."

I felt a pang of jealousy. It came from out of nowhere, hitting me hard, surprising me fully.

"But then we'd lead different lives," Austin went on. "We'd be forever apart. Forever separated by divergent paths."

351

He paused for a moment. "Yet with you..."

"With you'd we'd remain together," Maddox finished for him. "As a unit. The unit we've always been."

"The unit we're *best* at," Kane added.

A hand touched my cheek. Maddox was kneeling now, turning my face toward his.

"We already love you Dallas," he said. "And you love *us*. It could work, the four of us together. We'd be more inseparable than any couple ever could. We'd be a team."

Together. Inseparable...

The words hung there in my mind, glowing brightly.

"And if anyone knows a team its us," smiled Austin.

"*Be* with us," said Maddox. "Forget everything, forget everyone else. Be ours, and we'll give you the world. And in return you get *us*."

My heart soared. I felt it open... and the warmth poured in.

"And we'd have a Winters on our team again," said Kane solemnly. "Just as we always did." I could see his face contorting, trying to choke back powerful emotions. "Just like before."

I sat there stunned. Elated. Jubilant.

You complete them, Dallas.

Excited. Thrilled beyond belief.

And there's nothing wrong with that.

Slowly I stood. I crossed the kitchen halfway, grabbed

the wall clock, and smashed it against the floor. The moment was almost apocalyptic: it exploded into a *thousand* plastic shards.

"We can move, right?" I ventured. "Get the hell out of here?"

All three of them were dumbstruck, staring back at me in awe. Kane let out a short, barking laugh.

"You mean leave Vegas?"

I nodded.

"Fuck yes," they all said at once.

I was holding back the mother of all smiles. Now I let it go. It broke across my face, splitting me from ear to ear.

"Then I'm all in," I said, spreading out my arms.

Less than three seconds later, I was being crushed in a triple bear-hug.

Epilogue

DALLAS

"One..."

I stood helplessly sightless, my pulse racing with the anticipation of being able to see again.

"Two..."

My whole body felt charged and alive. Burning hot. Sizzling.

"Three!"

The blindfold dropped, and for a moment everything was fuzzy. Then I blinked three times in rapid succession, and clapped both hands over my mouth.

"Oh my GOD..."

The room was breathtakingly beautiful. Decorated in perfect feminine style, but with a distinctive, man's touch.

Or should I say *men's* touch.

"Holy shit! It's... it's..."

"Perfect?" Austin offered.

"YES!"

From the silk drapes just kissing the hardwood floors, to the Persian rug squared off against the four-poster bed, it was everything and anything I could've ever wanted. My boys had done good. *Very* good.

"I love it!" I practically shouted, spinning in a slow circle. "Oh wow. You guys... you *really* outdid yourselves."

It was our first day in the new house. Our first night in my new bedroom! Or more accurately *our* new bedroom, because we'd converted the master into an area big enough, and wide enough, to accommodate the four of us.

And now it was actually decorated too.

"Sort of makes you forget the rest of the house is still in boxes, doesn't it?"

"YES!" I shouted again, still soaking it all in. The room was soft and comfortable. Probably because the lights were off, and a dozen or more lit candles had been placed strategically around the room.

But who was keeping score anyway.

"You guys are the—"

The rest of my words were lost as Maddox's mouth closed over mine. He began kissing me softly, sensuously, his warm tongue sliding erotically into my wet, willing mouth.

Oh!

Three sets of hands went to my body at once. They began pulling off my clothes. Sliding everything but my panties downward and away.

YES...

I stepped forward and out of whatever was left. I'd

been horny all week. Horny throughout the move, clear across the country to our gorgeous new home, nestled perfectly on our twelve-acre lot in the woods.

New Hampshire had been one of our choices; one of four different dart-throws against a map on the wall. As random as that seemed, it turned out to be an amazing decision. The four of us wanted a brand new start. Someplace cozy, that had seasons and snow. Someplace fresh, that none of us had ever been.

And the house...

The house was a gorgeous old mountain-style home, with pillars and gables and warm, wood-stained trim. Big enough for all of us... and then some.

We each had our own rooms, our own space, but my room was special. My room was *this* room, cozy enough for whenever I wanted to retreat to it, large enough to accommodate two... or three... or four...

Hey, a girl's gotta do what she can to stay warm.

And I'd heard the nights up here could get very, *very* cold.

Suddenly Austin was kissing me, and then Kane. One by one they shared my lips, turning my head this way and that. Leading me ever closer to the bed while their hands roamed my body, touching me everywhere at once until my tingling senses overloaded with pleasure.

"Oh fuck..." I murmured softly.

"Soon enough, yeah," one of them chuckled.

I jumped as something dripped onto my shoulder;

something wet but warm, something vaguely familiar but not unpleasant. It took me only a moment to realize what it was.

They're covering me with oil...

They were, and it was absolutely magnificent. Four hands rubbed up and down the left and right sides of my body, totally coating me with warm, Jasmine-scented oil. In the meantime, Kane was still kissing me. His hands were on my tits, kneading them softly, cupping them in his big hands until someone poured oil there too...

"Mmmmmm..." I cooed in contentment. "Oh *shit* that's nice."

It was beyond nice, actually. I felt enveloped by warmth. Coated all over in a deep, soothing heat that seemed to be radiating through my skin and into my body. I knew right away that the more they rubbed, the hotter everything would get.

"Turn her around."

They did, and soon they were getting my back as well as my front. If there was anything nicer than a pair of hands smoothing motion-activated oil all over your ass, it was two or three pairs working simultaneously. Their palms dove down, to do my legs. Closed tightly around my thighs, dragging their way agonizingly upward...

Oh wow.

I felt like a princess. Like a queen.

This is living.

My eyes slowly closed, dulling out all the rest of my senses except for the sense of touch. Their touch was growing bolder now, their fingers more insistent. Somehow they'd moved me, too. I was standing at the edge of the bed.

"Lay her down."

I was tipped backwards, and they cradled me as I fell. It was the ultimate trust fall. The most sensual thing I'd ever experienced in my life.

"Gently..."

A pair of lips brushed my ear. Another closed over my left breast. Someone whispered something hot and dirty to me, so husky and faint I could only barely understand it.

Then a pair of hands went to my legs... spreading my thighs wide.

"Do you want this?"

I nodded eagerly. I could feel a tiny pool of warm oil settled in the hollow of my throat.

"Take it then."

A hand guided mine, and suddenly I was stroking a long, thick cock. Maddox's, maybe. Or Kane's, judging by the size and head. Someone dumped oil into my palm, and everything became a lot easier... and more fun.

"Me also."

A second set of hands guided my other palm, my fingers closing over another cock. I was stroking them both now. Pulling them through my oil-soaked hands as a third lover buried his tongue inside me.

HOLY SHIT.

Everything was so fucking *hot.* So wet and slippery. I

kept kissing and stroking, writhing on my oil-soaked back into the oil-soaked sheets as whoever was between my legs devoured me expertly. I knew it had to be Austin, just from the technique. But I kept my eyes closed. Played along with the glorious anonymity of the whole unbelievable fantasy.

"You'd better fuck her soon, or I will."

Maddox that time. Off to my right. Playing with one nipple while the guy on my left played with the other. Kane, of course. I could tell by the thickness of his hands, the roughness on the pads of his fingers.

My legs were spread, and I opened my eyes. Austin was standing there, pushing his manhood against the oil-slick petals of my throbbing flower. Inching himself past the entrance... stretching me full of his hard, pulsating cock.

I gasped as he slid into me. Then he shifted forward... upward and *onto* me as well. The copious amounts of oil from my body coated his, and soon we were sliding against one other. Fucking like rabbits in full view of the others, who were pinning my knees back to my ears as I stroked them off in turn.

"Jesus," I grunted, although it was more of a moan. "You're *deep.*"

The oil wasn't just acting as a lubricant, it was helping to create a frictionless surface as well. Austin's chest was hot against mine. My own stomach slid deliciously against his washboard abs, creating warmth and heat between us as he drove *all* the way into me on every upthrust.

FUCK...

Austin stared into my eyes, taking full control. He was

359

fucking me every bit with his gaze, as he was with his cock.

"Welcome home," he said, smiling down at me. Then his eyes rolled back...

... and he came right in my pussy.

Awww, fuck!

It was lasciviously dirty, the way he just silently let go. His hands screwed mine into the bed, his fingers clenching and unclenching as he pumped me full of his cream.

I was helpless beneath him. My shoulders pinned firmly to the bed by the grip of Maddox and Kane.

Over and over he drilled himself into me, working the oil and come into a hot, heated mixture that coated his shaft and balls. We both looked down when he finally withdrew, admiring the sheer obscenity of what we'd just done.

"Who's next?" he smirked.

Kane stepped up, sliding from the bed and taking my ankles in his hands. His big cock stood out like a railroad spike, strong and beautiful, all glistening with oil.

Holy shit.

My legs were still trembling, my shallow respiration causing my stomach to go concave and convex with each alternating breath. Kane and I locked eyes, and every butterfly in my stomach took flight at once.

Then he flexed... and with one twist of his massive arms I was flipped instantly onto my stomach.

More oil was applied, this time from my other lovers. They poured it copiously over my ass. Massaged it in with their hands, kneading my supple cheeks and spreading them wide.

I sensed Kane as he leaned forward, his fingertips probing me gently. Somehow I was still wearing my G-string. I'd been fucked in. Filled in it. Now it went abruptly tight, digging in around my waist as he took it between his thick fingers...

SNAP!

It broke like a flimsy rubber-band, sending a shockwave of pain and arousal rocketing through my body. The pain only lasted a few brief seconds. The arousal hung around...

The pad of Kane's thumb pressed forward, against my tight little asshole. Between the heat and the lubrication and how relaxed I already was, it slipped past the opening and pushed slowly, deliciously inside.

Ohhhhhhhh...

"I've wanted this for a long time," Kane growled, leaning over my back. He was practically doing a push-up over me now. His thumb slid into my ass another inch. "Now I'm taking it."

I felt so warm and full beneath him. So incredibly, beautifully dominated.

"It's yours," I gasped.

He pressed his face against mine for a moment, kissing my cheek tenderly. Then he withdrew his thumb and replaced it with the thick, mushroom-shaped head of his cock.

Oh my God...

It felt absolutely insane as he pushed forward. Like trying to fit an apple into a garden hose. Yet somehow, I

361

stretched to accommodate him. My whole body sunk into the bed as my asscheeks parted and my sphincter relaxed to let my lover inside. I jumped only once, when the head snapped in. And then Kane was pushing himself... ever so slowly... all the way up my tight, glistening ass.

Fuuuuuck!

My hands were high overhead as they clenched the sheets, screwing them into my palms. Every inch was sweet, blissful agony. Every centimeter, a magnificent victory.

When he was fully inside, totally in me, I felt like we'd *won* something. I let out a small, raving laugh into the oil-soaked sheets... and then Kane began fucking my ass with strong, deep strokes.

"Holy shit that's hot," breathed Austin. The tone in his voice told me he lamented letting go so soon.

Kane grunted, squeezing my ass in his hands. His fingers slipped everywhere as he struggled to maintain his grip, all while plowing me into a series of breathless whimpers and not-so-soft moans.

We screwed for a long while, developing the most awesome of rhythms. Pleasure took the place of discomfort. Recklessness edged out caution as we continued to pick up speed.

I was yelling now. Saying things — some of them incoherent — all of them dirty. An oil-soaked hand went into my hair, and suddenly I was face to face with Maddox's beautifully ripped torso. He had his cock in one hand, and was smearing it all around my face. Sliding it under my chin, against my cheeks... over my nose and forehead in wide circles, smearing oil everywhere that it went.

I was soaked all over. Totally filthy and hopelessly wild. This was beyond hot — it shattered the limited scope of every wanton thought or dirty fantasy I'd ever had.

"Fuck..." Maddox was groaning. "Holy shit that's so... fucking..."

I opened my mouth and his cock slipped in. It was wet and slippery, hot and throbbing. I closed my lips and focused on milking it, on dragging my mouth tightly up and down his shaft while Kane drilled me from behind. I was bucking backward now. Embedding him in my ass as his balls slapped against my pussy and Maddox's balls grazed my chin.

Holy. Fucking. Shit.

They were using my body... and I was using theirs. A familiar heat rose inside me as I writhed and twisted and shoved myself back and forth between them.

"FUCK ME!"

The words were mine, but they also weren't. They were foreign. Alien. They belonged to someone else.

"OH *GOD...*" I gasped, screwing my eyes shut. "FUCK ME!"

Kane speared into me, touching all new places, bringing me all new pleasure as Maddox's thick cock filled my throat. I was lost in euphoria. Completely consumed by lust. I would've gone on forever. Done anything...

"Here," Kane said, his hands going under my belly. "Get *inside* her."

He lifted me back and upward, as Maddox popped from my mouth. I was pinned tightly against him. My asshole throbbing and convulsing around his cock, as if desperate for still more.

Then Maddox slid his whole body under mine... and I knew in an instant what they intended to do.

"Oh God..." I panted, trying to regain my breath. "I don't know..."

They held me together, and that made it simple. Positioned my body exactly where they needed it to be, as Maddox's legs slid through mine.

"Guys... oh fuck... oh holy sh—"

My eyes flared wide as Maddox impaled me, entering me smoothly from beneath. His cock slid snugly into my come-soaked pussy. Embedded itself wonderfully in my warm pink flesh, touching that one last spot inside me that hadn't yet been reached...

"OH GOD IT'S *GOOD*," I smiled, my face split in a rapturous grin. My brain flooded with pleasure, euphoria, relief. "SOOO GOOD!"

Austin stood over us now, holding me by the chin. Kissing my neck. Chewing my shoulder...

"OHHHH..."

Every last ounce of worry drained away. I was right where I needed to be. Exactly where I belonged.

"OH GOD..."

I was pinned between my three incredible lovers. One big cock sheathed comfortably in my pussy, the other buried balls-deep in my ass...

The intensity had me floating on the very edge of

consciousness. Austin's lips rotated against mine, drawing me forward in hedonistic abandon. Down below, my glistening thighs straddled Maddox. I rocked forward and back against his rippled stomach, controlling the angle of penetration. The depth and pressure of having them both inside me...

"UNNNGGHHHH!"

My orgasm didn't just hit, it tore through me like a cyclone. My body twisted between them, my pussy squeezing down hard around one lover while my ass clenched the other so tightly it was only a matter of seconds before I felt him flooding me from within.

OHHHHHH...

Kane ravaged me with one final thrust, his cock twitching wildly as it drained itself into my forbidden channel. Again and again it went off, filling my bowels with thick jets of his warm, soothing come.

My own climax raged on, contraction after exquisite contraction, sending my sex-starved brain on a blinding white tour of heaven. I screamed. I cried. I clawed at Maddox's chest... running my nails down his perfect pectorals just as his own cock went off in sweltering pussy.

"Come!" I yelled, only vaguely aware I was even talking. "Oh God, oh baby... come!"

He pumped himself into me, squeezing my hips with his hands until his balls were dry and empty. I bucked and rolled. Screwed downward, until the sounds and smells of our combined sex permeated my virgin bedroom...

"Mmmmmm..."

My sigh of contentment was orgasmic itself; like a

runner taking her first deep breath at the end of a marathon. I kept on moving, even after Kane left me. Grinding myself in slow circles against Maddox, while my other two lovers looked on in serene amazement.

"*Fuck...*" Kane whispered.

They were all looking down now, and I could feel it too. My lovers' come, seeping from my body. Oozing out of my well-fucked holes, as I collapsed forward on Maddox's chest.

We were face to face, breath against breath. Since our lips were touching I smiled and kissed him, although I don't think I had the strength to do anything else.

In the end I fell sideways, into the warm, oil-soaked blankets. Surrounded on all sides by heat. By muscle. By love.

"So what do you think?" Maddox asked eventually, when we could all speak again.

"Of *that?*" I wanted to punch his arm.

"No silly. Of your bedroom."

I looked up at the ceiling and giggled. "It's my favorite room in the house so far."

"Same here," Kane grunted. He was screwing the cap off a large bottle of water.

Maddox was tracing a finger over my chest, drawing lines through the shimmering pools of oil. He circled one of my nipples, teasingly, as Austin played with my tangled hair.

Three lovers, Dallas. Three sexy Navy SEAL boyfriends.

It was unreal. Beyond unreal.

All for you.

I shook my head in disbelief, like none of this was even possible. Like I was dreaming, and I'd wake up at any moment.

Holy shit.

I shook my head... and yet the guys were still there.

A new life. A new start.

Memories of Las Vegas drifted to mind. Of my family, my brother. Of my previous life.

They were all good ones now. All happy memories.

A brand new beginning.

Memories I would take with me into the future.

Kane was standing over me, smirking downward. He offered me some water, and I took it gratefully.

"So..." I asked innocently, letting the cool liquid slide refreshingly down my throat. "Are we going to do this in *every* room of the house?"

Austin laughed out loud, pulling on his boxers. Kane was already half dressed. One of them hit Maddox in the face with a shirt, causing him to finally sit up.

"After we finish unpacking a hundred damned boxes?" Kane shrugged.

My lovers' arms and shoulders were all pumped and full, their skin still glistening with oil. It made them look like a trio of chiseled, Roman gods.

"I don't see what in the fucking world could possibly stop us."

Protecting Dallas - Krista Wolf

~ Protecting Dallas ~
Bonus Epilogue

DALLAS

"You *sure* you're ready for this?"

I purred the words more than said them, stretched comfortably out across my bridal bed. Still draped in the sheer silk of my wedding dress, as a fragrant tropical breeze blew through our bungalow.

"The question is are *you* ready?" chuckled Maddox.

"Oh I'm always ready."

"That's generally true..." Austin theorized. "But this?" He began unbuttoning his shirt. "This is a little different."

I flipped onto my stomach, pushing up on my hands into a downward dog position. Stretching my back because I knew firsthand how important stretching was, especially with three Navy SEAL boyfriends.

Now Navy SEAL *husbands.*

"*Way* different," Kane chimed in.

The wedding had been beyond gorgeous; a private

ceremony at an ancient stone altar, nestled deep in the lush jungles of Kaua'i. A five-hundred year old Polynesian artifact, worn smooth by rain, wind, and time.

The sky had been the most beautiful cerulean blue. Our only witnesses: a wisp of tiny white clouds, stretching high over us like a long string of pearls.

That, and the smiling native priest who performed the ceremony.

I still wasn't sure where they'd gotten him, but the sweet old man seemed to know and love all three of my husbands. He spoke the most beautiful words in our secluded little clearing. Blessed the four of us in both our language and his, while standing around the crumbling altar, holding each other's hands.

When it was over my husbands kissed me, one by one, as deeply and passionately as the first time our lips had touched. For two solid years they'd kissed me as both friend and lover. As a girlfriend... and even a fiance.

And now, they kissed me as their *wife*.

"Last chance to back out," said Austin. He was down to his boxers already. "Once we do this there's no going back."

I rolled over again, scissoring my legs. Smiling and stretching like a cat. "Umm-hmm."

"It's not like we can *un*-impregnate you," said Maddox.

I laughed musically. "Yeah... I'm pretty sure I know how it all works."

It had been their request to consummate our marriage in my wedding dress. To make love to me — for the first time as their wife — while still wearing the beautiful silken gown they'd married me in.

It was *my* request that they be naked... except for the crisp, white, button-down shirts that looked so damned good on them. Chests open and exposed of course.

But it had been *everyone's* idea — all four of us — to get me pregnant on our honeymoon.

"So who drew the longest straw?" I giggled.

Maddox rolled his eyes. "Who do *you* think?"

"Kane."

He and Austin nodded bitterly. "He's always been the lucky one."

That much was true. Whether we were playing cards or rolling dice or generally doing anything that required any degree of randomness, things just always seemed to work out in Kane's favor.

"Well you're *all* lucky," I assured them confidently. "Because you all have *me*." I lay back, spilling my golden marital hair over my virgin marital pillow. I couldn't stop smiling. "He just gets to go *first.*"

Our bungalow was absolutely breathtaking. Everywhere I looked I saw flowers and candles and all things pretty. It was a far cry from our little farm in New Hampshire, where we'd taken to tending horses and generally enjoying the solitude. And the weather was a *definite* change from the cold, snowy winters... not that I didn't mind being snowed in with my three sexy SEALs.

No, our lives had been picture perfect since the

craziness in Vegas. Everything had worked out for once, and the people responsible had been held accountable for their actions. New Hampshire was like a never-ending vacation for us. Woodward sent us Christmas cards. Hell, even Dietz came up to visit.

"Just because he's going first doesn't mean he's got the strongest swimmers," said Austin, cracking his knuckles.

"Or the fastest," said Maddox.

All three of my warriors were retired now. Inactive duty. Sure, they still did consults and outside work that had them traveling quite a bit. But in two straight years, I was never alone. Never without at least one or two of my lovers to keep my bed constantly warm.

And to protect me, of course. I *always* liked that part.

Kinda missed it, actually.

"It's not exactly a race, guys," I laughed. "In fact when it comes to—"

"Don't go all technical on us now," said Austin. "We don't need to hear the biological details. This is a straight-up *competition*. Like everything else we do."

I laughed and rolled my eyes.

"And we've got a lot riding on this," agreed Maddox. "Bets. Secondary bets."

"Third party side bets..." said Kane, dropping his belt.

"What?"

They all smiled and looked at each other, but none of them said anything more. I threw them a sideways smirk.

"Just SEAL things?" I quipped. It was our common inside joke.

"Yeah."

Starting a family was something we'd all wanted, and we couldn't think of a better time than now. We'd agreed I'd stop taking my birth control right before the honeymoon. That from them on we'd let the chips fall... wherever they may.

"You know," I said, "impregnating me first isn't exactly all that great a prize."

Maddox sank down on side of the king-sized bed. Austin sat on the other.

"Oh no?" asked Maddox. "And why's that?"

"Because whoever gets me pregnant first is down to blowjobs and money-shots for the next couple of years," I pointed out. "While the others catch up."

It was yet another thing we'd obviously determined beforehand: that I'd father a child from each of them. Strong sons. Beautiful daughters. At least one from Maddox, one from Austin, and and one from Kane. In whatever order mother nature decided.

After that, any *other* kids we had together would be determined by chance. All bets would be off. But for now, once one of them got me pregnant? The others would have to refrain from shooting inside me, at least until I had a child by each of them.

"She makes a halfway decent point," said Austin. "I sure as hell would miss that pussy if—"

"Oh you can still *have* my pussy," I chuckled. "You

373

just can't finish inside it."

"I know, but—"

All talking ended as Kane grabbed me by the waist and pulled me to him. My dress rode all the way up, revealing thigh-high bridal stockings of pure white, with sexy lace trim.

And of course, my cute little white thong panties. Embroidered with the words 'just married.'

"You ready for husband number one?" Kane grunted.

I hooked one finger into my mouth and nodded, breathlessly.

He leaned forward, burying his face beneath my dress. His tongue was warm and wet against my flesh, licking in slow circles that were uncharacteristically gentle, especially for him.

Maddox and Austin were on either side of me now, their faces nuzzling into me. In no time they were kissing me wetly, drinking from my lips. Alternating between dragging their hot tongues up and down my most sensitive flesh, circling around my ears, pulling my hair aside to kiss and nibble at my neck and shoulders.

My God Dallas...

Already the room was spinning. Kane was lapping away, eagerly devouring my pussy while holding my panties to one side. They were already sopping wet. Drenched since the moment all three of them took turns carrying me over the threshold.

Three husbands.

I sighed, sifting my fingers through my lovers' hair. Pulling Maddox hard against one breast, while Austin inched the fabric down on the other side.

You must *be dreaming.*

It was a thought I had over and over again, and more times than I could even count. But this couldn't be a dream. No dream would ever come even *close* to this.

You're their wife now, Dallas.

I was! That part was thrilling. The word seemed utterly meaningless the first dozen or so times I'd said it, but it was slowly gaining traction in my brain. Not to mention the triple-banded wedding ring on my finger, right alongside my already-gorgeous diamond...

You're going to be the mother of their children.

The thought was amazing, frightening, exhilarating — all at the same time. Children. With *each* of them. Raised by four loving parents. A mother, and three strong fathers. A double-sized family that, unlike my old one, could never be broken.

I couldn't fucking wait.

"OH!"

I gasped as I was lifted; two strong hands planted firmly beneath my ass. Kane pulled me against his body, spreading my legs. In moments he was pushing himself between my thighs, pressing the head of his bulging manhood right up against my dripping entrance.

"My wife," he murmured...

Then plunged all the way inside me.

OHHHHHH...

The joy, the pleasure, the sheer gratification of him filling me from within. It was like this every single time, no matter how many times we did it. Only this time was different.

This time it was as husband and wife.

The concept overloaded my senses. Drove my mouth open as my chin tilted back. My gasps were louder, my arousal magnified as Kane began screwing me with a slow, steady rhythm. I could see him staring down. Watching me writhe beneath him, my white gown all bunched up around my waist.

He's taking pictures in his mind, I knew right away. *Mental photos, to remember this moment.*

I knew, because I was doing exactly the same. My *husband* was fucking me. Penetrating me as his wife for the very first time. In a little while he'd flood my pussy with his warm, delicious seed... and then my *other* husband would take his rightful place between my legs... and do the same thing all over again.

Three of them, Dallas.

It was too hot for words. Too hot to think about them coming inside my now-fertile womb... the rush of heat and wetness filling me up, maybe even impregnating me right here on our very wedding night.

Not two, but three.

If I concentrated, I could climax right now. I could let it all go — just contract around Kane while raking my nails down his shirt-covered back — drain him immediately and irrevocably inside me. I knew all the dirtiest tricks. I'd been with my lovers long enough to know what each of them liked, what they loved, what ultimately got them off.

Instead, I kept on screwing him. Kept on kissing Maddox and Austin, even reaching out to stroke them as I bounced on my first husband's cock. I wanted Kane to take all the pleasure he wanted between my legs. After all, this was our wedding night. It needed to be slow, and hot, and steamy. I needed each of them to remember it forever.

Holy... holy shit...

I let my thoughts wander, spinning happily over the last few years of my life. I'd finally found *love* with someone... and multiplied that love by three. Best of all it was with the three men my brother was closest to in the entire world; men *he* loved and trusted as well.

Just knowing that made it even more special for me.

Together, we made up both sides of my brother's life. We had him in every one of our memories. His legacy could live on through us, for as long as the four of us lived. And now, with children on the horizon... he'd live on in *that* way too.

Especially since the first son I gave birth to would be named after Connor.

That was something we'd all decided unanimously, hands down. That no matter who was the father, or how quickly it happened, the first baby boy of our new family would be named after my brother.

Or to be more accurate, *our* brother.

"Fuuuuuck..."

I looked up at Kane just he climaxed. I wanted him close. *Needed* him close...

"Baby, come here..."

Taking his face in my hands, I pulled him down against me and whispered into his ear how much I truly loved him. I told him how much he meant to me, and how much I hoped he was giving me a child...

The words spurred him on, causing him to throb and pulse and fill me all the way up from within. His orgasm lasted twice as long as usual. It held twice the intensity now. Twice the importance, as husband and wife.

Kane held me for a long while, kissing me tenderly before leaving my body. The others held back a bit, knowing enough not to rush things. Giving us the gift of this moment.

"Alright," Kane said when he finally withdrew. "She's pregnant now, so you guys can all go hom—"

Maddox laughed and shoved him aside. By the way he was already spreading my legs, I could see he'd drawn the middle straw.

"We'll see about that."

It would be interesting, to say the least. To not know who the father was, throughout my pregnancy. We'd decided to find out only afterward, through testing. Although all three of my lovers — now husbands — claimed they'd be able to tell just by looking at our child for the first time.

"Jesus..." groaned Maddox, sinking inside of me. "She's already a mess."

"I think Kane was holding off the past few days," joked Austin. "Stacking the deck."

Maddox hooked my legs over his shoulders and swore

under his breath. "Cheater."

I laughed inwardly at their constant competition. That part was always fun. It extended well past me of course, and into just about every aspect of our daily lives.

In no time Maddox was digging me out, his beautiful abdominals rippling as he pumped me hard from above. My hands were on the thickest part of his upper arms.

Fuck.

I could feel the striation of every muscle, taut and surging, beneath my grasp.

God, he makes me so fucking hot...

Again I could've come at any time. It would've been instant, like opening the floodgates. All I had to do was let go... give myself over to the deliciously submissive sensations of being plowed hard and deep. But it was Maddox who let go first.

"Shit," he said suddenly. "Ah, shit..."

The others laughed, knowing their friend was already past the point of no return.

"*Dammit,* Dallas."

He looked at me disappointedly, almost angry that he couldn't last longer. I smirked up at him and blew him a kiss.

"Not my fault," I shrugged.

"It's too fucking hot in there," Maddox complained. "Like a goddamn volcano."

"Maybe that's because I put lava in there," Kane jeered.

His arms tensed and locked as he let go, pumping me

with his seed. He drove himself deep first, though. Held his body as tightly against mine as he possibly could, as if attempting to shoot past Kane's already significant deposit.

"How long do we have to get her pregnant, again?" grunted Maddox.

"On our honeymoon?" replied Austin. "Two weeks."

Maddox looked down through the delirium and laughed. "She's not gonna last two *hours.*"

Like Kane, he withdrew slowly. Kissing me as a husband kissing his wife. It was sweet. Romantic. Beautiful.

"Alright," Austin said finally. "Glad to see you saved the best for last."

He was already shifting me his way. But the others were teasing him.

"Best for last?" grunted Kane. "Isn't that just euphemism for sloppy seconds?"

"More like dirty thirds," Maddox chimed in.

From my position on my back, I threw a pillow at them. Austin was nudging my knees apart now. Rubbing the head of his thick cock through my swollen, come-smeared pussy.

"God you're wet..."

I nodded up at him, smiling. Our eyes met, and our lips drew together at the exact moment he entered me.

Mmmmmm...

Austin pushed himself deep, screwing his balls against my ass. He stayed there for a long, beautiful moment, kissing me hotly, letting his cock marinate in my wet, sultry depths.

"Are you going to me pregnant?" I whispered sweetly.

"Damn straight."

"Do it then," I smiled. "Let's see you show them both up."

The others hung back, watching as Austin put me through the paces. He fucked me slowly at first, building momentum gradually through a series of deep, rolling grinds. It was like he was churning butter. Or stirring a pot. Or any number of other analogies that slipped my sex-soaked brain, as I finally broke down the last of the barriers between myself and a violent orgasm.

"*OHHHHHHHH!*" I screamed, pulling him into me with two hands. My fingers was digging hard into his tight, muscular ass. "Oh... OH FUCK!"

My third husband came savagely, just after I did. Or maybe *because* I did, and Austin was the most visual of them all. Many times my own orgasm would trigger his, simply because whenever I talked or screamed or cried out it turned him on to the point of ultimate release.

Just like Maddox, Austin held me tight when he came. He kept pumping and grinding though, as if trying to spray every square inch of my insides with every possible ounce of his thick, white seed.

"So did you get good coverage?" joked Maddox, laughing from beside us.

"You'll find out in nine months," Austin shot right back.

Down between my legs, everything was a swampy mess. Warm, wet come lay seeping from pussy. It was soothing. Comforting...

"God, look at it all."

It ran down from between my thighs. Dribbled onto the sheets, soaking the entire area between my legs.

"If you're not pregnant by the end of this trip..." Maddox swore.

I shook my head incredulously, wanting to laugh. Only I couldn't laugh. It was too relaxed to even move. Utterly and completely satiated.

"Two full weeks?" Maddox asked.

The others nodded.

"Damn. This is going to be fun."

Now I did laugh. Even the slightest movement set my whole body quivering. "You don't even know the *half* of it."

I stretched back into the softness of the sheets, wondering if the resort staff had *any* idea how much in the way of linens and bedding we'd be going through. Probably not, I decided. But they'd find out soon enough.

Not exactly how you envisioned your wedding night would go, is it?

I laughed even harder, and this time I couldn't contain it.

No. Definitely not.

"What?" asked Maddox.

"Nothing."

"It's about Austin, isn't it?" poked Kane. Austin reached out to shove him and missed.

I smiled and stretched some more. No, this was definitely not the wedding I'd imagined. Or the honeymoon. Or the husband... much less *husbands* I'd always pictured in my mind's eye.

Sometimes though, as I well knew, life threw surprises your way. Bad ones. Worse ones. And then...

Well, then sometimes life could come through in a clutch, too.

"Anyone else hungry?" asked Austin.

Two weeks of this, my inner voice reminded me.

"Famished," said Maddox.

Two weeks... and then a whole lifetime.

"Starving," I added.

God it felt good.

We all turned to look at Kane. With a wide, glorious smile, my biggest husband gave a single shrug of his mighty shoulders.

"Yeah," he grinned at last. "I could eat."

Need *more* Reverse Harem?

Thanks for checking out *Protecting Dallas - A Military Reverse Harem Romance.* Here's hoping you absolutely LOVED it!

And for even *more* sweltering reverse harem heat? Check out: *Unwrapping Holly - A Holiday Reverse Harem Romance.* Below you'll find a preview of the incredibly sexy cover, plus the first several chapters so you can see for yourself:

Protecting Dallas - Krista Wolf

Unwrapping
HOLLY
A HOLIDAY REVERSE HAREM ROMANCE

KRISTA WOLF

Chapter One

HOLLY

"So.... I– I didn't get it."

My lip quivered as I told him. It was a humbling admission, a shit end to a very shit day. But I felt better in saying it. Much better now that it was finally out.

"Oh honey," Malcolm said, laying his hand over mine. "That really stinks."

I took as much comfort as I could from my boyfriend's touch. The promotion was mine, by every right. Among my team I had seniority, and I was certainly doing the best job. I'd even been working tons of extra hours for it, sitting at my desk late into the evening, until my ass was asleep long after I should be.

"They gave it to Louis," I sniffed, choking back tears. All the way here, I'd promised myself I wouldn't cry. "Can you believe that? Fucking *Louis...*"

Malcolm nodded sympathetically. It was all he could

do — his mouth was already full of another bite of cheeseburger.

"I—I mean, how the hell do you pick *Louis,* when he hasn't even been—"

"Holly, stop."

I looked up at him as Malcolm squeezed my hand. He handed me his napkin, which wasn't exactly clean. I dabbed the corners of my eyes with it anyway, wondering if anyone else at the greasy little diner was looking at me.

"Please, give me your keychain."

Keychain?

I blinked rapidly, driving the tears away. What could he possibly want with my—

Oh my God.

My heart soared. My whole body started to tingle. Suddenly all that nasty business at work seemed inconsequential.

He's going to ask you to move in with him!

For the first time all day, a smile cracked my lips. I reached into my bag almost reverently, pushing past my phone. The screen was still shattered of course, from when I'd dropped it earlier in the day. But none of that mattered now.

Malcolm smiled as he took my all-too large keychain from my trembling, outstretched hand.

"I— I want you to know this means *everything* to me," I said, trying once again to keep the tears at bay. But they were tears of joy this time, so I wasn't trying all that hard. "Especially after the day I've had," I sighed. "Especially after—"

I watched anxiously, waiting for him to bring it out — the key to his apartment. I'd been staying there three out of four nights a week, anyway. It only made sense for us to move in together.

Thank God.

After nearly two years of dating, of living alone in the concrete jungle of New York City, I'd *finally* have someone to come home to. And to think of all the rent money I'd save! Even after kicking in half with Malcolm, an offer I knew he'd take me up on because he was so frugal, I'd still be coming out ahead each month. Shit, this was even *better* than a raise.

More than that though, it was a sign of big progress. The advancement of our relationship. The next logical step in —

"I'm sorry you didn't get that promotion Holly," Malcolm said pityingly. "But if I'm being honest, I didn't think you would."

My eyebrows knit together. It was a cold thing to say. But that was Malcolm: brutally frank about everything, to the point of unflinching honesty. I'd thought it was heartlessness at first, but later on I realized it was only his personality.

Truth be told, I was used to it by now. Marcus approached life the same way he approached our accounting jobs: everything was all business.

"It makes this whole thing a little... harder."

I watched, trance-like, as he manipulated my keychain. Instead of *adding* a key to it, he twisted it counter-clockwise and took one off.

"W—What are you doing?"

"Taking back the car," he said simply.

"*My* car?"

My boyfriend suddenly looked uncomfortable. And he *never* looked uncomfortable.

"Holly I'm sorry," he said. "This... this isn't working out."

The words didn't register, no matter how many times my brain repeated them. I shook my head as if to clear it.

"*What* isn't working out?"

"This," he said, motioning casually back and forth. "Us. Our relationship."

The realization finally hit me — like a brick being dropped from a 90-story building. The same building we worked at together. The building where we'd met and fallen in love... or at least I *thought* we'd fallen in love, and—

"It's difficult for me to do this on a day you're already disappointed," he said.

"Difficult for *you?*"

He nodded, completely oblivious. "Yes. And that's why I feel so badly. But Holly, please, search your feelings. If you do it honestly, you'll come to the same realization I did."

A hard lump formed in my throat. "And what's that?"

Malcolm sighed gently. "This just isn't worth it anymore."

Isn't. Worth. It. Anymore.

My heart dropped into my stomach. All of a sudden I felt sick.

"B—But why are you taking my *car?*"

"It isn't your car," Malcolm shrugged. "It's a lease. A lease with my name on it."

"Yes, but I've been making the payments!"

He nodded. "You have. And on time too. I appreciate that, but—"

"You *gave* me a car for my birthday," I said, slowly raising my voice, "and you gave me a *payment book* along with it! Don't you remember?"

"Of course."

"What kind of a boyfriend gives his girlfriend a fucking *payment* book?" I practically shouted. "Who the hell *does* that?"

Now we *did* have an audience. Half the diner was staring at us, like the bloodthirsty crowd of a gladiatorial coliseum. Waiting for whatever entertainment came next. Hoping for me to slap him, or throw a drink in his face, or—

"What do you *mean* this '*isn't working out*'?" I yelled. "How long have you known? And you take me *here?* To the shittiest diner in all of Manhattan?"

The waitress topping off coffee halted mid-stride. She glared at me angrily, one dirty pot clutched in each of her hands.

"You break up with me today of all days? And now you're taking my *car?*"

"Not *your* car," Malcolm repeated simply. "It's—"

"I KNOW WHAT IT IS!"

A thousand different emotions went surging through me at once. Heartbreak. Rage. Remorse. Stupidity, at not having seen this coming. Embarrassment at having to do it in a room full of strangers.

Malcolm pushed the keychain back across the table, minus my car key and remote fob. He also pushed something else: a pair of what looked like pamphlets or brochures.

"What the hell are these?"

"City bus schedules," he offered helpfully. "And subway maps, for all the lines near—"

"You brought me *bus schedules?*" I growled.

"Mmm-hmmm," he said, almost cheerfully. "And subway maps. Look, if you leave your apartment ten minutes earlier each morning, it's real easy to just..."

His voice droned on, but I was no longer listening. My shoulders slumped. My head hurt. I couldn't believe any of this was actually happening.

Malcolm laid his hand over mine again, but now I was repulsed by it. I jerked it back like I'd just gotten bitten by a snake.

"Holly, I want you to know—"

I leapt up and threw my napkin down on the table. The tears were coming again. There was no way to stop them this time, and I didn't want anyone else to see.

Especially *him.*

The diner's bathroom was just as tiny as the rest of it. I spent two minutes bawling my eyes out, another minute feeling sorry for myself, and another staring into the dirt-streaked mirror while telling myself to buck up. By the time I finished washing my face and putting drops in my eyes, I was ready to go out there and give that piece of shit a piece of my mind.

But when I returned to my table there was just one problem with that plan: Malcolm wasn't there.

Son of a bitch!

Silently I kicked myself. I really should've known. My boyfriend was never good at conflict; he usually dealt with problems by ducking out and skulking away.

Like a coward.

I grabbed my keys, which were the only thing still on the table. They felt much smaller now. Lighter and emptier. Like my life.

I stomped past the front counter and toward the exit, wondering if my now *ex*-boyfriend were already on his way to repossess my car. If I knew him he probably was. Or better yet, he'd get someone *else* to do it. That seemed more like—

"Miss?"

The word came haltingly, almost meekly, as I pushed on the glass door. I turned around.

"You still have to... well..."

I knew the answer before even asking the question.

"Don't even *tell* me he didn't pay."

The man behind the counter shrugged apologetically. "Sort of," he said, his voice hesitant. "He, uh..."

"Let me guess," I offered, with a mad chuckle. "He

only paid for himself?"

"Well... yeah."

Fuck you Malcolm.

I opened my bag mechanically, paying with my last twenty-dollar bill. It should've been a good day. I should've gotten a raise, a well-deserved promotion. I should be celebrating with a handsome, loving boyfriend at some beautiful restaurant uptown. One who loved me enough to move in with me after nearly two *years* of dating.

Instead I was in some greasy diner, crying like a baby, paying my own bill. I'd missed the promotion, and now I didn't even have a car anymore.

Oh yeah, and my boyfriend had just dumped me. *Right* before Christmas.

Fuck my life.

I went to look down into my phone's cracked screen, to see what time it was. But when I pressed the button, all I saw was the darkness of a fully-drained battery.

Hell, fuck everything.

I pushed on the door so hard it bounced back and nearly hit me in the chin. My eyes dropped to the big PULL sign. Just as the guy behind me said the word needlessly over my shoulder.

It was just one of those days. The ones that kicked your ass, and kept on kicking you even after you were down.

At least it was almost over. At least nothing else could go wrong.

Right?

Finally opening the door, I stomped outside... into a cold, freezing rain.

Two

HOLLY

"No calls, no texts... no *anything?*"

I shook my head from the other side of the couch. The coffee shop was crowded for a Thursday. This close to Christmas, in New York City? I'm surprised we got a seat at all.

"Nothing," I said proudly. "Two whole, beautiful Malcolmless weeks."

Jocelyn pursed her lips approvingly. She took another sip of her latte.

"And you haven't even run into him at the office?"

"Nope. Remember, he works three floors above me. And it's not like I saw him a lot to begin with."

That part was a flat-out lie, and Jocelyn knew it. I saw Malcolm all the time, as much at work as outside the office. She didn't call me out on it, though. It was the mark of a good friend.

"Good for you, Holly," she smiled, raising her mug.

Very carefully, I clinked mine against it. "I'm proud of you."

In truth I was proud of myself. I'd actually gone out of my way to avoid my ex, taking a different bank of elevators and avoiding the exit near the parking garage. Hell, it wasn't like I had a car to park there anymore, anyway.

A sadness crept over me at that last thought. I really missed my little hatchback.

"So what do you think about Sunday?" I asked. "About Lincoln's... invite?"

"Sure sounds like a date to me," Jocelyn grinned.

"*Really?*"

My best friend in all of Manhattan swept a stray blonde lock over one ear. "Tell me again how he asked you."

I relayed the story one more time. The story about how Lincoln Wallace, my first and oldest personal shopping client, had asked to meet up with me on Sunday.

"Shopping and *lunch?*" Jocelyn repeated thoughtfully. "Well has he ever asked you to lunch before?"

"He's never even asked to go *shopping* before," I said. "Come to think of it, he barely makes suggestions. He's always just handed me his credit card and left everything to me."

That part was true, and it was also what I loved most about my little side business. Being a personal shopper was like getting paid to have fun. You went shopping with someone else's money, and you got to buy things you wouldn't normally buy yourself.

"How'd you meet him again, anyway?"

"I took the business over from a woman I worked

with," I said, "back when I first came to town. She was moving away and left me about a dozen clients. Lincoln Wallace was the best of them."

"You mean he *pays* the best," Jocelyn added shrewdly.

I sipped off the last of my foam. "Oh yeah. He's the CEO of his own advertising firm. And he's got four sisters and plenty of nieces and nephews. Not to mention two adorable parents back in Maine... all of whom he showers with gifts."

Jocelyn sighed wistfully. "Rich. Successful. Loves his family..." She squinted back at me. "And you said he was handsome, too?"

God, is he ever.

"Tall, dark and gorgeous," I nodded.

Jocelyn stared back at me enviously. "Well shit, Holly! If he's *not* trying to take you out, mind if I have a crack at him?"

I laughed, but my laughter came out nervous. Suddenly there was a little knot in my stomach.

Jealousy? The little voice in my head taunted. *Really, Holly?*

A huge part of me *did* want him to be asking me out. If for no other reason than to feel wanted again — to feel desired in ways I hadn't felt in almost two years. The fact that it was someone like Lincoln Wallace only made it ten times better.

But if he *wasn't* asking me out...

"Holly? Earth to *Holly?*"

I snapped back, just in time to avoid spilling my coffee

all over my own leg. It sloshed dangerously close to the lip of the mug, causing me to overcompensate and almost drop it entirely.

"Easy," Jocelyn chuckled, laying her hands over mine. "He's all yours, honey. I was only kidding."

She handed me a napkin, which I accepted gratefully. At the rate things were going, I might need a towel.

"And to answer your question, yes," she added, "I *do* think he's asking you out. Just look at yourself. You're beautiful and amazing, and now you're single to boot. He'd be a fool not to take a crack at you."

I blushed, even though it was just the two of us. "Thanks."

When it came to friends, Jocelyn was one of the better ones. Cute, funny, level-headed... and tough. New York tough. The kind of tough I learned all about when I moved out here two years ago, from my sheltered little town in Southern Texas.

"Treat it like a date," Jocelyn advised. "You haven't had one in a really long time. A good one, anyway."

"You don't think that would be unprofessional?"

"Do you really care?" Jocelyn smirked.

I thought about it for a second. "I care about losing him as a client."

She waved me away dismissively with one hand. "Shop with him. Flirt with him. Enjoy yourself for a change. If he flirts back, you know the drill. And if not?" She shrugged. "He's gay."

I laughed so hard I almost spit my coffee. "He's *not*

gay!"

Jocelyn threw me her most seductive wink. "Then go have fun with him."

Three

HOLLY

"C'mon, three more reps!"

I pushed hard, through the pain, feeling the burn in my thighs as the platform above me moved smoothly up and down. I always loved the leg press machine. The sheer amount of weight on each side made you feel like you could put up really big numbers.

"Two more..."

Except today, when I was doing it for the first time in months.

"Another two..."

"Hey!" I grunted. "You said that *last* rep!"

"Yeah, well you half-assed that one," Donovan barked. "I don't accept half-reps. If you followed through you'd be done by now."

I reached down into my core and pushed, shoving the weights away and finishing out my set. My perfectly-sculpted trainer engaged the locking clamp just as my legs went limp.

"There you go," he smirked back at me. "That wasn't so bad now, was it?"

I gave Donovan my dirtiest playful look. "No. It was absolutely perfect."

"Perfection is when I can bounce a quarter off your ass," he shot back. His look went stern. "But you already know what I'm going to say next, don't you?"

"Yeah yeah," I acknowledged. "It wouldn't hurt this bad if I came on a regular basis."

He nodded as he threw me my towel. "Damn straight."

I mopped my forehead as I looked Donovan up and down. As always he was flawless, from his square jaw and handsomely stubbled chin right down to his powerful biceps and rock-hard abs.

Jesus, did his arms get bigger?

It was the first time I'd actually seen him since my breakup. The first time I could really drink him in without feeling guilty, as if I were doing something wrong. Our playful banter was something I looked forward to during our sessions. It was cute and funny, and it also kept me in line.

"Fitness is like a relationship," he finally winked. "You can't cheat and expect it to work."

In reality I wasn't cheating. I'd been coming the last few weeks, I'd just been avoiding him.

"You avoiding me, Holly?" he squinted.

Shit, it was like he read my mind.

"No sir."

"Then where have you been?"

"Around."

"Not around *here*," he said. "At least not while I'm in the gym."

"Why?" I flirted playfully. "You been looking for me?"

Damn. That was bold! It also wasn't like me at all.

"I look out for everybody," he smiled. "But you especially."

It felt good, being able to flirt with him like this. To be free of Malcolm, who'd always thought my personal training sessions were a huge waste of money. "Why pay for something you can do yourself?" he'd argued often. "You're already paying for a gym membership. Do you really need to throw *extra* money at someone to stand over you?"

With any other boyfriend, I would've chalked it up to jealousy. After all, Donovan was *gorgeous*. But with Malcolm... not so much. Like always, he was just being cheap.

"So when did it end?"

Donovan's deep, velvety voice brought me back to reality. I stared up him curiously. "Huh?"

"Your relationship. You broke up with your boyfriend, didn't you?"

My confusion was suddenly replaced with astonishment. I was stunned.

"How do you kno—"

"Because you didn't talk about him at all," Donovan

403

interjected. "Not once, during our entire session. Usually you talk about him a lot, whenever I work you out."

"I do?"

"Yes," he smiled. "Nothing good, usually. He sounds... well..."

"Go on," I smiled. "You can say it."

Our eyes locked. My personal trainer hesitated, sizing me up a little before continuing. "He sounds like a cheap, controlling asshole."

I laughed as I popped the top off my water bottle. "Bingo."

"So you broke up with him?"

I wish. Suddenly I felt very foolish. As if the other people in my life could see something obvious I was totally missing. Missing for a very long time.

"Something like that."

"So then tell me," he said. "If you're single, and you obviously have more time on your hands... why are you avoiding me?"

I stared back at him, feeling like a deer caught in a pair of steel blue headlights. There was no use lying to him. He'd know immediately, before I even finished constructing the sentence.

"I— I'm kinda strapped for cash," I admitted humbly. "I don't have a car anymore, so I'm saving up for one."

His expression softened. I saw a welcome understanding in his eyes, as all judgment went out the window.

"I can't afford too many sessions right now," I said. "So I was thinking of cutting back my sessions. Maybe only coming—"

"You're a personal shopper, right?"

I blinked. It was the last thing I expected him to say.

"Yes."

"Well Christmas is coming," said Donovan. "And I've got a ton of people to buy for. Friends, family, small gifts I usually give to clients..."

His voice had changed also. It was still beautiful, still wonderfully deep and sexy. But it was smoother now. Much more casual.

"How about we trade?" he smiled warmly. "Some personal training sessions for some personal shopping?"

He had the *best* smile. It brought mine out as well.

"You'd do that?"

"I'd actually *love* to do that!" he said excitedly. "Can't tell the gym though." Donovan rolled his beautiful eyes. "It's against policy, or something equally stupid."

"O—Okay," I stammered.

All of a sudden my heart was racing. The idea of shopping for this incredible man, of getting to know him on a more personal level... there was something as intimidating as there was appealing about it.

"Gotta do *something* to get you in here," Donovan laughed. "You need an excuse to show up more."

I had to stop myself from turning about ten shades of

red.

"Maybe I need a little more incentive?"

Holy shit! Did you really just say that?

"Then maybe I should just take you out on Saturday," he countered smoothly. "How's that for incentive?"

For a couple of seconds, time stopped. It was all I could do to keep my mouth from hanging open.

"I... I work on Saturday."

Stupid! Stupid! Stupid!

"Do you work at night?"

I swallowed hard. "No..."

"Then I'll take you out then. Unless you—"

"No no," I jumped in. "I, uh... I mean Saturday night is good."

Donovan set his hands on hips as I let out a relieved breath. I couldn't believe how close I'd come to screwing things up.

"Then it's settled. Dinner, you and me, Saturday night. We can discuss the terms of our trade, and—"

"BURKE!"

We both whirled in the direction of the voice. Behind the front desk, the gym's owner — a man I knew only as Eddie — was staring daggers at us. Or more specifically, at Donovan.

"You've got an eight O'clock who's been waiting five minutes already," the owner growled.

"Yeah, we'll she's ten minutes early," Donovan shot

back.

Eddie's return scowl told me everything I needed to know next. Donovan's shoulders didn't slump an inch. He remained defiant in the face of the big, red-headed man. They stared at each other for a long moment, neither one of them willing to look away.

"It's okay," I said, pulling Donovan's attention back to me. "Go. Do your thing."

"You're my thing," he said. "At least until I'm done with you."

I smiled sweetly. "Well, are you done with me?"

"For now," he grinned back.

My stomach felt like a butterfly zoo. I couldn't believe this was happening. Donovan! Asking me *out!* And this time there was no doubt about it. This time it was most *definitely* going to be a date...

I couldn't wait to tell Jocelyn.

"I'll text you," he said, before turning away. "But remember: Saturday night, you and me."

I nodded mechanically. Like a schoolgirl being talked to by her biggest crush.

"Okay."

"Be hungry," he ordered. "But for right now? Treadmill. Thirty minutes. And I'd better see sweat when you leave."

Damn. I was hoping he'd forgotten.

"I'll do my best," I said. "Been a few weeks though, so

I'll have to go slow."

Donovan chuckled as he walked away. "No matter how slow you go, you're still lapping everybody on the couch."

Four

HOLLY

It was one of those rare glorious days, where the weather tells the current season to fuck off. In this case the skies were a pristine, cerulean blue. Totally unblemished by clouds, they were full of sunshine and warmth and promise.

Despite full winter being only days away, the temperatures had somehow climbed into the sixty-degree range. I had my ass firmly parked on a bench in Washington Square Park. Surrounded by sprawling green grass and skeletal trees that, just a few short weeks ago, had been exploding with fiery fall color.

Little things like that had astonished me the first year I was here. Simple things the locals always took for granted, like golden leaves and thousand-foot skyscrapers. Underground tunnel systems, flinging metal tubes packed wall-to-wall with people in every conceivable direction.

I had my face buried in the most boring of all possible literature: my CPA prep-book. The NYU campus loomed over my shoulder, a constant reminder that I had no less than three big finals coming up next week.

But that was okay. It was Friday. And Friday was *my* day.

Yes, it was the day I'd chosen to take all my classes. But once the morning was gone, I had the rest of the day all to myself. Friday was when I walked the streets of Manhattan, dipping randomly into shops and coffee houses and bookstores along the way. I went to museums. Saw plays on Broadway. Did anything I wanted, really, once I got my side work done and my studies out of the way.

Even then, shopping the City was like homework for my second job anyway. It gave me ideas on clever gifts to buy. I kept current on the latest fashions, just as eyeballing the millions of colorful people teeming the streets kept me up to date on the latest trends.

Most of all I loved the freedom. Malcolm worked late on Fridays — presumably so he could golf all weekend — so while we were dating I didn't even have to be home at any particular time. School aside, Fridays were my day off from everything. Especially days like today, which I considered a rare, precious gift.

I flipped the page, trying to keep my focus on more of the mind-numbing jargon. Accounting wasn't my first choice in life. It wasn't like every little girl grew up hoping to stick a pencil in her ear and maintain spreadsheets on profit/loss statements.

No, I'd wanted to do other things of course. Accounting was what happened when I took something I was already good at and added the pressing need to pay an exorbitant rent... even in a rent-controlled building.

Right now though, I didn't want to think about any of those things. I just wanted to inhale the crisp, fresh air. Enjoy the feeling of being surrounded by grass and dirt again — if only for a little while — rather than tons of glass and rebar and concrete.

I'd been on the bench nearly an hour when I saw him looking; the cute guy on the other side of the clearing. He was leaning against a tree, eating an apple. Staring at me... but not creepily. Almost as if he were looking with a certain, permissible familiarity. Which—

"*OOOF!*"

My heart nearly leapt through my chest as the jogger fell sideways against me. He came seemingly from out of nowhere. His body bounced from the bench, his momentum barely slowing as he spun away from me with an apologetic grunt and continued to run.

"I—"

Only now he was running away with *my bag*.

"HEY!" I yelled. "HEY, STOP!"

I looked around, but I'd chosen one of the more private areas of the park. The only person nearby was my apple-eating colleague, who I noticed was already sprinting full speed in my direction.

"HE TOOK MY BAG!"

The cute guy nodded as he flew past, his dirty-blond hair flowing behind him as he sprinted in the direction of the jogger. He was moving unbelievably fast. Taking long,

411

powerful strides with what looked like long, powerful legs.

Oh my God!

A half-eaten apple went spinning to the ground at my feet. I'd never been purse-snatched before! But of course I'd read about it. Hell, I'd seen it in a dozen movies, but none of them compared to the feeling of it actually *happening.*

I whirled, looking around helplessly. There was no one else. Only the jogger and his pursuer, who was slowly gaining on him.

What if he's armed?

The thought sent shivers through me.

What if he has a knife, or a gun, or—

"*UMMPH!*"

At the edge of the clearing, both men were now on the ground. My would-be savior had made a last-minute jump, tackling the jogger around his ankles. It looked painful, the fall. The jogger landed hands first to protect his face, skidding along the cement path with a scream of pain.

The apple-eating cute guy was crawling his way onto him.

Don't just stand there Holly! Go help him!

My legs moved on their own. I was walking at first, then running over to where the two men wrestled in the grass at the edge of the path. There was a grunt of exertion, then a cry of pain as the thief kicked my would-be hero square in the jaw. He scrambled to his feet and dove into the next wooded area, stopping only once to glance back in my direction.

I gasped as we made eye contact... and then he was

gone.

Holly, move!

Impotently I realized I was frozen again. By the time I ran up to help my champion, he was already on his feet.

"A—Are you *okay?*"

The cute guy, now minus the apple, was rubbing his jaw with one hand. In the other, at the end of his outstretched arm...

"My bag!"

I took it and hugged it to my body. Then I rushed forward and hugged *him*.

"Thank you so much!" I cried. "Oh my God, you saved my *life!*"

He laughed. "Well not your *actual* life," he replied breathlessly. "But your purse at least."

"But my whole life is in here!" I shot back. "Besides, I got paid today. I just cashed my check."

He started brushing himself off, and I moved to help him. Leaves and dirt fell away as my hands rubbed his chest, his arms, his back. Every surface I touched was hard with muscle. Every bit of him was in spectacular shape.

"You really carry cash?" he grinned. "I figured everyone has direct deposit these days, and—"

Our eyes met. From this distance, I recognized him immediately.

"I *know* you!"

My hero grinned back at me. "I was hoping you'd say

that."

"You're in my *class*. My psych class. My—"

"Statistics for Behavioral Sciences," he grinned. "Yeah."

"That's why you were looking at me. That's why you were staring."

He laughed out loud. It was one of the better sounds I'd heard in a long time. "Was I really staring?" I watched as his skin flushed red. "Sorry, I— "

"No no," I smiled. "Please don't be sorry. You're my hero! You saved me. Saved my *stuff*."

He nodded back to the bench, where my book lay face down on the ground. "If the thief were smart he'd have left your bag alone and grabbed one of our textbooks," he joked. "They're like a zillion dollars each anyway."

He stuck out his hand. I took it, and he squeezed me firmly but gently.

"I'm Brody by the way. Brody Valentine."

"*Valentine?*" I smiled. "That's really your last name."

He frowned immediately, but I could tell he was only pretending to be offended. "Why? What's wrong with—"

"Nothing," I said quickly. "Actually it's kinda cool."

Brody guided me off the path protectively as another pair of joggers ran by. Innocent ones, this time.

"Well," I said after an awkward pause, "you have to take something."

I began rifling through my bag, but he laid his hand

over mine.

"You have to take a reward for—"

"Are you kidding me?" he said. "A reward? For what? For tackling that asshole?" He grinned boyishly. "Anyone would've done that. Although I will say you got lucky. Instead of some slow, heavyweight stranger, you got one who ran cross-country all through high school."

I chuckled. Damn, he was even cuter close up.

"And on top of that we're not strangers," he said. "We're classmates."

His sparkling green eyes were almost mesmerizing. They were an incredible emerald color, flecked with the most beautiful streaks of black.

"T–That's true," I stumbled. "But you still have to take *something* as a reward. Let me at least buy you coffee or —"

"Wanna reward me?"

I nodded quickly.

"Then go out with me tonight."

It took a good three seconds for his words to sink in. "Wait, what?"

"Let me take you out," he said simply. "Or if you want, you can take *me* out." He smirked back at me proudly, and even that was cute. "You *did* say you wanted to reward me, right?"

"Yes," I said hesitantly. "But I, uh... I don't have a car."

"Then I'll pick you up."

I felt a wave of heat. Suddenly it seemed a lot more like ninety degrees than sixty.

"Unless you have a boyfriend, or—"

"No," I said.

"Or hate devilishly-handsome men with superhuman speed, who—"

"No," I giggled. "Nothing like that."

In one swift motion he pulled out his phone and unlocked it. "Text yourself," he said, handing it over. "So I'll have your number."

It all happened so fast. So boldly, yet naturally as well.

"Uh, okay."

Before I knew it I was doing what he asked, and handing his phone back to him. Surprisingly, I found that I *wanted* to! My handsome savior looked so well put-together. So roguishly hot. So charming and sexy, and—

"And your name?" he grinned, looking down at his phone.

"Oh, sorry. That might help, right?" I extended my hand nervously. "I'm Holly."

My classmate leaned in and wrapped his strong arms around me instead. He gave me the biggest, most satisfying hug.

"Text me your address, Holly," he smiled, before walking away. He left the scent of leather and a delicious hint of cologne in his wake. "I'm picking you up at seven."

Five

BRODY

She looked absolutely adorable, standing on the corner in a pair of pre-ripped jeans and a tight white sweater. Not to mention her little lace-up black boots, which looked unfortunately new.

I could tell by the look of surprise on her face that she hadn't expected me this way. I figured that much as I pulled up. I hadn't really told her.

"A *motorcycle?*"

I smiled through my open visor and handed her a helmet. She was wearing her hair straight, so I didn't think it would be an issue.

"Ever been on one?"

"I'm from Texas," Holly chuckled, throwing one leg over the back with practiced ease. "What do *you* think?"

A minute later we were speeding uptown, her boots on the footpegs, her arms wrapped pleasantly around my waist.

Her coat was thankfully short, and buttoned up tight. Though it was dark, it was still unseasonably warm.

"Where are we going?" she shouted over my shoulder.

"For a ride," I called back.

It was incredible, being out on my bike this late in the year. Even so, I knew it was probably my last ride until spring. My last chance to get out before the snows came and everything iced over, and the dirt trucks spread enough sand over the roads to make them virtually unrideable.

Damn, she feels good!

I zipped up 5th Ave, feeling Holly lean tight with me on the lane changes. She definitely *had* ridden before. She was a great passenger, and one who didn't fight the turns.

Saving her in the park today had been thrilling. Not only did it give me an excuse to talk to her, but it made me a temporary hero in her eyes. The cute little brunette in my psych class was no longer just someone I saw on campus or studying in the park. She was on my *bike* now. Her legs spread, hugging tight against my body.

We skirted the Park, continuing north through Harlem. Christmas decorations flew by — colorful lights and wreaths, dangling from streetlights and doorways, all the way up Amsterdam Avenue. It was beautiful. Always was. Maybe even more so that I could enjoy it without freezing my hands off.

"I've never been up this far," Holly said, as we turned onto Broadway. She laughed musically. "Where the hell are you taking me?"

"Connecticut!"

I felt her thighs squeeze deliciously against mine. It gave her enough leverage to punch me playfully in the ribs.

"Alright, alright," I laughed. "Hang tight. We're almost there."

It was another half mile before Fort Tyron Park came into view. We parked and continued on foot, me pulling Holly along excitedly by her warm, feminine hand.

"Wow, this place is gorgeous!" she marveled. Her head moved like it was on a swivel. "I never even knew it was here."

"Not many people do," I said. "It's so far out of the way, it's almost not even in the City."

Cobblestone paths lead us deeper into the heart of the wooded preserve. The sounds of traffic and car horns seemed to fade with every step we took.

We walked the paths for a while, still holding hands. The two of us enjoying the silence, marred only by the steady sounds of our booted feet.

"Are you cold?" I asked, pulling her into me.

"No... I'm good."

I could see her blushing, even through her rosy cheeks. Our fingers were interlocked, and when I squeezed she squeezed back.

"If you get cold, just tell me," I said.

"Why, are you gonna give me your jacket?" she teased. When I didn't answer she shrugged. "Hmm, I guess chivalry isn't dead after all."

I couldn't help but chuckle. "Funny you should say 'chivalry'."

The path we were on opened up, and a long series of castle-like structures came into view. Holly's eyes went adorably wide.

"Oh wow..." she breathed. "What are—"

"These are the Cloisters," I answered. "A bunch of Gothic hallways and monasteries from Europe, dismantled in the 1930's and brought all the way here."

Her bright eyes scanned the ancient stones. They looked so foreign, so out of place, especially tucked away deep within New York City.

"C'mon," I said. "Let's go!"

For the next hour or so we wandered through all four of the open galleries, interconnected to form a square. In the center of the quadrangle was a lush garden that would undoubtedly be amazing in the summer. Right now it was still beautiful, but in a wintery way.

It was amazing to me, that such history could be taken apart and put back together half a world away. The interior was a breathtaking array of arches and pillars. Of colorful tapestries, stained-glass windows, frescoes and sculptures. Much of it had been decorated for Christmas, lending what could've been considered a cold place a warm, holiday feel.

Holly was a good sport, even when I made her stop several times to take different photos. I even took one of us — an adorable selfie, smiling cheek to cheek while I held the camera at arm's length.

Eventually we stopped at their tiny cafe, for a pair of coffees. Relaxing at our little table, I was able to really give her the once-over. Unapologetically, too.

"This place is adorable," Holly smiled. She threw me an accusatory look. "Maybe a little *too* adorable."

"Oh?"

"I can only imagine how many first dates you've brought here," she laughed. "I'll bet it charmed the pants off every one of them."

I pretended to look under the table.

"No wise-ass," she giggled. "My pants are *not* coming off."

"Not yet anyway," I confirmed. "But please let me know when they do."

She laughed again, and that was a good sign. Holly wasn't just pretty, she was sexy too. There was a smoldering sensuality about her that I really liked, hiding just beneath her witty surface. All I needed to do was break through.

"So how many?" she shot back. "Two? Four? Six? A girl's gotta know."

"Actually," I sighed, leaning back in my chair, "this is my first time here."

My cute little classmate furrowed her brow. "C'mon..."

"No, really. This is just one of the many places on my list."

Now she actually looked intrigued. "Your *list?*"

"Yeah, I have a list. It's... well, it's a little complicated."

"Try me."

Her eyes looked almost turquoise in this light. So pretty. So bright, even in the cafe's dim light.

"Alright," I said. "So I have this list of things to do and places to go, in and around New York City. Each month I choose one and force myself to visit. No matter what I'm doing, I just go."

She stared back at me over her mug. "That... actually sounds kinda cool."

"Right? It's my grandmother's idea," I admitted.

"Your grandmother?"

I nodded. "My grandparents raised me. My sister too. Our parents got divorced when we were eleven, and they both just sorta took off in different directions."

"Holy shit."

"That's what *we* said," I laughed.

There was a moment of silence, but for some reason it wasn't awkward. Holly's look was more one of admiration than pity — something I appreciated immediately.

"Anyway, the whole 'go someplace new' thing was my grandmother's idea. It was something she used to do, back when she could still get around."

"And you took it over."

"Yup. She's still sort of living vicariously through me now. That's why I bring her lots of photos of everything."

Holly was abruptly quiet. I couldn't tell if she was weirded out, or—

"Brody?"

"Yes?"

Her eyes looked glassy. "That's one of the most

adorable things anyone's ever told me."

Now it was my turn to blush. All of a sudden I was glad for the bad lighting.

"It's kind of silly, I guess. I mean—"

"No," Holly said sternly. She reached across the table and took my hand. "It's *not*."

Six

HOLLY

The ride downtown was a lot cozier, somehow way more intimate than the ride up. I snuggled against Brody's back, trusting him implicitly as we zipped through the streets. My hands were locked even lower around the warmth of his abdomen, which felt scrumptiously hard and rippled beneath my interlaced fingers.

God, he's so... cute.

Yes, he definitely was. But lots of guys were cute, and Brody went well beyond that. He was sexy too, carrying himself with a cool, casual confidence that made me feel safe and protected, even in the middle of nowhere. And the Cloisters had been a charming little oasis. The perfect place for a quiet cup of coffee with a broad-shouldered stranger, one with a bright, beautiful smile.

And he's definitely not a stranger, I reminded myself. *Not anymore...*

We'd walked halfway back to his bike when Brody had

pulled me against a lamppost. His kisses had been sensuous, so unspeakably hot, they'd practically melted me right there in his arms. It had been a long time since I felt passion like that. Far too long since I'd been held in a way that made me feel *wanted...* and not just superficially but with a desperate, pressing need.

We'd continued making out in the middle of the park for what seemed like a long time, oblivious to our surroundings. His hands wandered downward, over my back, sliding dangerously below my hips. I'd gasped into his mouth as he cupped my ass, pulling me hard against him. Brody merely responded with a smug smile, nibbling sexily on my lower lip.

Our mouths churned hotly, our tongues dueling as they rotated slowly against each other. All around us, the world stopped. The lamppost became our own private island; a glowing steel beacon in the darkness of the empty park. No one came down the path we were on — not a single, solitary person. It was the most solitude I'd had since leaving Texas, and for some reason it felt utterly magnificent.

Back on the motorcycle, we arrived at my apartment all too fast. I was left standing in front of my building, handing my helmet back to Brody as he comfortably straddled his bike.

"Wanna come up?" I asked boldly. "For a drink?"

I really didn't know who this new Holly was. But I knew I liked her a lot.

"Sure."

We were in my apartment all of two seconds before we were all over each other again. This time there was nothing stopping us — no inhibitions or worries about being walked up on by anyone else.

No, it was just us, Brody's rock-hard body pressing me hard up against the back of my door. His sweet mouth trailed kisses down my neck, as I helped him drop his leather jacket to the floor.

Oh wow. This is going to happen...

I swooned, clutching his head against me. Pulling him further downward, toward my breasts, even as his hands worked their way beneath my clothes to find warm, naked skin.

"I want you."

It was all he said. It was all I needed. Two strong hands rolled up along my ribs, and I raised my arms for him as he pulled my shirt and sweater over my head.

We couldn't get undressed fast enough. Clothes flew everywhere, and my eyes went wide as his incredible chest came into view. It was full and strong and hairless... and so unlike Malcolm. His shoulders were broad, tapering down to two big arms that were corded with muscle.

His face was in my chest now, buried in the perfumed valley between my breasts. I felt the welcome relief of my bra being unclasped, and then the warmth of his hands smoothing over them, my nipples stiffening in his two open palms.

"I... It's..."

He nuzzled me, dragging his lips upward. His mouth closed over my areola, and I felt the slow swirl of his tongue.

"It's been a while since..."

Brody responded by cupping me from behind. He pulled me tightly against him, our bodies molding into each

426

other so perfectly it was like we were made for each other.

"It's okay," he murmured into my breast. An electric shiver ran through me as his palm slid downward along the flat of my stomach. Instinctively I was on my tiptoes, gasping, as his fingers pierced the waistband of my thong...

"We'll go *slow*," Brody grinned.

My mind was spinning, but my body was responding feverishly to his every touch. In a flash of clarity I realized I *needed* him, and not just his body against mine. I needed him *inside* me. Spreading my legs wide. Filling me up the way I loved and craved, the way I hadn't been filled in ages, not since before my ex-boyfriend's lame attempts at satisfying me.

I took his zipper down, and slipped my hand through his boxers. My fingers closed over his manhood, all warm and thick and heavy. The heft and weight of it was thrilling, even before it began coming alive in my palm...

Our eyes met, and Brody smiled mischievously.

"OH!"

In a whirl of speed and motion he lifted me over a massive shoulder. With one hand clamped tightly over my ass, his fingers slid deliciously through my thigh gap as he walked me across my living room.

"Bedroom," he said simply.

I was already wetter than I'd been in my entire life.

"Door on the left," I grunted.

It was slightly ajar as he kicked it open, carrying me over the threshold and into semi-darkness. Only a dim swath of moonlight filtered in through a single window. It bathed

427

everything in a blue-hued, spectral glow as Brody tossed me onto my own bed.

Oh my God...

He stood at the edge for a moment, staring down at me like some hard-won prize. Then he dropped to his knees, rolled my panties down my thighs...

... and lowered his beautiful mouth into my warm, wet sex.

UNWRAPPING HOLLY IS NOW ON AMAZON!

Grab it now — It's free to read for Kindle Unlimited!

ABOUT THE AUTHOR

Krista Wolf is a lover of action, fantasy and all good horror movies... as well as a hopeless romantic with an insatiably steamy, dirtier side.

She writes suspenseful, mystery-infused stories filled with blistering hot twists and turns. Tales in which headstrong, impetuous heroines are the irresistible force thrown against the immovable object of powerful, alpha heroes.

If you like intelligent and witty romance served up with a panty-dropping, erotic edge? You've just found your new favorite author.

Click here to see all titles on Krista's Author Page

Sign up to Krista's VIP Email list to get instant notification of all new releases: http://eepurl.com/dkWHab